The Gideon Files, Book One

# Red Lotus

Ande Li

ROOM 808 PRESS

Copyright 2019 Ande Li at Room 808 Press

ISBN-13: 978-1-951575-09-0
ISBN-13: 978-1-951575-08-3

Source: Digital copy

Cover image: Max Acronym, Stock photo ID: 152292131, Sep 1, 2013. Photograph. Shutterstock. Web.

## Acknowledgements

For the survivors, the fighters, and those still
struggling to find their strength...
As long as there is life, there is hope.

# Chapter 1

"Leave it! You'll grow another."

Mina Gideon brandished the blackened dagger dripping tar-like blood down her arm, staring down the demon until it retreated through its portal, back to its own realm. She took a step back, taking her boot off the severed demon's hand, which still twitched and writhed, as the portal snapped closed, leaving a brimstone smoke in its wake.

With the dagger still in her grip, she spun around and faced the other hulking, char-skinned demon, looming over her, the red glow from its eyes illuminating her. She held up the dagger with a chastising glower. "Ba'ermun-ti, you know better than to run off with those kids. New York is no place for you," she scolded gently.

The demon lowered its head abashedly, and Mina severed the coarse rope that had bound its wrists. Once the rope was cut, a summoning portal yawned open behind the demon, and through the opening, Mina could make out the smoldering crags and bubbling, steaming pools of its home.

"Go on. Your parents have been worried sick."

Mina watched the oversized briquette

shamble through the portal before it closed, as she fixed her ponytail, whipping her straight black hair back into place. She pulled a zippered plastic bag from her jean jacket pocket to collect the severed demon's hand, which had thankfully stopped convulsing, and tossed it into her canvas sling bag, along with her dagger, which she cleaned off with a cleaning wipe.

Mina looked down at her all-black outfit, to make sure there were no tell-tale blood spatter or scorch marks from her brief encounter, then vacated the empty warehouse and headed towards the nearest subway station.

Once homeward bound on the train, she let her mind drift for a moment, to think of happier things. She thought of her big brother Adam, who had returned recently after years of working abroad. She thought of her friends, the Crain twins and Cindy, who supplied many of her leads and referrals. She thought of her new dog, who always made her smile with his beautiful ice-blue eyes and luxuriant, black-marked silver coat, no matter how awful or exhausting her day had been.

Sure enough, her Siberian husky was waiting at the door when she got back home to her apartment, sitting patiently, with his vulpine tail sweeping back and forth like a flag. She gave him a quick scratch behind his ears and a kiss on his forehead, as she did for most of the past month since she took him in, took off her shoes and went to her bedroom to change.

She had just pulled her clean tee shirt over her head when she heard a knock at the door. Not the security buzzer from the front entrance downstairs, but her actual apartment door. Suspiciously, she tiptoed to the door, and she reached for the deadbolt but paused momentarily when she heard her old classmate's voice: "Hey, Mina. It's Jack. Jack Mackay, from high school? I know you're in there, and I really need your help. Didn't you get my message?"

*Yeah, I did, you creep.* She threw the deadbolt and backed away from the door when Jack started banging his fist furiously against it. He may have even started kicking it, but she wasn't waiting by the door for him to break in. After the evening she had had, she was not in the mood for uninvited guests.

She ran back to the bedroom and grabbed her baseball bat, gripping it tightly, only loosening her hold slightly when the banging at the door stopped. She stepped to the peephole and peered through it, to make sure that Jack had really gone, as she didn't trust the silence. She only released the breath she was holding when she was satisfied that she wouldn't be bothered again.

How had he even found her, anyway? Her home phone number wasn't listed, and she didn't do business either by phone or at home, anyway, so when her land line rang late the night before, she had let it go to voicemail, expecting some telemarketer or robocall message. Honestly, when she listened to Jack's frantic message, she had been more than a little disturbed by it. He sounded manic and distracted, nothing like the Jack Mackay she knew from high school, the popular class president who barely talked to the misfits like Mina. Still, she wasn't convinced that it wasn't just one of his childish pranks: *hey, let's leave the wannabe chink witch a vague, cryptic message about demons and curses, and have a good laugh when she calls back.*

Mina looked at the silver and black husky stretched out on her couch. "Big help you are, doofus."

The dog raised his head and stared at her with his black-lined ice-blue eyes, answering her with a low muttering growl. He barely moved except to flick his tail and back paws a smidge, as she settled next to him on the couch.

For a rescued stray, he certainly acted like he had always enjoyed the comforts of a cozy home; perhaps a more spacious one than a small one-bedroom apartment, too, guessing from how his brush tail or lanky frame was always knocking something off her bookshelf or coffee table during his first couple of weeks living with her. He had even been trained at some point to use the toilet, apparently.

"Why are guys such jerks?" she asked, resting her head on the back of the couch, her long black ponytail hanging off the cushion. "Not all of them, but most," she mumbled tiredly, thinking of the handful she knew who were decent and smart. "If you were human, would you be one of the good ones, or would you be an ass, too?"

Mina picked up her head at the sound of her phone buzzing with an incoming text. As the husky lay back down with a relaxed, rumbling sigh, she glanced and frowned at the message from her brother: *The axe has fallen … I've been let go.*

She called her big brother back immediately, her own troubles forgotten. "Adam? Are you okay?"

"Yeah, just...you know?" Adam said, his voice as tired as Mina's. "I should've known that this was coming, after being recalled to New York. I've been back for all of what...two weeks?"

"You'll be okay," Mina said, hearing the frustration in her brother's voice. She was the *mei-mei*, the little sister, and he was the *ge-ge*, the big brother, and he had always been the more secure and responsible one, both financially and emotionally, so this had to be a jarring upset for him, despite how calm he sounded. "Your company's a cesspool of shit, and you're better off away from that soul-sucking place. Did you want to get a drink, or something?"

"No, not tonight, thanks. I'll probably turn in early, since I have to go into the office and turn in my security badge and equipment first thing in the morning," Adam replied. "I just wanted to tell you, to psych myself up before I call Mom and Dad. Maybe we can do drinks tomorrow night?"

*Drinks sound awesome.* "Sure. Text me when you get off work," she said, then cringed at her misstatement. "Sorry, I meant..."

Adam was laughing. "How was *your* work today?"

"Not bad. I did a sage smudge for a family moving into a place in Williamsburg, and a consult for a woman in Hoboken who thinks her upstairs neighbor is a werewolf. He's not; he's just very hirsute and leads wildlife tours during full moons, so he keeps weird hours on those nights."

"Any recent run-ins with demons or devils?"

She knew he was half-teasing, but she always answered him honestly, because he was the closest she had to a confessor. "Had to send a bunch of demon spawn home tonight," she said, thinking of the young hooligans she had shooed off earlier. "Oh, met a banshee last night. I let her vent a little and bought her a drink, and we went on our separate ways."

"Sounds like you're keeping busy. I'm glad *one* of us is."

Mina thought of Jack Mackay showing up on her doorstep uninvited. "Oh, yeah, it's great. I have potential clients beating down my door. Get some sleep, tell Mom and Dad I said 'hi.' We'll talk tomorrow."

*SCREECH!*

Then a stomach-churning crunch of metal and the deafening crash of shattering glass, followed by a blinding flash. *Shit, is this how I die?*

Orbs of glowing white light danced around Adam's head, drawing him towards a brighter doorway in front of him, just out of reach.

*No, Mister Xing*, whispered a sweet, child-like voice. *It isn't time.*

Adam Xing awoke with a start, gasping for breath, his body stiff and aching with tension. The visceral shrieks of crumpling metal continued to echo in his head, long after he had awakened and released his balled fists. The white lights that had blinded him in his dream slowly faded to black.

Sitting up in the darkness, Adam slowly

remembered that he had fallen asleep in front of his television, with his phone still in his hand after disconnecting with his parents. He was safe, and the sounds that haunted him in his dreams were from weeks ago. He was back in New York City, where he was born and raised. His little sister, Mina, was about forty blocks north and west of his apartment, and presumably sleeping.

The television was still on, on a channel with some talk show guest boasting about his endorsement for a "testosterone-boosting male enhancement" supplement. *Whatever the hell that is.* Adam had no inkling of the people on the television, whether they were athletes, actors or something else—he hadn't paid attention to celebrity or entertainment news in years, focusing whatever spare energy he had on work.

At least, the television distracted him from his dream, where he had been replaying the accident that had left him with a concussion and a broken finger. Back in Singapore, the hospital doctors had told him that he was lucky to walk away from the car crash with just minor injuries, unlike his colleague, who had been driving and had died at the scene of the head-on crash.

More than the crash itself, Adam was haunted by the memories of seeing his closest friend from work pinned to the driver's seat, trying to speak while blood burbled from his mouth and the gash across his neck, a chunk of wiper blade embedded in his throat. From Adam's angle, his friend had looked nearly decapitated, and given the grotesqueness of the mortal wound, that would've been a quicker, more merciful end.

Adam had been recalled to the home office in New York after his overnight stay in the hospital, then summoned into his supervisor's midtown office, where he was notified that he was being transitioned off his projects so that he could begin a mandatory medical leave.

For the two weeks that Adam was back in New York, his days and most evenings were filled with meetings to update his team members and business liaisons about what was still outstanding from his work load. He attended his colleague's funeral during one of the weekends and was uncomfortably aware of the stares and whispers from friends and his colleague's family: how was it that Adam was barely hurt, when his friend had died so horribly that the services necessitated a closed casket?

Sensing the growing professional and personal distance from his colleagues, and without his regular involvement in his projects, Adam watched his role diminish, so that when his manager had called him that evening to let him know that his group was being downsized, Adam had felt little sentiment or resentment in his company's decision. He listened to his supervisor's standard speech and summary of termination benefits with detached numbness and few comments or questions.

Adam sat in the dark, with his knees drawn to his chest, still feeling alien in his apartment. He had spent more time abroad in the past three years than he ever had spent there, which was a shame. It was a nice, compact unit, a junior-four one-bedroom on a high floor, with a partial view of Washington Square Park, mostly paid for with savings accumulated through years of frugality, his dad's ferocious negotiating skills, and a loan from his younger sister that Mina was unlikely to ever ask him to repay.

*Mina Xing Gideon, married at twenty-two, divorced at twenty-three.* She had gotten married shortly after college, to Adam's college roommate who had graduated with him a few years earlier. Both sets of parents had been upset by Mina and Malcolm's rashness, and Adam had tried to talk Mina out of her decision to settle down so quickly, but her mind was set, so Adam wished them the best. Mina and Adam's parents had been more troubled by Malcolm Gideon's drinking and partying ways than the young couple's age, and when Mina and Malcolm divorced, amicably, less than six months after their nuptials, the Xings accepted the news with more relief than disappointment.

Neither sibling fit the traditional roles their Chinese family had envisioned for them. Mina was always the nonconformist rebel, who followed her heart more than her head. Four years older, Adam was her polar opposite, more intellectual and level-headed, but he was too busy with his career to bother with relationships. *How's that working out for you, moron?* he berated himself. *Thirty-one and never even had a serious girlfriend.*

Knowing the day that lay ahead of him, Adam was tempted to stay up, but he got to his feet and trudged to the bedroom for a last few hours of sleep. He passed the picture window with its view of the New York skyline at one end and a sliver of Washington Square Park at the other, the twinkling glow of the park lamps illuminating the arch. *Things could definitely be worse.*

He knew that he would be in a funk for a while, but he and Mina had endured far worse, and it was always easier when they had each other for emotional support. For the past two weeks, he had barely seen or talked with her; even though his office was within walking distance of her building, she was hardly ever home, but he still liked knowing that she was close by, geographically. They weren't on different ends of the globe anymore.

So what, that he was losing his job? He was back home in New York City, his favorite city in the world, with his tough, sassy little sister in his corner, with more time now to reconnect with her and really find out how she was spending her days and her life. Things were going to change for the better. *I can feel it.*

*This is going to be a good night. I can feel it.*

A few blocks from Pennsylvania Station in midtown, Malcolm Gideon was feeling great, as he was sipping his fourth scotch. He had forgotten about the three beers he had during happy hour, while he was watching the evening's band set up, but he usually didn't keep track of how much he drank, anyway.

He brushed back his overgrown, chestnut-colored hair and closed his tired blue eyes for a moment, just relaxing and listening to the band's cover of some late-80's power ballad. The sound system wasn't great, but the band was decent, and he was feeling jovial.

Malcolm opened his eyes and caught the glance of a cute brunette who was just his type: golden skin, dark almond-shaped eyes and a short, straight black bob.

"What are you drinking?" he asked, as the girl perched on the stool next to him.

"Cosmo?" she ordered, and Malcolm nodded to the bartender.

"Never seen you here before?" she shouted over the deafening drums and wailing guitar.

"Just in town for a few days," Malcolm smiled, his blue eyes twinkling. "I'm heading back home to Boston after the weekend."

"Oh, you're from Boston?" she asked, as she took a sip of her cosmopolitan.

*Jesus, isn't that what I just said?* "Yeah. Where are you from?"

"Me? I'm from the Island," she said.

Malcolm was unfamiliar with the New Yorker vocabulary. He was sure that Mina had told him something about the areas of metropolitan New York City, but he couldn't remember any of the details, if he had ever really paid attention in the first place. "Which island is that? Staten Island, or Long Island?"

The girl laughed, and he was surprised that he could hear her shrillness over the music of the band. "Long Island, duh!"

The more he heard her talk, the more grating he found her voice, and he was disappointed in himself, that he had been taken in, once again, by the features that had originally attracted him to his ex-wife. His melancholy and his judgment were always worse after a few drinks, but he couldn't help himself. Mina was one in a million, and he was an ass to give her up without making more of an effort. In his fondest fantasy, he would meet her by chance on the streets of New York or Boston, and she would remember that she still loved him and was willing to give him another chance...

"Thanks for the drink, but I gotta go," the girl said, pulling him back to reality. "I have to catch my train, so I can get my beauty sleep and get up early for work."

"It was nice to meet you," he said, ironically, not bothering to ask her name.

"What?" she shouted back.

He shook his head. "Have a good night," he shouted back dismissively, and watched her leave with her friends.

*Well, that was a waste of time and ten bucks*, he said to himself, as he slipped a twenty across the bar for the last drinks.

"Do you need me to call you a car?" the bartender asked, looking at him with concern.

Malcolm shook his head. "Nah, I'm good."

He felt a little better once he was outside in the bracing evening air. He liked New York. It was dirtier and more crowded than Boston, but it was glitzy and shiny, especially at night. With the blinding billboards and marquees lighting up the midtown buildings, one could almost overlook the piles of garbage and garbage-like makeshift shelters that crowded the sidewalks.

Walking down towards his hotel across from Penn Station, Malcolm felt his pace slowing and his heart racing, as his breathing became more labored. As he saw the crosswalk light change, he followed the lights in a daze, as they blurred

12

together and took the shape of an angel in glowing white, with dark almond eyes and a short black bob.

*You're doing so well, Malcolm*, the angel smiled, beckoning him closer with a wave. *She's so close now, and she'll cry when she sees you!*

Malcolm paused mid-step, and the pedestrians behind him shoved him aside roughly with rude reprimands, but he was focused on the angel. *Happy crying?*

The angel stopped floating and stepped closer to him. *Remember why you're doing this. Quickly, now, before you lose your nerve!*

Spurred by the figure's encouragement, Malcolm found newfound energy. Although he had already reached the other side of the street, and standing just a few feet from the revolving doors of his hotel, Malcolm spun unsteadily on his heel and ran back into the street, into the path of a rushing yellow minivan cab.

Malcolm heard the crack of his bones, and of his skull slapping down on the asphalt crosswalk, but he didn't feel nearly as much pain as he would've expected. He heard car horns, and screaming passersby.

As his eyes began to dim, he thought he saw the angel figure darken, until it was a black silhouette, clutching its sides in hysterical laughter. He couldn't see its features, but he heard its low, cruel chuckling, then a familiar, shrill female voice, from the opposite end of the crosswalk, above the other noises.

It was the girl from the bar, standing with her friends, snorting her disgust. "Fuck it. You guys can stick around and watch this shitshow,

but if I don't catch this train, the next one to
Ronkonkoma won't be for another hour, so I'm
out! Bye-eee!"

# Chapter 2

Near Madison Square Park, Alexandra Crain—
"Alex" professionally, but "Xani" to her close
friends—was lost in her thoughts, peering out the
window of her office on the 20th floor. It felt as
though she had been standing there for hours,
just marveling at how quiet and still New York
looked from her window. She could almost ignore
the bustle of cars and trucks far, far below, still
in the throes of the morning rush hour.

Xani had awoken that morning alone, just as
she had every day for the past four years, ever
since Cyril left. For some reason, however, this
morning felt different. Even with her brother
sleeping in the other bedroom, the apartment felt
eerily empty and quiet. So much, that she left
earlier than the usual eight o'clock and sought
refuge here, in her office of glass, steel and
leather.

"Good morning, Miss Crain," Morgan greeted
in his bright, cheerful tenor voice, setting a sheaf
of correspondence on her desk. "You left the
apartment early; I only woke up when I heard
you lock the door."

"I didn't want to disturb you," Xani smiled at
her twin brother in turn. His long, flame-red hair
was shaggy and unkempt, and Xani combed

through her own curls instinctively, as though the effort would miraculously fix Morgan's mop. "The Blackstone Group reps have confirmed for lunch at Union Square Café at twelve-thirty. You want to take that one?"

Morgan nodded. "While I do that, you can text Mom back. She's going to Saint Petersburg this morning and asked if we wanted her to bring back anything."

"We should say something, otherwise, she'll just bring us back some garish tchotchke." She glanced at the news scrolling across her workstation, including an announcement about restructuring and downsizing of Global Pacific Trust's Private Equity research division. She was only familiar with the company because she had heard Mina mention it in the past, as where Adam worked. *Used to work.*

Morgan's green eyes didn't miss the quick diversion. "You read about Global Pacific?"

"Yeah, sucks for Adam," Xani grimaced, her own green eyes hooded. "But he's smart and ambitious, so he'll be fine." She caught Morgan's sly grin. "What?"

"Now that he's back in town, and has some free time, you're dying to ask him out," Morgan said, perching on Xani's windowsill and deliberately ignoring the urgently ringing phone. "Well?"

Xani glanced at the phone, her attention torn between Morgan and work responsibilities. "You're imagining things."

"Bullshit!" Morgan laughed. "Let it go to voicemail," he said, glancing at the number on the display. "It's just the lawyer from Garrison

Brothers again. He said he needed an answer by end of day yesterday."

Xani sighed. "Then he shouldn't have messengered the contract over at four-thirty. He can sweat a little."

"Agreed, especially since he was supposed to send it over last week," Morgan said blithely. "His lack of planning is not our emergency." He crossed his lean, freckled arms and smiled at his older twin. "You can lie to yourself, if you want, but we both know you've never completely gotten over Adam Xing."

Adam could tell that Mina really wanted to fling his phone across the lounge, but she refrained and just slid it back towards him, after she reviewed the details of the severance package that he had received from his company. "So, that's what your pound of flesh is worth to them," she remarked coldly.

Adam laughed at his little sister's protective outrage, as he tucked the phone in the pocket of his jacket. "It's fine. It's a more generous package than other companies give during their layoffs." He lay his head back on the red velvet settee, admiring the crimson pumpkin lanterns dangling overhead.

The Red Lotus was certainly a quieter, more elegant establishment than the dive bars they used to frequent in their college days, and the margaritas were made to order—top-shelf white tequila, simple syrup and plenty of fresh lime juice—not the slushy, day-glow concoctions mixed and served out of plastic pitchers. Instead of tacos, Adam dined on ceviche and crispy cubes of

Spanish tortilla, as well as Mina's order of potstickers and arancini balls.

Adam had wanted to stay away from his old company's hangouts, where he risked encountering former colleagues, so Mina had recommended the Red Lotus. With most of the nearby Broadway shows and musicals already underway, the lounge would remain quiet until the arrival of the post-theatre crowd later, so it was nice to be able to talk without having to shout.

"It might have been expedient and what the shareholders wanted, but that doesn't make it right," Mina frowned.

Adam smiled patiently. "That's how companies work. The corporate life isn't for everyone, but it suited me, for a while. Now, I think I just need a break."

"That, we agree on," Mina rejoined, nudging the last potsticker towards him. "Go spend some time with Mom and Dad in San Francisco—a week with them, and you'll forget all your adulting skills."

"Do the touristy stuff, like stare at sea lions and ride the trolley, then come back and start the job hunt?"

Mina shrugged. "Look, your package covers your bills for the next year. Why don't you take a couple of months to really relax? You haven't taken a real vacation since you started working," Mina said, raising her vodka and cranberry. "Here's to a fresh start and a clean slate."

"*Ganbei, mei-mei*," Adam toasted his little sister, and finished his gin and tonic. "Maybe I can just forget that the last three years at Global ever happened."

"You don't want to do that," Mina warned.

"Why not?" he asked.

"We learn from mistakes," Mina said. "Move on, but never forget."

Adam heard the lingering pain in his sister's soft voice. "You're right. I don't want to forget what I did wrong."

"Or the wrongs that were done *to* you," Mina reminded. "Not everything that happens to you is your fault." She pointed to the scab over his eyebrow. "That's looking better. How's your finger?"

Adam wriggled his splinted left ring finger. "I'm tempted to take the bandage off already. It itches like crazy." He steeled himself to ask Mina something that had been preoccupying his thoughts. "You deal with ghosts and spirits from time to time, right?" The waiter delivered another gin and tonic for him, and vodka and cranberry for Mina. "Excuse me, we didn't order another round?"

"Compliments of the lady at the bar," the waiter said and withdrew.

Mina shrugged and finished her drink and reached for the second, without even a glance at the bar.

"You're not curious about who sent us drinks?" Adam asked, eyeing the gin and tonic with suspicion.

"The drinks came directly from the bar, not some rando, so they're safe," Mina said, taking a sip from her fresh glass. "You were asking about ghosts and spirits. Yes, I deal with a few different types. Why?"

"I'm trying to figure out if my concussion knocked something out, or back in," Adam said. "Since the crash—"

A tall, curvy redhead in a fitted white blouse and dark gray pencil skirt, moving with a manager's authority, approached the table. "How are you both doing this evening?" she greeted warmly.

Adam took a slow sip from his gin and tonic, as Mina laughed, "Since when are you so formal?"

"I'm always formal with new customers," the flame-haired Amazon said with a teasing lilt.

"Thank you for the drinks," Adam said. "I'm presuming that these came from you?"

The woman giggled, and Adam stirred at the familiarity of the sound. Aside from her glorious red curls, her features were hard to discern in the dim glow of the scarlet pumpkin lights, and he was trying not to stare.

"Yes, the drinks are from me. I hope that wasn't too presumptuous, but you guys looked like you needed another round," she admitted. "Remind me or Morgan later, we have something for you," she said to Mina, as she strolled off to greet the next tables.

Adam admired her curvy silhouette, outlined by the fitted contours of her tailored clothes. "How do you know her?"

"You know her, too," Mina cajoled, then laughed at Adam's befuddled look. "That's Xani Crain. I know I told you about her; she and her brother helped me get settled when I came back to New York. You *must* remember," she prodded. "Alexandra and Morgan, from high school, the guidance counselor's office?"

Adam didn't have to think long, but he was surprised by his realization. "Alex Crain?" *Holy crap!* He remembered her and her younger twin as quirky, slightly awkward college students who worked at the school as peer counselors. Her hair was red and curly back then, too, but her grooming efforts had usually left her looking like she had tangled copper wire atop her head...

"Yeah, *that* Alex Crain," Mina murmured with amusement at Adam's wide-eyed reaction. "It's crazy how people can change in a few short years, isn't it? She and Morgan are both doing well as functional adults. They helped me find my building."

"Didn't you tell me she was working for a security firm somewhere?" Adam asked. At the time, he hadn't thought anything of it—it was just one of several updates about mutual acquaintances that Mina had looked up when she returned to Manhattan.

"No, you idiot," Mina shot back, flicking a drop of ice water at him. "I told you she was *starting up* a security firm, with Morgan. They do corporate and private events, safe room installations ... the full range of services."

"So, they do security for this place, too?"

Mina shook her head. "No, they co-own the Red Lotus with Cindy McManus."

"McManus," Adam mused. "I remember *Cyril* McManus from your class: tall black guy, captain of track and field... You had a crush on him, as I recall. Any relation?"

"Sort of. Cyril and Xani were together for a while, then Cyril decided a few years ago to transition and now goes by 'Cindy,'" Mina said.

"It's fine, they're all still friends, and Cindy's actually, really, super-model hot. Too bad I didn't graduate with the class—the ten-year reunion promises to be pretty lively."

Adam grunted. "I completely missed my ten-year reunion."

"It was pretty staid," Mina answered readily. "Crain Private Security was working that event, too. It was three years ago, this past summer." At Adam's inquiring glance, she shrugged. "What? It's my job to know things. Besides, the Crains keep me on retainer, just in case."

Adam laughed. "For what? An emergency faerie infestation or a demon attack?"

Mina grinned wryly. "This is New York City. Anything can happen, at any hour."

The hours passed remarkably fast, and when the Red Lotus started getting busy again, Adam looked down at his phone and saw that it was half past eleven. The lounge's late-weeknight crowd consisted mostly of theatre talent and fans, with a line out of the door of revelers waiting to get in.

Out of consideration for their hosts and the Lotus's other customers, Mina and Adam decided finally to vacate their table, but they stayed under the Red Lotus's illuminated awning to feel a draft of the warm air from inside, as they decided where to go next. As the early October evening breeze slapped against him, Adam noticed that Mina had ducked behind Micah, the brawny, deeply-tanned bouncer. Micah didn't seem to notice or care, as he continued to check IDs and bags at the door.

"What are you doing?" Adam asked.

"He blocks the wind for me," Mina said, huddling behind Micah, as the bouncer laughed, his shaved head reflecting the overhead glow. "You should stand here. He's like a space heater."

"No, I'm good. Thanks." Adam checked the time on his phone. "How are the subways running at this hour?"

"Why don't you stay over?" Mina offered. "I've barely seen you since you got back from Singapore, and you haven't even met Arkady yet."

"I've hardly spent any time in my own apartment," he said. "I think I've only used it to sleep, shower and change, since I got back."

"So, you can do that at my place," she said. "Come on, get a change of scenery."

"Yeah, no offense, but Washington Square Park is prettier than your neighbors' garbage piles and fire escapes."

"Ha-ha, funny," she said dryly. "My place is still better than where you lived in Hong Kong: it doesn't reek of dried fish or have a view of the neighbors' drying underwear. Come on, it's just a few blocks up."

"You guys alright?" called a voice over Adam's shoulder. "Just loitering?"

Adam recognized Morgan Crain's light, lyrical voice. "Wow, I haven't you in ages!" Morgan had grown taller over the past ten years, but he was still boyishly lean.

"It's been a few years." Morgan and Adam exchanged a handshake. "Welcome back to New York, buddy. You should've popped into the back office to say hello. Cindy and I were just going over the Lotus's books for the month."

"'Going over books,'" Mina said with a doubtful smile. "Is that what you and Cindy are calling it now?" A bright pink hue flooded Morgan's fair skin at once. "I'm just teasing, Morgan. Cindy's *way* out of your league."

"God, you're just like the bratty little sister I never wanted," Morgan quipped. "Does she do this to you, too?"

Adam shrugged, as Mina chortled. "I'm trying to convince Adam to come up to the apartment."

Under the bright lights of the Red Lotus's awning, Morgan's features looked as Adam recalled, just a little more mature. His red hair fell in crisp curls, and his green eyes were just as piercing as Adam recalled, and he imagined the same was true for Alex—*Xani*. "It's not that bad," Morgan joked, "apart from all the chanting and incense—"

Mina slapped his arm. "Shut up! You're not helping."

He laughed. "Xani has the files you wanted, by the way, somewhere," he said. "You want them now, or should we slip them under your door later?"

"I probably won't look at them till later, so there's no rush. Thanks for looking into it," she said.

As they left the Red Lotus, heading towards Mina's apartment, Adam bumped her shoulder. "So, are the two of you, like…"

Mina laughed. "With Morgan? No, he's too good for me." At Adam's scolding look, she amended, "I don't mean he's better than me, or anything like that. I mean he's a genuinely *good* guy: nice, thoughtful, volunteers at shelters... half the stuff I do would scare the shit out of him."

As Xani tucked the envelope under her arm and rushed up Tenth Avenue towards Mina's apartment building, her thoughts kept returning to Adam. She was a little thrown at seeing him, more than she had expected or wanted.

Xani recalled when she and Morgan had met the siblings the first time, in the guidance counselor's office where the twins volunteered. She and Morgan were sophomores in college, Adam was a college junior in Boston and home on break, and Mina was four years behind him, a junior in high school.

Mina had been there to talk to the counselor about an issue with one of her teachers, with Adam there for emotional support. From what Xani had overheard of the hushed conversation, it sounded as though Mina had been propositioned and wanted the school to address the teacher's inappropriate behavior.

The school had dragged out its investigation over weeks, over which time the four of them became friends, and Xani started developing a crush on Adam. He was more mature and poised than most guys she knew, and he treated her like a lady; maybe because Mina was usually around when they spoke and he wanted to show her what a gentleman was, he was always respectful, funny and sweet.

In the end, despite Mina and Adam's efforts, no one was disciplined. If anything, Mina was ostracized for accusing a well-liked, tenured teacher, as no one else stepped forward to corroborate her claims. Mina transferred to another school over the winter break, while Adam returned to his school in Boston. End of story.

Until four years ago, when Mina Xing—now Mina Gideon—called Crain Private Security out of the blue. Xani and Cyril had just broken up, as a couple, and Mina had just ended a brief marriage and had returned to New York to get a fresh start.

Their friendship was rekindled easily, as it felt as though Mina had never been away. She was still as feisty and independent as Xani had recalled her, with Mina's teenage idealism tempered a little by a more worldly cynicism. Mina had seemed more solemn and focused than most young adults in their twenties, which Morgan found appealing, but Mina was careful to keep their relationship a platonic one.

Xani wondered if she could manage the same with Adam. Over the years, she had seen him in pictures that Mina shared, so she recognized him at once, but his actual, physical presence elicited a familiar flutter in her stomach that she hadn't felt in ages. Morgan was right, damn it. She had never really gotten over her crush.

She rang the doorbell and waited a couple of seconds for the buzzer before she went inside. The door release felt a little hesitant, so she made a mental note to have one of the guys check the mechanism in the morning. Since she had done the original security system installation, she actually had her own master code for building access, but she had rung the doorbell as a courtesy, so that Mina knew she was coming in.

The building was a three-story brownstone, in one of the few areas in Manhattan where such quaint little buildings still existed. The owner had been a friend of Xani and Morgan's parents, who wanted to sell it quickly for cash and move down to Florida without putting anything extra into upgrading the outdated electrical wiring, removing the last traces of lead and asbestos from the late 19th-century building, or inconveniencing the existing tenants. At the same time, Mina was looking to find a place to live and had some cash from her divorce settlement, and was fine living with lead and asbestos in her floors and walls, as long as she didn't have to deal with roaches, rats… *or people sleeping outside her door?*

Xani reached the third-floor landing ready for a fight, as she spied a vagrant lying outside Mina's apartment. As she got closer, though, she noticed the pristine condition of the man's expensive sneakers and crisp, clean lines of his designer jeans. *This isn't a homeless guy*, she realized, as she tapped the man's foot with her shoe, to try to rouse him. The man remained unmoving, and Xani realized what she was seeing. *Shit!*

She crouched down by the man's head and didn't see any marks or blood, but the man's open eyes were dull and unseeing, and his skin had started to take on a gray pallor. The features looked slightly familiar, but Xani was trying very hard not to stare at the dead man's face.

Mina's door opened, as her laughter floated out into the hall. "What's taking you so long,

Xani?"

Instinctively, Xani got to her feet and tried to block her view. "Call 911! We need police and an ambulance," she shouted, holding up her hand to keep Mina from coming out. "Stay in here, you don't need to come out for this."

"Oh, my God!" Mina cried, as Xani spied Adam in the background, calling emergency services. Mina looked past her. "Shit, is that Jack Mackay?"

*Jack Mackay. Fuck.* That was why she recognized the man. Xani had photos of him inside the envelope that she come to deliver, which suddenly felt very heavy. The door to the second-floor apartment opened, and Xani moved to block the stairs. "It's alright, Missus Krantz," she called down gently to the white-haired tenant in her pastel housecoat and fuzzy slippers, staring up towards her. "Mina and I will take care of it."

"It's that troubled young man, again, isn't it," the old woman said sadly. "He was coming here all week, and I told him to leave Miss Xing alone. How did he even get in the building?"

"I don't know, Missus Krantz," Xani said, more calmly than she felt. "The police are on their way. You can go back inside." Once the door closed and she was confident that Millie Krantz would not be venturing out of her apartment again, Xani stepped around the body and stood at Mina's door.

"You asked for information about Jack Mackay," she said, clutching the envelope. "You didn't say he was stalking you."

"I didn't know what he was doing," Mina

said, holding out her hand solicitously. "I thought he wanted to hire me, but I didn't want to take the job without knowing more about him. So, do I get the file, or not?"

"If you know too much, the police may start wondering about your connection and interest," Xani said, holding it out of Mina's reach.

"Give me the file, Xani," she said grimly. "He died outside my apartment, in the building I own, and there are witnesses to the fact that he was looking for me, so they're going to wonder anyway. Let *me* worry about the police."

# Chapter 3

Adam heard the panting and felt the steamy breath against his ear for a moment, and he blindly shoved the massive beast off his pillow before he was able to sit up on Mina's couch. The oversized silver and black wolf-like creature simply rolled over to give him some room but gave no indication that he would be yielding the sofa to him.

"Oh, good, you're awake," Mina called from the kitchen. "I made some tea, and there are some bagels on the counter, butter and cream cheese in the fridge. I took Arkady out already, so don't let him sucker you into another W-A-L-K."

Adam glanced at the husky. "He doesn't even have a collar. Aren't you afraid he's going to take off?"

"He doesn't need a collar when he's in here, just when he's out, so it's attached to his leash," she said, pointing to the woven leather leash hanging by the door. "He's never shown an interest in leaving on his own, so I've never bothered forcing him to wear it inside."

Adam got to his feet and stretched, glancing at his phone, and he marveled that Mina was already dressed to go out, despite it being before eight o'clock. "Where are you off to, this early?"

"I got an early morning text. I have to go down to the medical examiner's office for an identification," Mina said, pouring a cup of tea for Adam.

Adam wondered about his sister's mysterious business network, that she should be summoned to the morgue by text. "I thought all the stuff with Jack Mackay was cleared up last night," Adam said, perching on one of the counter barstools and reaching into a brown paper bag for a soft, warm bagel. Sesame, their favorite.

"It was," Mina said, pulling her long black hair into a ponytail. "I've been asked to go ID someone else."

"Someone else just died, that you know?" Out of the corner of his eye, Adam noticed that the dog had parked his furry rump on the floor next to him, gazing up plaintively with his icy blue eyes. "Who?"

"Malcolm Gideon," Mina answered quietly.

Adam was speechless, and even Arkady seemed to stare blankly, for a moment. "Malcolm's dead? But wait, you're not his next of kin."

"His family is in Boston," Mina said. "Once I confirm that it's him, the police will notify his parents."

"I'll go with you," Adam offered, taking a sip of the tea. "Let me just get dressed."

"Are you sure?" Mina asked. "For your first official day out of work, wouldn't you rather binge-watch some TV or play video games or something?"

"I'll have plenty of time for that, later." Adam lobbed a chunk of bagel over Arkady's head, and he caught it effortlessly. "If you need moral support, I want to be there for you. Besides, I knew Malcolm longer than you; if anything, *I* should be the one doing the identification."

First to arrive in the office, Morgan set a cup of Xani's favorite almond milk caramel latte on her desk on his way to his desk. He was halfway through his unread emails before he heard the familiar jingle of his sister's keychain. He heard her happy squeak before he saw her appear in his doorway.

"Thank you, Morgan. You're feeling generous?" she asked, raising her latte to him.

"You deserved a treat after dealing with Jack Mackay outside Mina's apartment last night," he said with a worried glance. "Are you okay?"

Xani nodded soberly, taking a quiet sip of the hot, sweet coffee. "It was a shock to find him, but at least it wasn't gruesome, if that makes it any better. There didn't look to be any signs of an assault or struggle, but the ME still has to determine cause of death."

"I should've been the one to drop off the file with Mina, instead of you, but at least one of us was there first," he said. He knew Mina was tough, but seeing a dead body was never easy.

"Yeah, finding him was bad enough," Xani said. "The police and paramedics were there in the hallway and stairwell for a long while, and it was all a little overwhelming, but Adam and Mina both seemed okay when I left."

"That's good. They know they can call or text if they need anything?"

"Of course," Xani replied. "They probably

won't, but I made the offer."

"Thanks. Bob just texted, by the way," Morgan said, glancing at his workstation. "He'll try to get to Mina's building today to look at the doors, like you asked, but depending on what it is, he may have to finish it tomorrow?"

"The sooner, the better," Xani said. "I don't like that Mackay was able to sneak into Mina's building without permission, so I'd like to make sure it's secure."

"Agreed," Morgan said. He didn't like that Mina was so exposed in her own house, either.

They were interrupted by a buzzer from the lobby, and Morgan answered. "Yes?"

"Hey, Crains," greeted Mina's voice. "Finished up with the ME and found myself in the area. Got a minute?"

"For you, always," Morgan answered, a little too eagerly. He winced, as he disconnected, and Xani laughed.

"You hypocrite! You're teasing me about Adam, but you still can't work up the courage to even ask Mina out, and she's been here four years." Xani cut her lecture short, as Morgan buzzed Mina through the reception door. "To be continued," she muttered.

Mina took a seat in Morgan's guest chair. "First of all, thanks for sticking around last night, Xani. I usually just see the spirits, not their empty mortal coils," she said, the lightness of her voice concealing an edge.

"It was the least I could do," Xani replied. "How's Adam this morning?"

"Fine. He went back to his apartment after the appointment."

Morgan remembered the text that he and Xani had gotten that morning from Mina, about where she needed to be. "How did it go with the medical examiner?" he asked gently.

Mina shrugged. "Okay, I guess. It was sad to see Malcolm like that, but at least it didn't look like he was in pain or anything, when it happened. He was apparently hit by a minivan, but his blood alcohol was so high, his probably didn't even feel most of his injuries."

Morgan grimaced, recalling Mina's account of how Malcolm Gideon's drinking had affected their marriage, but recognized from her deep breath and roll of her shoulders that she had moved on, mostly. "They're sending him home to Boston?"

She nodded. "Probably over the weekend. His family will want to start arranging services for him, and there's no reason for him to stay in New York."

"Did you get a chance to look at the file for Jack Mackay?"

"A little. Dropped out of college, in and out of rehab. Traffic stops, multiple assault charges but never convicted. He lived out in Jersey, though, and we hadn't spoken since high school, so I'm still not sure how he found me, or why."

"Maybe he really was looking for supernatural help," Xani suggested. "He might not have known who you were."

"No, he knew," Mina frowned. "When he was banging on my door the other night, he asked if I remembered him from school. If he had just given me some details on what he needed, instead of stalking me and leaving nonsensical messages, I might have been able to help him."

"Well, he missed his chance," Morgan said. "I do feel bad for him and his family, but he was a bit of a jerk to you."

"A lot of people were, but high school is always like that," Mina said. "As for missing his chance," she said, "you know as well as I do, that life isn't always that linear."

Nearly twenty blocks south of Crain Private Security's offices, Adam got a pepperoni slice and a bottle of unsweetened iced tea from a pizzeria on Eighth Street and found a shady spot on a park bench near the fountain in Washington Square Park. He spent his lunch time watching the flow of the neighborhood, in and out of the New York University buildings that surrounded the park.

He missed New York-style pizza when he was away, almost as much as he missed the tap water. There was something magical about the thin, crisp, chewy crust under the tangy sauce and slightly toasted cheese, that very few places in the world could replicate. Pizza in Italy was sublime, of course, but Manhattan and Brooklyn were still his sentimental and personal favorite sources to get his fix.

He finished his pizza and dropped bits of crust on the ground for the quickly amassing sparrows and pigeons. The wild animals of the city were as impudent and cheeky as the people, judging by how close the birds and squirrels ventured for their chance to grab a morsel. Adam's stillness didn't help, as his calmness and quiet merely encouraged the animals to come closer.

After he had parted ways with Mina at the medical examiner's office, Adam had returned to his apartment to call their parents in California, three hours behind. As the phone rang, Adam had regarded his sleek modern furniture, that suited his high-rise apartment and his own preference for simplicity and efficiency, but he had to admit that there was something homey and comforting in Mina's deliberate clutter and soft, cozy furnishings.

Adam's chat with their mom had been brief, as they often were, but he felt better for the opportunity to hear their parents' voices, with their dad interjecting his thoughts in the background while their mom was talking. Their door was always open, they had wanted him to know, and they wanted him to visit…but only if *he* wanted to visit *them*.

Mina was right: it had been a really long time since Adam had gone on vacation. Since graduation, he had worked steadily, going from one company to the next. When he had been recruited for Global Pacific's research group, he thought he had found his perfect job; he enjoyed the work, the travel and the company of his colleagues. He didn't mind working strange hours to accommodate different time zones, and his lack of close relationships helped to simplify his work-life balance.

Adam didn't necessarily envy Mina's life, but he saw the appeal and advantages of setting down roots in a place, even a place as hectic as Manhattan's Hell's Kitchen. Adam knew that his sister's life was fraught with dangers and stresses that were intangible and unfathomable to him, but he also recognized that Mina had found her calling and was happy. And that part of Mina's life, maybe he did envy, just a little.

Sitting under the gold and copper autumnal canopies of the park's shade trees, Adam passed the day people-watching. It was something that he hadn't done in…ever, but he really didn't have anything better planned. He observed parents and nannies with their children, the NYU students who preferred studying and doing their homework in the brisk autumn air to spending their hours in their dorms, and the octogenarians playing chess as though they also had all the time in the world. Adam could tell the end of the school day by the throngs of adolescents who converged on the playground with their skateboards to practice their shredding and half-pipe maneuvers.

He noticed something else in the air, something that he wanted to ask Mina about the night before, but then Xani had distracted him, and he had completely put it out of his mind. He ignored it for now, reminding himself to ask Mina later, but he disregarded as a brief side effect of his concussion. Everything would probably be fine in another week or so, just like with his broken finger.

In a moment of restlessness, he unwound the dressing from around his ring finger, fully intending to rewrap his injury once he had a good look at it. He had only broken his finger a couple of weeks earlier, but it felt fine, and he was able to move and bend it without any pain or soreness. To his surprise, his finger looked like all the others on the hand, as though nothing had ever happened. Just to be safe, he rewrapped his finger and forgot about it.

He started back to his apartment when the sun started dipping towards the Hudson River. In the lobby, he spied a gorgeous bouquet of long-stemmed, peach-colored roses in an arrangement that overwhelmed the doorman's station. "Pretty, but not really your style, is it, Dave?" he quipped as he went to check his mailbox.

"Don't let my wife see it, that's for sure," the doorman muttered. "I'd never hear the end of how I never do anything that romantic for her."

Adam chuckled, but his thoughts went immediately to Xani Crain. She seemed the practical, self-reliant type, based on how she had taken charge the night before when emergency services arrived at Mina's apartment to collect Jack Mackay, but she also seemed genuinely concerned and fond of Mina. Plus, Xani was smart, funny and absolutely, breathtakingly gorgeous.

"You're brilliant, Dave," Adam grinned, heading for the elevator.

"Now, that's something I'll never hear from my wife," the doorman muttered. "Have a good night, Mister Xing."

Jonah, also recently called "Arkady," picked up his head from the sofa cushion and pricked his ears. It was an old, creaky building, but he had learned over the past month to distinguish between old building noises, live people noises and dead people noises. The dead didn't move air the same way and carried a different kind of smell.

He jumped off the couch where he spent most of his day, making an effort not to dislodge the fur-covered blanket that Mina tossed over the couch to keep it relatively clean. He might have been a dog, presently, but he still liked to be fastidious and polite. Mina was a cool roommate, and he did his best to make the arrangement an equitable one; he couldn't hold a job or clean house, in his current form, but he could help Mina in other ways.

*If she knew who or what I was, I wonder how she would take it.* He didn't understand what he had become, either, or whether he would be that way forever. Some days, he felt very canine and primal, and other days, he recalled very lucidly how it was to be human, but most days, his thoughts were a disorganized jumble of recollections from another life, and more recent memories of decimating a scrumptious knot of smoked rawhide on Mina's couch.

He knew his name was "Jonah", and he had agreed to check up on Mina as a favor to a cousin, when he was still human. At some point during his trip down to New York, he had been transformed into a dog, and he was still piecing the details of that night together, but he did somehow find his way to Mina Gideon's doorstep. He would eventually get around to figuring out what had happened to him, but in the meantime, he found that he liked his untroubled, simplified life.

Without a collar or a microchip, he was effectively a stray, but Mina apparently had a soft spot for big, fluffy, blue-eyed dogs like huskies, so she let him stay in the apartment with her while she checked "lost dog" flyers and posts around the neighborhood. By the end of the month, she had decided to keep him around.

Jonah didn't particularly like the name "Arkady"—the name was ruined for him by its association to an obnoxious old neighbor—but he could deal with it. When Mina had decided to keep him, she had tossed out a whole bunch of names, and this was at least a dignified, human-sounding name.

Navigating the floorboards that creaked less than the others, he cantered to the bedroom and saw the intruder: glowing and translucent, as with most spirits, with his back to the door as he looked over Mina's dresser of jewelry and trinkets. The apparition had some color, like a muted watercolor of what he had been in life. *Her rings aren't here*, the spirit was saying to himself. *Did she sell them, or does she still wear them?*

*Shit!* The fur on Jonah's back stiffened, as he recognized the voice and the dark mop of hair, and he bared his wolf-like fangs. *What the fuck are you doing here?*

*Wait a second. You can see me?* The ghost of Malcolm Gideon straightened. *I know that voice.* Malcolm turned around and stared at him in shock. *Holy shit, Jonah! You're a dog!*

*And you're dead*, Jonah snipped. *Aren't we a pair?*

Malcolm's ghost crouched to get a better look at him. *How long have you been like this?*

*Well, let's see. We last saw each other a little less than a month ago, so... almost a month.*

*You've been here all this time? How did this*

*happen?*

*Where can I go? I can't exactly go back to Boston looking like this,* Jonah said. *Even if I could talk, I couldn't explain what happened*, he said, trying to speak, but only able to emit a plaintive howl. *I fell asleep human and woke up like this.*

*And now you're living with my Mina,* Malcolm said, with a tinge of resentment, as he looked around the bedroom.

*Dude, look at me!* Jonah snapped. *I'm a fucking husky! And she's not 'your' Mina, by the way. You blew your chance with her years ago.*

Malcolm stood and crossed his arms. *Jonah Gideon, you piece of shit. You're in love with her, aren't you? For how long now, you bastard?*

Jonah didn't want to get into it with him. *What are you doing here, Malcolm? Mina said she had to go down to the medical examiner's office to identify your body.*

Malcolm looked anxious and troubled. *I needed to find Mina. I missed her. I was just having some drinks Wednesday night, you know? Just unwinding after the long train ride, and I was going to look her up in the morning. But then I got into an accident.*

Jonah stretched out across the doorway. *What aren't you telling me?*

*You're going to think I'm crazy*, Malcolm said, shaking his head.

*You're dead, and I'm a dog*, Jonah said. *This whole situation is jacked. Just tell me.*

Malcolm started, hesitantly. *I started having hallucinations. Like, dark, demonic visions, and voices telling me to kill my folks and people at work. Now that I'm dead, I don't get the visions anymore, but I think that Mina's still in danger.*

*Stop bullshitting me, cousin,* Jonah snarled.

*I'm not, I swear it! We have to find a way to tell her!*

*Lucky for you, she can talk to dead people,* Jonah said acridly, getting back to his feet, *so you can tell her yourself. In the meantime, get out of her bedroom. You may not be able to touch her, but that doesn't give you the right to be here, either.*

Malcolm laughed harshly, as he followed Jonah to the bedroom door. *Why the hell do you care what I do in her room?*

*You asked me to come to New York to keep an eye on her, so I'm doing what I promised,* Jonah said, quickening his pace as he heard familiar footsteps by the front door. He sat attentively by the door, and he greeted Mina with a soft stare and a wagging tail.

"Hi, handsome," she cooed, giving the top of his head a quick peck before she shut the door and slipped off her shoes. "Did you miss me?"

Jonah glanced down the hallway, where Malcolm's spirit loomed in the doorway of Mina's bedroom, his ghostly features twisted into a jealous glower.

To his surprise, Mina followed the direction of his gaze, and she started. "What the hell?" she gasped.

*You really can see me?* Malcolm seemed stunned.

"Yes, I can see and hear you," she said, her eyes narrowing. "Why are you in my bedroom?"

Jonah glared at him, too. *I warned you to*

*stay out of there.*

"And you," Mina said speculatively, glancing down at Jonah. "Your hackles are usually raised, and you're a little more restless when there's a spirit in the apartment, so do you know who he is?"

Jonah flashed his ice-blue eyes at his cousin. *Malcolm, don't—*

*He's my cousin, Jonah,* Malcolm announced with a smirk.

*You son-of-a-bitch,* Jonah said.

*That would be you,* Malcolm shot back nastily. *Literally.*

"Jonah," Mina said, taking a step back. "Jonah, your best man?" she shouted, her eyes going back and forth between them. "What the hell are *either* of you doing here in New York?" She dropped her phone and keys on a shelf by the door and took off her jacket, eyeing Malcolm. "I can't converse with Jonah, so you'll have to translate."

*I asked him to check on you,* Malcolm confessed. *When he didn't come back, I came to see you myself. I was worried about you.*

*You were a jealous, controlling bastard who couldn't let her go,* Jonah snarled.

"What did he say?" Mina asked, noticing Jonah's bared teeth.

*He thinks I should've stayed away,* Malcolm said. *But I think you're in danger. I can feel that something is wrong, that something is coming, and I came to warn you.*

"You should've stayed in Boston," she said. "You'd still be alive."

*You still care about me?* Malcolm asked

hopefully.

"You were my brother's best friend," she said bitterly. "Seeing your dead body today was really tough for him. I never told him what a total dick you were to me when you drank, or how you made me shut up when you got tired of hearing my voice."

*Did you hit her? You never told me about that*, Jonah said, his eyes on Malcolm.

Malcolm ignored Jonah and was trying to defend himself: *You were always nag—telling me that I drank too much. You knew, when I was buzzed, I wasn't in the right state of mind to listen to anyone.*

"So, you still think it's my fault that you hit me," Mina said coolly. "Great, even dead, you're still an asshole. Don't worry, Adam still remembers you as a nice guy."

She grabbed her keys and the woven leather leash with the collar already attached and crouched in front of Jonah. "Jonah, eh? You want to go for a walk with me? I need some fresh air, and you look like you could use some, too."

Jonah got to his feet and shook his coat and waited patiently as Mina fastened the collar around his neck. He could see Malcolm's derisive smirk at seeing him in such a docile, degrading situation, but he couldn't care less. As much as he had loved his cousin in life, right now, he was pretty pissed at Malcolm, too.

*I thought you wanted me to translate,* Malcolm called after Mina.

Mina paused with her hand on her doorknob. "I think I need a break from you. When we get back, we'll discuss how to help you move on." She opened her door and gave a disgusted snort. "What the fuck!"

Standing on Mina's doorstep was the spirit of Jack Mackay. Jonah had never met him, but he recalled the designer jeans and sneakers on the body in the hallway the night before, and the inquiries about his identity while he was being processed. Then, his growling, threatening voice, which Jonah recognized from voicemails and hearing it through the door.

*I told you I needed your help, you bitch!* Mackay screeched at her. *Now, it's too late! Are you happy?*

"Jack," Mina greeted, nonplussed. "If it's too late, then you don't need to be here, do you? Both of you," she said to Malcolm and Jack, "you can stay and wait for me, or get the hell out. But if you're still acting like assholes when I get back, you can fuck off and find yourself another medium to help you."

Mina let Jonah walk out ahead of her and shut the door behind her, and Mrs Krantz's door opened as they reached the second floor. Jonah liked Mrs Krantz: she reminded him of his maternal grandmother, smelling of simple white soap, old paperbacks and snickerdoodle cookies.

"Are you okay, Mina?" she called. "That sounded like a lot of yelling up there."

*Shut the door, Millie! She's fine,* came Mister Krantz's gravelly, wheezing voice from inside the apartment. Even though his widow couldn't hear or see him, Arthur Krantz's spirit stayed around to keep her company, and Jonah often heard her speaking aloud to him, too.

"I'm okay, Missus Krantz, thank you," Mina

said. "Do you need anything from the store, since I'm going out anyway?"

*How about some of those chocolate cherries you used to like so much?* Mister Krantz offered, even though his wife couldn't hear him. *Remember how I used to hide them in the fridge to surprise you when I left for work?*

Mrs Krantz shook her head, wistfully. "No, thank you, Mina."

Jonah stepped forward and grazed the hem of Mrs Krantz's seersucker housecoat with his muzzle, and the gesture made her smile. "What a well-behaved pup," she said. "I never hear him barking during the day."

"Yeah," Mina said wryly, as he glanced up at her, "he's definitely one of a kind."

Mina walked down Ninth Avenue lost in her thoughts, and during those moments when she remembered that she was holding a leash, she was trying reconcile the memory of Jonah Gideon, her dead ex-husband's handsome, thoughtful older cousin, with the confident, charming silver-coated wolf-dog that was staying by her side and matching her long stride, sniffing the delectable food aromas wafting from the numerous Ninth Avenue restaurants and cafes.

"I wish I had known earlier," Mina whispered. "I wouldn't have made you walk through gross puddles or endure a vet checkup. Oh, God, I made you eat dog food!" *Shit, I'm glad I put off getting him neutered.*

Jonah shot a look over his haunch at her, and he didn't seem upset with her. If anything, he seemed embarrassed to have his secret discovered, and he was trying his best to stick to his dog persona.

"I'm going to assume that you don't want to stay like this, so we'll need to figure out how to change you back," she said, slowing to a stop in front of a grocery store. "Maybe if you tell Malcolm what you remember, he can relay the details to me."

She tied the leash to a bike rack outside the store and went inside to pick up some food, wondering about what was going on between the Gideon boys, that their exchange in her apartment had seemed so contentious. She knew that Jonah was older by a few years and was like an older brother to Malcolm, but something had happened to strain their relationship...

"Can I help you?" she called when she exited the store, noticing a police officer looking at Jonah's plain collar.

"Is this your dog, Ma'am?" the officer asked, his expression inscrutable under the brim of his hat, a few stray wisps of blond hair peeking out from underneath.

"Yes, Sir," she said, loosening the leash from the bike rack. "Is there a problem?"

"How long have you had your dog, Ma'am?" he asked, looking Jonah over for any distinguishing marks.

"About four months," she lied easily.

"If your dog is more than four months old, he's required to be licensed. If he's already licensed, he should be wearing his tag on his collar. Is he neutered?" he asked trying to look under Jonah's belly.

"No, he's not," Mina answered shortly, seeing

47

a bare-toothed twitch of annoyance by Jonah's muzzle. "I'll get on that right away…Officer," she said diffidently.

The edge of the police officer's lips rose a little at the softness of her voice. "Okay, I'll let you off with a warning, this time." He scribbled onto a pad. "Someone recently reported a missing husky about a month ago, matching your boy's description. If you spot a stray that looks like him, maybe you can give us a call?"

Mina took a step closer and saw that the paper only had a name and cell number. "Thank you," she said. "I'll certainly keep an eye out and let you know, but I'm sure you have more exciting things to do than to chase lost dogs."

She reached over his hand and took the sheet with a gentle, lingering tug. "If I see anything, I'll be in touch. Good night, Officer."

As they started on their walk back, Mina sensed a kind of stiffness in Jonah's posture, and saw that his brushy tail was held a little lower. "You're not annoyed that I flirted with a cop to get out of a ticket, are you?"

He had his eyes forward, his muzzle stiff and pointed straight.

"Oh, my God, you are!" she laughed. "Did it occur to you that I also want leads to find out who's looking for you, in your present condition? A shape-shifting curse like yours isn't easy or cheap to commission, so whatever happened to you was done intentionally."

His pricked ears pinned back a touch with chagrin, but he still refused to look at her. His nostrils flared intermittently, as he caught an occasional whiff of the savory items that Mina had picked up from the store, but he remained aloof and generally avoided eye contact with her, as he explored and marked the neighborhood, as any other independent-minded dog would.

That was fine, as Mina was lost in her own thoughts about the situation in which she had found herself. She had two spirits and a cursed man requiring her help, in addition to checking up on her big brother Adam. Thankfully, she had finished up with a couple of clients earlier in the week and had time to spare in her schedule.

Mina stopped in the doorway of her apartment but did not unbuckle the dog collar, as she normally did. Instead, she led Jonah into the bathroom and asked him to get into the bathtub, setting the bag of groceries on her counter as they passed the kitchen.

Malcolm's snickering towards Jonah irritated her. "I'm still busy," Mina snipped, seeing Malcolm's spirit on her couch. "Until I'm done, I don't want to hear a peep out of you." She looked at Jack Mackay, sitting next to Malcolm on the couch. "*Either* of you."

## Chapter 4

Mina picked up her head from her desk at the vibration of her phone, inches away. It felt like she had put her head down for just a moment, but her incoming texts indicated that she had passed out an hour ago. Groggily, she put Adam on speaker.

"You didn't answer my texts, so I got worried," Adam said.

"Sorry, I got busy, then I fell asleep," Mina said, seeing that she had missed a few texts from Adam, and one from Xani. "I had to give Jonah a bath and make him dinner."

"Who's Jonah?" Adam asked. "Are you babysitting for someone?"

Mina slapped her cheek a little to wake up. "Too much to explain over the phone. I'll tell you when I see you next." She skimmed her messages, which included a photo from Adam of an ad for long-stemmed, apricot-hued roses. "Why are you sending me a picture of... Oh, you want to send flowers to Xani!"

"Yeah," he said sheepishly. "As a thank-you for sticking around last night. I texted you because I don't have her number or address."

Mina's lips curled mischievously, as she looked at the text from Xani, and she was glad

Adam couldn't see her expression. "Very smooth, bro, but Xani's not the 'long-stemmed rose' type of girl. You'll need to try a little harder."

"For crying out loud, I'm not making a play for her!" Adam exclaimed. "I just want to tell her 'thanks.'"

"Uh-huh," Mina dismissed, firing off a quick reply to Xani. "Tell her in person, then. It'll mean more. You don't have to ask her out to dinner or anything; she'll be at the Lotus tonight, if you want to 'happen to stop in' and chat with her."

"And you're babysitting this Jonah kid, so I'm on my own, tonight."

"Yep, go practice flapping those little wings, baby bird!" Mina teased. "You'll be fine. If it goes to shit, you can swing by afterwards, and we'll cry and swear together over whisky and chocolate."

As Mina disconnected with Adam, she met Jonah's chastising blue eyes, as he rested his chin on the couch armrest. "Yes, I'm using you as an excuse to get them alone together. I didn't exactly lie, did I? I did wash your feet and cook for you."

Jonah gave a loud, fulsome exhale and returned to his stretched-out sleeping position. Malcolm and Jack's ghosts were pacing across her living room rug, impatient but careful not to disturb her.

Wide awake now, Mina returned to her laptop and skimmed over the information she had pulled up before she had fallen asleep. Between the ghosts and the shape-shifter crowding her living room, she expected a long and busy weekend ahead of her.

◇◇◇

At the Red Lotus, Xani sat the bar nursing her watered-down scotch and soda, casting a watchful glance at the door every few minutes. Her phone was in her bag, in the back room, but she remembered her last text exchange with Mina vividly.

*Coming by the Lotus tonight?* Xani had texted.

Mina had replied, an hour later: *Can't make it. Adam will be there.*

Xani had texted back, *What time?* but never got a reply, so she had decided to just put her phone away and stop thinking about it.

In the meantime, she straightened the drape of her emerald-green silk shirt and black skirt and was starting to regret not going home to change first. She liked to look professional for the office and kept an arsenal of tailored skirts and blouses at home, ready to mix and match at a moment's notice, but in her downtime, she preferred t-shirts and jeans, and she eyed the dressed-down patrons a little jealously. At least, she was able to unpin her hair and let her fiery red curls do whatever they damn well pleased.

Cindy, though, was even more dressed-up than Xani was: in a corseted, sleeveless black bodysuit that covered her neck and torso, and leather pants that hugged her modest curves. With her tight curls worn close to her head, and a perfect complexion like polished mahogany, she was beautiful and sexy without showing any cleavage or back. There were multiple reasons for Cindy's modesty—her transitional changes, scars and other distinguishing features—but her covering up didn't make her any less stunning.

Xani looked over to the door as Cindy floated over to greet a customer. While Cindy was taller than the average man, the customer was above average, himself: broad-shouldered, with full, jet-black hair that grazed his collar. *Wait a minute...* Xani finally recognized Adam by his clean-shaven profile when he turned aside for Cindy's playful kiss on the cheek. He gave Cindy's hand a glancing peck and whispered something that made her giggle.

Cindy took Adam by the hand and led him over to Xani, leaving him on a barstool as she circled behind the bar counter. "It's so good to see you, Adam. It's been too long. What can I get you?"

"Gin and tonic?" Xani recalled.

"Good memory," Adam smiled, impressed that she remembered.

Cindy's warm brown eyes flashed between Xani and Adam, and she simpered. "You got it. I'll go mix it up *way* over at this end," she said, moving down the counter.

Adam and Xani laughed at Cindy's total disregard for subtlety, as Xani stole a peek at Adam's idea of casual attire: dark slacks, fitted dress shirt, black woolen jacket and dark boots.

Adam caught her critiquing his outfit and grinned sheepishly. "Sorry, I haven't carved out the time to shop, and I didn't want to show up looking too schlubby. Am I overdressed, or underdressed?"

Xani smiled. "Neither, you look great. You always look great." She bit down on her lip for letting that last bit slip out. It was true, but she hadn't meant to say it out loud.

Thankfully, Cindy had returned with Adam's drink. "It's on the house, for helping us class up the joint."

Adam flashed a handsome smile. "You don't need me for that. You ladies make this place shine, all by yourselves."

"Damn, Mina never told us you were so cute or charming," Cindy said.

Adam gave her a speculative look over his glass, as he took a sip. "That'd be weird for a sister to say about her own brother."

"Would it be weird?" Cindy asked, looking pointedly at Xani. "You mean sisters don't usually try to talk up their brothers to their single friends?"

Xani wanted to reach across the counter and throttle Cindy. "Morgan needs all the help he can get, okay? Adam doesn't need any such..." *Again, you've opened your mouth and inserted your size nine foot, dingbat!*

Adam was trying very hard not to react to Xani's off-hand remark and took another sip of his drink. "Anyway, Xani, I wanted to thank you for staying around last night, and on Mina's behalf, too. It was reassuring to have your company and support."

"Of course," Xani said, fighting the impulse to set her hand on his. "She's like a little sister to us, too. She told us about having to go ID Malcolm this morning. Are *you* okay? I know you and Malcolm used to be close, before he started getting abusive towards Mina."

"Yeah," Adam said tersely, a furrow forming on his brow, as he dropped his eyes. "It was definitely unexpected news, but there's never a convenient time for stuff like that, is there?"

Xani noticed his sudden remoteness, and she wondered if she had spoken out of turn. "I'm sorry. Maybe I shouldn't have said anything."

Adam looked at her again, and his expression had brightened, just a little. "No, you didn't say anything wrong," he said soothingly. "I was just remembering him, the way he seemed to get along with everyone. I guess it just shows that, even when you think you know someone, they may be hiding a darkness inside them."

Xani nodded, feeling a little relieved. "Can we get you another drink?"

Adam peered into his glass of ice. "No, I'm good, thanks. I should get going." He noticed her brief frown of disappointment before she relaxed her brows and lips. "Would you like to have dinner with me, sometime? We could go out, or I can cook."

She was speechless at the unexpected invite, and her answer froze in her throat.

"If that's too awkward, we'll make it a siblings' dinner," he suggested, "and we can ask Mina and Morgan to join us."

Xani finally recovered her voice. "That sounds awesome!" she managed, actually accepting his original offer, but she would accept the latter, too, if it meant that Morgan would finally have a moment to speak with Mina one-on-one.

"Great," Adam smiled, looking relieved, himself. "Does Sunday work for you? I know it's already Friday night, but if you want to come up to the apartment, that would save us the trouble of making reservations."

Xani blanked on what was on her calendar, but she didn't much care—she wasn't passing up this opportunity. "Yes! That sounds... that's just... wow."

"Okay," he said bemusedly, saving her the effort of struggling for words. "It's a date, then. Should we exchange numbers, or coordinate through Mina, so we can confirm the details?"

"Oh!" She looked around for her phone, then remembered with dismay that she had left it in the back room.

Cindy cleared her throat discreetly and held out her hand. "I'll give you the number," she offered, with a side-wink at Xani. After she saved the number in Adam's phone, she simpered flirtatiously, "You want Xani's, too?"

"Hey!" Xani cried indignantly, grabbing Adam's phone to see what had been saved. "Cin, this is *your* number!"

Adam laughed, as Cindy took the phone back. "Okay, I'll put your number in here, too," she bemoaned melodramatically. "You can memorize ten-digit security system codes for your clients but not your own damn phone number. Serves you right."

Adam glanced at his phone before he rang Mina's apartment from the front door. It wasn't quite midnight, and in New York City on a Friday night, the night life was hitting its stride, so Adam was fairly sure that Mina was still up.

Sure enough, Mina buzzed him in promptly, and Adam sprinted up the first flights with an extra spring in his step. Not only had he gotten

Xani to agree to come to his place for dinner, but he had gotten Cindy's number, too. He recalled how Cyril McManus had looked—and that Mina had a little crush on him back in high school— but Cindy was a knockout. Between Xani and Cindy, Adam couldn't remember the last time he had garnered such enviable female attention, but it was definitely an ego boost, and it had temporarily distracted him from more troubling thoughts...

The door to the second floor apartment opened, and Mrs Krantz opened it partway.

"I'm sorry, I didn't mean to disturb you," Adam whispered.

"It's okay, I was actually listening for the door," Mrs Krantz said unabashedly.

When Mina opened her door, Mrs Krantz called up: "Thank you for the chocolate-covered cherries, honey! What a nice surprise! They're my favorite, how did you know?"

Mina leaned over the third-floor railing. "I just heard a little voice, Missus Krantz. I'm glad you like them. Good night," she said, as Adam reached the top floor and slipped inside the apartment.

As Mina shut the door, Adam looked around her living room at the assortment of books and jars of herbs scattered throughout, and the blue-eyed husky sitting in the middle of the floor, staring at him inscrutably, surrounded by a chalk circle and a ring of candles.

"What the..." Adam muttered under his breath. "I'm going to guess that your babysitting is over for tonight?"

"I know, it looks a little eccentric," Mina said,

returning to her desk, where she had multiple windows open on her laptop screen, then back to her collection of jars.

"Eccentric doesn't begin to describe this," Adam said. "You look like you're in the middle of…something, so I'm just going to start talking, and you can join in, if you'd like, okay?" Adam took a seat in Mina's vacant desk chair.

"Sounds good," Mina said distractedly, mixing and grinding a mixture of dried herbs with a mortar and pestle. "Everything go okay at the Red Lotus tonight?"

"Everything went great. Xani's coming to my place for dinner on Sunday night, and you and Morgan are welcome to join us, so that it doesn't feel like a date." Adam watched Mina closely, as she began to light the candles around the dog, who seemed strangely relaxed amid the open flames so close to his fur.

"Sunday, hmm," Mina said, adding a pinch of some kind of spice to her mixture. "Depending on how things go tonight and tomorrow, Sunday may not work for me, but you should still definitely stick with your plans."

He asked what had been on his mind since leaving the Red Lotus: "Mina…did Malcolm ever hit you?"

She paused a couple of beats, then returned to grinding her concoction. "Does it matter?" she asked, her eyes focused on her task. "He's dead, and we were only married a few months. It was over in the blink of an eye, relatively speaking."

By not answering him directly, she gave him the response he needed. It wasn't what he wanted to hear, but it was truthful. "Why didn't you tell me? Why didn't you come to me?"

Mina didn't answer, giving all her attention to her mixing.

"*Mei-mei*, I need you to say something!"

"I need a few minutes, please. The timing of *this* part is critical," she said. "If this doesn't get done by midnight, I lose my window, and I have to start all over during the next waxing half-moon, which might be too late."

Adam glanced at his phone. It was ten to midnight. "Okay, I can wait."

He watched as the candles burned down nearly half-way, and Mina mixed some water into the mortar with the spices and knelt in front of the dog.

"I'm sorry," she said to the husky, "it's going to taste awful, and it is slightly toxic, so you're going to feel pretty sick afterwards, but if you don't drink it all, I can't help you. If you have to vomit, keep it on the hardwood or the tile, okay?"

She held out the mortar holding the soupy concoction, and to Adam's amazement, the dog lapped up the entire mixture. He didn't seem to enjoy it, but he finished it, and Adam heard the sandy brush of his tongue against the rough interior of the granite bowl.

Mina gave a sigh of relief. "That part's done, with a minute to spare. Now," she said, looking at the empty couch. "Let's figure out what's going on with you two."

Adam followed Mina's line of sight, as the dog left the circle of candles and flopped down next to him, under the desk. The husky glanced at Adam and lowered his muzzle to the floor, closing his eyes, as two glowing white figures rose out of the floor. "What the hell…"

"I know it may not look crowded in here, but it's like Grand Central Station right now," Mina said, setting the mortar and pestle on the desk behind her.

"Terminal," Adam corrected automatically. "Grand Central's where everything comes to an end, so it's a terminal, not a station." He stared at a figure that reminded him of Malcolm Gideon, hovering in front of Mina with another ghostly figure.

"Yes, this place is certainly that," Mina smiled grimly, lighting a stick of incense with of the burning candles and sticking it into a brass holder, which she placed into the center of the circle where the dog had been.

The wispy smoke from the incense began to move in jerky, deliberate patterns, despite Mina's stillness in the midst of it, and began to form shapes around her and the apparitions. Not blobby, imagined shapes like clouds in the sky, but actual figures, faces and scenes, like projections.

"You bastard!" Adam snarled, finally recognizing Malcolm through his slouchy clothes and twitchy mannerisms. "It's actually him, isn't it? That's Malcolm's ghost."

"Yes," Mina said in surprise, looking at Adam. "You can see him? Can you see Jack, too?" She pointed to the other figure.

"Yes," he said, noticing the movements of their mouths, "but I can't hear them."

"That's probably for the best," she muttered.

"Why are they here?"

"Something or someone sent them to me,"

she said. "Someone drove them to kill themselves, but their spirits are bound to me."

"Someone, like an actual person, or something supernatural?"

He could tell from Mina's smile that she was gratified that he was tracking with her so easily. She focused on the spirits briefly. "The spells holding you in place were cast by the same human entity, as far as I can tell. You both came here, but from different locations, and you don't know each other."

"You're a common link, somehow," Adam said.

"Possibly," Mina said. "I went to school with Jack and was married to Malcolm. So, who else do you both know? Give me names." She seemed to be listening intently, as the spirits seemed to both be speaking at once.

The husky picked up his head suddenly and gave a gruff woof, and both spirits stopped to look at him, and each other.

"The dog can talk to the ghosts, too?" Adam asked in amazement.

"Full disclosure: he's not a regular dog," Mina confessed. "He's under an enchantment, so yeah, he sees and hears them, too. Unfortunately, I can't talk directly with him." She looked up at the spirits and frowned. "We're almost out of time. What was the name he picked out?"

The ghosts seemed to repeat the names, and Mina shook her head. "I don't know anyone by that name.'"

The spirits stopped speaking, and the smoke dissipated, and them with it. Adam looked at the incense and noticed that it had burned completely to ash.

"So, what happens now?" he asked. "Are the spirits coming back?"

"They're spent for the night, but they'll be back in the morning. In the meantime, I have to find out who this 'Sophie' is, and why she cursed Malcolm and Jack and drove them to me." She blew out the candles and picked them up from the floor.

"You don't think it's just an odd coincidence that they both showed up here?"

Mina shot him a look. "I've discovered that coincidences are much rarer in life than one would think, in general. With spirits and curses, hardly ever."

Adam noticed for the first time that she had everything laid out on a bamboo-slat mat, like the ones they had used in the summertime for sleeping, when they were children. "Does Mom know you use your sleep mat for your rituals?" he asked, as he helped Mina roll it up.

"No, does Mom know that you used to smoke and sneak nips of her rice wine?" she shot back. "Some things are better left unsaid."

"Except between us, right?" Adam asked, tucking the rolled-up mat next to her desk where she pointed. "We never used to keep secrets from each other." At her tired scowl, he pressed, "I'm your brother. I've done a shitty job sometimes, but I'm supposed to protect you."

"You've protected me plenty of times, *ge-ge*." Mina leaned against her desk and took his hand. "And you've never done a shitty job, ever."

"So, what was different with Malcolm? So why didn't you say anything?"

Mina's eyes darted to the husky napping on the floor, before she spoke again. "I didn't tell you about Malcolm, because I handled it," Mina resumed. "You taught me to stand up for myself, and also not to give up without a fight for what was important. I fought, I didn't give up, and then I walked away when I finally realized I was more important than the effort I was putting in."

"That's not the same as my protecting you," Adam retorted.

"It was my decision," she said resolutely. "But you know what? Even though I didn't tell you, it meant everything to me, that I could, if I needed to. I knew you would always have my back, that you would always take care of me." She dropped his hand and snapped her fingers. "I promised you whisky and chocolate!"

Adam thought back to their brief phone conversation from earlier in the evening. "You said if the evening went to shit. It didn't go badly."

Mina opened a box of truffles and reached for a bottle of Japanese whisky. "So, we'll celebrate with whisky and chocolate, instead." She poured out two glasses and passed him one. "Do you think I'm crazy? Doing this for a living?"

"I don't understand enough to know what to think," he said, savoring the fine, aged single malt on his tongue. "I can't fault your taste in liquor, though."

Mina clinked her glass with his. "You taught me that, too: if I'm going to drink, know what's in my glass at all times, drink moderately, and only the good stuff. See, I pay attention to everything you tell me." She took a sip. "At the Lotus last night, were you asking me about spirits because you're starting to see them yourself? From your reaction, it didn't seem like Malcolm and Jack were your first sightings."

"They weren't," Adam said, swirling his glass. "It started in Singapore, when I woke up in the hospital after the crash. At first, it seemed like just a vision thing, like a shadow or floater out of the corner of my eye. Because I had a concussion, the doctor ordered an MRI, and that came back clean."

"But then you started seeing spirits more clearly." Adam nodded, and Mina looked into her glass thoughtfully. "You were hurt worse than you told us, weren't you?"

"Why do you say that?" he asked, taking one of the truffles.

"The sight usually follows a near-death trauma," she said, pouring a little more whisky into Adam's glass. "Let me guess: you didn't want to worry Mom and Dad."

"Honestly, I don't know what happened, myself, even after seeing some of the crash scene photos," he said, trying not envision the images again. "My seat was soaked with blood, there was glass and metal everywhere. I shouldn't have sustained just a broken finger and a bump on the head," he scowled.

"The details don't matter. The important thing is that you're alive," Mina said. "You told me that, after I almost drowned."

Adam didn't have to be reminded of those details, as he recalled them as well as she did; it was the summer Mina turned fourteen, during a family vacation in upstate New York, when they had gone out rowing on the nearby lake. "You scared the shit out of us, and for days after," Adam recalled. "You weren't breathing when we pulled you out. It took almost fifteen minutes to get you out of the water, like you were snagged on something. Then, when we got you back to the cabin, you kept talking about wanting to remember everything that had happened."

"Because it felt surreal to me," she said. "It felt to me like I was under for only a minute or two. Do you remember what I told you I saw?"

"You said you saw mermaids," Adam said. "You were delirious. I told you there were no such thing as mermaids."

"Well, you're partially right. Mermaids don't do well in freshwater lakes and ponds," Mina said matter-of-factly. "I did see something down there, but after you blew me off, I just kept it to myself and didn't tell anyone."

Adam was struck that she still held onto his dismissal of her from years ago. "What did you see?"

"They were spirits," she said. "They showed themselves to me because they thought I was a witch, like them, and that I was being dunked."

"A witch like them?" He frowned. "You're telling me that you saw ghosts of dead witches, and they thought you were being tried, like in the old days?"

She nodded. "They thought I was being tested, just as they all had been before they died. They felt it would be more merciful to drown me than to let me die at the stake, so they held me down. They were trying to protect me from floating up to a more horrible death."

"What made them release you?"

"You did," Mina smiled. "You jumped into the water and fought to save me, and they realized that I wasn't a witch, but I had been close enough to death that I was able to see them, just like you do now."

"So, that's what kicked off your obsession with becoming a witch." Her odd teenage goth and Wiccan fascinations made more sense now.

Mina laughed. "Of course, being fourteen, I was probably more fixated than I should have been. My weird phase started just in time for freshman year of high school. Had I been older when it happened, I might have been a little more discreet with my hobbies."

"You'll have to excuse me, if I don't follow in your footsteps," he said, as Mina refilled his glass. "You seem to have more of an affinity for this kind of work than I do."

"It's work," she said wryly. "It's never boring, and it pays the bills. Once in a while, I have to do a pro-bono job, especially if the client is deceased, but it's still work experience," she shrugged.

Adam grinned, clinking his glass with Mina's. "Mom and Dad always said we should start our own practices. They never specified that we had to be doctors or lawyers."

"Speaking of which, what's your next phase, now that you've escaped the corporate hamster wheel?" she quipped. "Close-up magician or fast-food cashier, maybe?"

He laughed. "I don't know," he admitted, with some relief. "It's nice to be able to say that. It's humbling to admit that I'm figuring it out, as I go along."

It was well past one in the morning by the time Adam left. While Adam seemed intrigued about Jonah's role and was not subtle about wanting to know more about him, Mina did not offer any details about who Jonah was or how he had come to be in her custody. With all the other revelations that night, Adam had also forgotten that she had promised him an explanation about Jonah when they had spoken on the phone earlier in the evening.

Mina deadbolted her door. "Malcolm and Jack are resting, for now," she said to Jonah, "so I'll find out what I can about this 'Sophie Lyons' in the meantime." She crouched and examined Jonah's eyes and paws. "Open your mouth, please. I want to check how you're recovering and how your color is."

Jonah dropped his jaw for her and sat patiently as she looked at his tongue and gum line.

"Good. The toxins should clear up by themselves by morning." She moved to pet his head and ears but caught herself. "Sorry, Jonah. I forget sometimes that this is a temporary state for you."

Jonah lowered his muzzle to the floor. The past month had certainly been a learning experience, between tolerating food scraps and kibble and teaching himself to flush and balance on the toilet to spare himself and Mina the indignities of her cleaning up after him. His thoughts were mostly uncomplicated and primal, but during the fleeting moments when he recalled his humanity, he tried to stay as clean and neat as possible.

"How did I not realize that you were under an enchantment?" she murmured, more to herself than Jonah. "I usually notice and pick up these things pretty easily, but you've been here for a month." She went to her laptop computer and returned to her research, as she had been doing for much of her evening.

He could tell she was tired, from her half-closed eyes and atypical slouch, and he appreciated her dedication, but he wanted her to get some sleep, too, more than just that hour-long nap she caught at her desk earlier. He nudged his muzzle under her elbow to pry her away from the keyboard.

She straightened in her seat, ignoring him. "Sophie Lyons was Mary Sophia Leone," she summarized from her screens. "Jack and I went to high school with her, but she used her old name then. It looks like she went to Boston for college after graduation and decided to stay. Same college as Malcolm and Adam, so there's that connection…"

Mina did an image search and found an assortment of photos of Sophie, over the past several years. "I remember her now. She was at the wedding when Malcolm and I got married. She seemed to know your family pretty well."

Jonah couldn't explain to Mina that by the time he had met Sophie, she had already ingratiated her way into the extended Gideon family, perhaps filling a void in her own family life with their ready acceptance—"the more the merrier" was the Gideon way. Sophie was canvassing most of the Gideon boys for a way to become a permanent part of the family, and Jonah had picked up on her designs early enough to steer clear of her, except to keep a friendly distance at the larger family gatherings.

"So, what happened?" Mina asked. "Did you play with her emotions once too many times, and she turned you into a literal dog?" She turned around in her seat and looked at Jonah. "You're going to start feeling different, as the elixir goes through your system, and your nausea should subside by morning. Until I can figure out exactly what she did to you, the best I can do is keep you in flux, so you're not forced to stay like this forever."

He didn't understand everything Mina said, but he trusted her. He didn't have much of a choice, as she seemed to be the only one who had any idea of what had actually happened to him. He was grateful for her extra considerations, like the foot bath and the seared sirloin that she had made for him—it was a well-marbled prime cut and not cheap, especially in Manhattan.

"Sophie has a different purpose for you," Mina said. "I'm not sure what, yet, but I don't think she expected you to get away. I think she's the one who's filed a report for a missing husky and has the police searching for you."

Instead of petting his head, she stroked the whiskers on his cheek. "You and I both need to get some rest. I have a lot to get done tomorrow...um, later this morning, and your nausea will be more manageable if you can sleep through it."

She shut down her laptop and went to get ready for bed, and Jonah hopped back up to his usual spot on the couch. She undid her ponytail, and he caught a whiff of her scent as she tossed her scrunched fabric band onto the side table behind his head. Tonight, she smelled like lavender soap, incense smoke and whisky.

"Good night, Jonah," she called, shutting her bedroom door with a quiet click.

*Good night, Mina*, he replied belatedly, not that she could hear him, anyway. He felt chills and a general achiness in his joints, as though he was coming down with a flu, but the discomforts helped to distract him from the churning in his gut.

He picked up her ponytail holder with his teeth and tucked it under his muzzle, as he curled his tail around himself, and with her scent soothing him with every breath, he drifted off to sleep.

# Chapter 5

Morgan awoke to the smells of cannolis, ricotta cheesecake and espresso, and he knew immediately that Xani had made a quick stop on the way back from her morning jog along First Avenue. Since their favorite pastry shop opened at eight on Saturday mornings, he knew it had to be later.

He trudged from his room, rubbing his whiskered face vigorously to wake up a little bit, and he growled at Xani's fresh, perky smile. "Why are you so happy?"

"You and I are going to Adam's tomorrow for dinner," Xani smiled, taking a sip of her cinnamon-dusted latte. "Mina will be there, too."

Morgan sat at the dinette across from Xani and plucked a vanilla cannoli from the red-printed white cake box. "Oh, yeah? When was this decided?"

"Last night, after you left," Xani said. "Adam came by the Lotus for a drink, and he invited us to dinner. You were passed out by the time I got home, otherwise, I would've told you then."

Morgan savored the crisp shell and the decadent vanilla ricotta cream as he tried to formulate a response, but it felt too early for that level of thought. He took a sip of black espresso from the tiny paper cup. "Why am I so tired?"

Xani shrugged. "Beats me. You were out cold last night, and sound asleep when I went out for my jog earlier. Are you coming down with something?"

Morgan shook his head, as he took the last bite of the cannoli. "No, I feel fine. After we left the office, I went to meet to have drinks with the rep from Garrison Brothers," he recalled. "She said they wanted to move ahead with an expedited schedule, that the extra cost for labor was not going to be an issue. They want it done by the end of the month."

"Garrison's the one with the brownstone that they want installed with the works: retinal and voice scans, all the bells and whistles?"

"That's the one," Morgan said, the fog lifting from his head. "There's a stone-walled cellar and vault that she was asking to have sage-smudged and purified, too."

"Okay, I guess we're bringing in Mina, also," Xani said. "When you see her tomorrow, you can ask her for a date…that works for everyone's schedule."

"You're so funny," Morgan said sarcastically. "I'm actually thinking of asking Mina to give the Garrison rep a quick look. Something seemed a little strange about her, that I couldn't quite figure out."

"Lawyers are always an odd assortment," Xani dismissed.

Morgan shook his head. "Yeah, but she wasn't one of their lawyers. She introduced herself as someone in their business development group. That's not someone we typically meet to discuss building security."

Xani gave a thoughtful scowl. "That does sound a little peculiar, but maybe she wears multiple hats. You can send Mina the name and contact info, anyway, just to be safe."

Morgan nodded, replaying the brief meeting in his head. They had met at the bar of a restaurant on 23rd Street, ordered their drinks and started talking. She looked young enough that she got carded, which was when she mentioned that she was flattered to be asked for proof of age despite being twenty-eight and wearing a suit. This apparently never happened in her Boston home office.

Aside from that, the meeting was brief and fairly unmemorable. He went home shortly afterwards, feeling a little tired, and went to bed without bothering to make anything for himself for dinner. He had brushed his teeth, but even that had seemed to take an exhaustive amount of effort.

Morgan reached for his phone and shot off a quick text to Mina: *Can you check someone, please. Garrison Bros on MacDougal. Sophie Lyons, Boston.*

"You look pale, almost anemic," Xani said. "Are you sure you're okay?"

"Yeah," he said. "I think I need to wake up a little, that's all."

As he set his phone down, Xani grabbed his hand and turned it palm-side up. "What the hell is that?"

Morgan looked where Xani was focused but just saw his pale, freckled skin. "What the hell is what?"

"*That*," Xani said, pressing her thumb against his wrist, and he jerked his hand away, feeling a sharp pain. "When did you get that bruise?"

Morgan looked at his wrists side by side. "What bruise? There's nothing there." As he turned his eyes to Xani, he caught a dull purple out of the corner of his gaze, which disappeared when he looked back down. He tried again, and realized that he could only see it out of his periphery. "What the fuck?"

"Yeah, no shit," Xani said smartly. "You'd have to be blind not to see it."

Morgan tried feeling the bruise himself, but couldn't. "I can't see it, and I can't feel it, either."

Xani reached over and squeezed his wrist suddenly, and he yelped. "I think your mind is playing tricks with your senses. You don't feel it when you do it to yourself because your brain is overriding your reactions. It's like trying to tickle yourself."

Morgan shook his head. "This is crazy!" He tensed as Xani took his arm, more gently, to look at the bruise.

"Relax. Have another cannoli, you big baby," she cajoled as she peered at his wrist. "You have a little scab over your vein. Don't look, you idiot! You can't see it, remember, but *I* can."

Morgan frowned, trying to remember when he could've gotten cut without his notice. He was distracted by the chime on his phone, from a returning text. He peered over to read Mina's reply. "Huh," he grunted with bemusement.

"What did she say?" Xani asked.

"She says to call her ASAP."

✧✧✧

Mina studied Sophie Lyons, as Sophie entered the diner and approached her table. Sophie looked as Mina remembered her from high school: pretty, slender, with wavy blond hair, blue eyes, a tiny sprinkle of freckles on her nose. Mina stood and extended her had in a greeting.

"You're not afraid I'll prick your finger or hand for blood?" Sophie asked warily, looking down at Mina's hand.

"No, and I wouldn't do that to you, either," Mina said mildly, smiling as Sophie took her hand. "It's a general courtesy among witches to refrain from that, at least in public." She sat back down and gestured to Sophie to do the same.

"I wasn't sure that you followed the norms," Sophie said. "You're reputed as more of a rogue or solitary practitioner."

Mina raised her brow, as she sipped her green tea. She wasn't aware that she had any kind of reputation outside of New York's five boroughs at all. "I don't belong to a conventional coven or an established sisterhood, but I do believe in acting honorably. Thanks for agreeing to meet me, especially on such short notice."

"Of course, Mina," Sophie said amiably, as though they were close friends. "I've been looking forward to seeing you again, for a long time. You're the reason I found my vocation, after all."

"Really?" Mina asked with genuine surprise. "How's that?"

The waitress came to offer Sophie a menu, inadvertently interrupting their conversation.

"The matzoh ball soup is excellent," Mina

suggested. "But if it's too early for that, they also make their pies in-house."

The waitress took Sophie's order for a slice of lemon meringue pie and a cup of coffee and retreated with the menu, allowing the women to speak privately again.

"Back in high school, do you remember Mister Harmon?" Sophie asked.

"Yes," Mina said shortly. He was the teacher whose advances she had rebuffed, about whom she had filed her complaint, and was never reprimanded.

"You're not the only one he approached," Sophie said quietly. "There was me, and a couple of other girls, too. I wanted to say something, then, I really did, but my parents advised against it," she said ruefully. "They said it was my junior year, and I shouldn't jeopardize my college chances by starting trouble or getting distracted."

Mina wasn't there to discuss the past, and she was annoyed by the reminder of her futile efforts. She had enough pestering reminders of her personal history in the form of Malcolm and Jack's spirits. "Whatever. It was ten years ago. I hear Harmon moved to Phoenix and died in a car crash last year," she said gruffly.

"I heard that, too," Sophie said. "Karma always finds a way, right?"

Mina took another sip of her green tea, as the waitress returned with Sophie's coffee and dish of creamer. "Did you or one of your friends have something to do with that?" she asked quietly.

"The point is," Sophie deflected blithely, "that you and I seem destined to work together.

When you transferred mid-year back in high school, I thought that would be the last time I'd ever hear about you, but then I got to college and met your brother and his roommate, and I thought, 'this can't be a coincidence.'"

*That's the very definition of a coincidence, unless you're a stalker*, Mina thought to herself, but she nodded without comment.

"It was fate," Sophie said. "We were destined to avenge the wrongs done to us, and other women."

*Not through killing and cursing.* "So, are you here to exact vengeance, or did you come to New York to reconnect with me?"

"Can't I do both?" she smiled, as the waitress set her slice of fluffy lemon meringue pie in front of her. "When I saw you at your wedding to Malcolm, you looked so beautiful and had a glow about you, and I envied your power. I wanted to be like that, so I studied and practiced. My sisterhood found me, mentored and supported me, and here I am," she said proudly. "I have everything I want, thanks to you."

"I never used my gifts to curse anyone," Mina reminded.

"But you could, against those who deserve it," Sophie said. "What Malcolm did to you was inexcusable, and he deserved to be punished then. He hadn't changed, you know, from when you left. Some people don't deserve forgiveness, because they'll never change."

"You talked to him recently?" Mina asked, feigning innocence.

"You know I did," Sophie said coyly. "I went out with him a couple of times, after you guys first split up, and he tried to explain what had happened, but I saw through his lies. Then, about a couple of months ago, we met up again. I could see his appeal, but he's still a mean drunk. He needed to be stopped before he hurt someone else, the way he hurt you."

Mina heard a tinge of accusation and resentment in her voice, as though Sophie blamed her for not taking Malcolm to task sooner. "And Jack? What did he do?"

Sophie smiled grimly, stirring sugar into her coffee. "Jack Mackay? Did he mention me? I'm surprised he remembered my name. We went out to dinner, and then he asked me back to his place. We had a few drinks, and then… then, he wanted to have sex. When I told him no, he called me a bitch and tried to force me."

*She's a liar!* Jack's spirit sprang up from the booth next to them and glared at Sophie. *It was her idea to come home with me, and she was totally into it. She only said no after we were already in bed, so what was I supposed to do?*

*You respect her decision, you stupid piece of shit,* Mina wanted to say aloud, so that Jack could actually hear her reply, but she had to keep her focus on Sophie, who wasn't admitting to killing anyone, but certainly showing motive and a vengeful inclination.

"Did you send their spirits to me, or did they find their way to me on their own?" Mina asked. "There's little I can do for them, now that they're dead, except to put them to rest and let them leave this world."

Sophie stopped stirring and frowned, and Mina realized that Sophie didn't know. "They're dead? Both of them?" she asked quietly.

"You did curse them, didn't you?" Mina confirmed.

Sophie put down her spoon with a trembling hand. "I cursed them, but I didn't kill them!" she said. "I swear. I wanted to scare them, make them hear voices and see hallucinations so that they would come to you, and then you could do whatever you wanted with them, but they're useless, dead," she grimaced.

Mina saw the panic and bewilderment in Sophie's face and heard the same in her voice. "I believe you, but that means that someone else knew what you had done and gave Malcolm and Jack an extra 'push' to finish them off." The insinuation was clear that someone in Sophie's sisterhood had completed what she had unwittingly started, and Mina hoped that Sophie would offer a name, but Sophie only shook her head.

"No, nobody in the sisterhood would do that. We support each other and respect each other's boundaries when it comes to our projects."

"Speaking of boundaries," Mina said lightly, sipping her green tea, "turning a guy into a dog without his permission is a bit overstepping, in my opinion."

"I don't know what you're talking about," she sniffed, but judging by her stiffness, she *did* know about Jonah's condition.

*She's lying again*, Malcolm's spirit piped up from the booth, sitting opposite from Jack.

"Okay," Mina nodded, in response to both Sophie and Malcolm. She had pressured Sophie enough and knew she was reaching her tolerance level. "If you can just let me know if there's anyone in your sisterhood who's acting strangely, I'll send Malcolm and Jack on their way."

"You're just going to let them go?" Sophie frowned.

"I don't need restless and tortured spirits haunting my apartment building," Mina said, shooting a passing glance at Malcolm and Jack. "It's crowded enough with the friendly and peaceful ones in residence."

"Well, that's your prerogative, I guess," Sophie said peevishly. "As for me, I'm not going to spy on my sisters for you. They help me, they're building me up. I was hoping you'd be more supportive, but I suppose there's a reason you work alone."

Mina shrugged off Sophie's sulkiness. "I don't socialize at networking events with other witches, if that's what you mean, but I know my craft, and I value my friends," she advised. "I'm not sure what you or your sisters intend with the blood you took from Morgan Crain, but I swear: any shit that befalls him is going to be returned a thousand-fold."

"Is that an actual threat, Mina?" Sophie asked.

Mina shook her head solemnly. "I don't make threats, just promises, that I always keep. It could only be taken as a threat, if there is some harm intended, so if Morgan is okay, then we have no issues."

Sophie took a bite of the fluffy, tangy lemon meringue. "My sisterhood's not going anywhere, you know. It would be unwise to make us your enemy."

"I'll keep it in mind." Sophie's tone was menacing, but Mina refused to react to it. "It's good to see you, Sophie. I'm glad we connected, and I look forward to seeing more of your work."

Sophie seemed to take a moment to discern whether Mina was being genuine or sarcastic, as her poker face gave nothing away. Everything Mina said was truthful, but perhaps not as innocent and trusting as it sounded.

"So, about this guy who got turned into a husky..." Sophie led.

Mina had never mentioned the breed. "Don't worry about it," she said, shaking her head. "You've got nothing to do with it," she reminded.

"Well, is he okay? Are you going to be able to change him back?" Sophie shrugged. "I'm just curious. This is just shop talk, between us girls.

Mina bobbed her head noncommittally. "Changing him back is not the challenge. He's going to want to know how and why it happened, so I'll do whatever I can to help him with that."

Sophie took a sip of her coffee. "Why? What if he's an asshole, and this is his punishment? It's a waste of your time and effort."

"Perhaps. I don't know what he's been up to, lately, but unless he understands why it happened, he can't change his ways, can he?" Mina posed, throwing Sophie a crumb of information.

"Lately? So, you know who he is," Sophie said, seizing on the tidbit. "Where is he, now?"

"Someplace safe," Mina said. "And yes, I make it a point to know who all my clients are."

"So, who is it?" The question was issued almost as a challenge, or a test.

"Sorry, I can't say," Mina demurred with a smile and finished her tea. "I maintain my clients' confidentiality, whether my clients are able to ask for it or not."

Adam got a text from Mina while he was getting his late-morning coffee; she was finishing up with an errand in the West Village and asked if he could swing by her apartment, since she had had to leave for an appointment and had left behind something "that I don't want to leave unattended for too long."

He hated when her messages were vague like that. It meant that there was more to the situation, but that she didn't want to get into details over text, so he would have to see for himself or wait until he saw her later. With Mina, it could be anything, ranging from a roast in the oven to live animals loose in her living room, or both, as had happened during Saturnalia almost two years ago.

He let himself into her building and apartment with a spare set of keys that she had given him, and he was immediately on his guard when he got inside.

Adam silently grasped the baseball bat that Mina had left by the front door and set his coffee cup on the floor, focusing his eyes on the blanketed, sleeping figure on the couch. He looked around for the husky, who was nowhere to be found, and stepped towards the couch, leaving the door ajar behind him to avoid waking the intruder.

Gripping the bat, Adam crept around the couch and heard a floorboard squeak underfoot, and the man immediately pushed himself up to sit. The first things Adam noticed about him were his wide, startled ice-blue eyes and streaks of gray in his black hair. Okay, those were secondary—the first was that the man was stark naked, draped in Mina's old *Star Wars* fleece blanket.

"Who the *fuck* are you, and why are you in my sister's apartment?" Adam demanded, standing like a batter waiting for a pitch.

"Shit!" the man replied, scooting away from Adam, as his eyes darted around. "Umm... wait," he said, pulling the blanket closer to himself instinctively. "Adam, it's me, Jonah. Jonah Gideon."

Adam acknowledged that the man bore a close resemblance to Malcolm's cousin, but that didn't explain why he was naked on Mina's couch. "Prove it."

Jonah seemed to wrack his brain to think of something. "Ah... We first met on moving day of your senior year of college. We went to play pool a few times at that place near Beacon Hill, even though their chowder sucked, because we both liked the waitress. We took Malcolm out the night before the wedding; he wanted tequila, and I said no more than two shots, and you watched them pour them out to make sure that it was really gold tequila and not the cheap *mixto* shit."

Adam smiled tightly, remembering the more innocent, happier days. "What did I ask you to include on your best man's wedding speech?"

Jonah met Adam's eyes. "You said to remind him that marriage was a joining of families, and that family is forever."

83

*Jonah Gideon.* As he was talking, Adam recognized the mannerisms and vocal inflections of Malcolm's older cousin. He then remembered Mina's comment from the evening before: *'I had to give Jonah a bath and make him dinner.'* He almost dropped the bat in his surprise.

"Holy crap, you're the dog! You're *the* dog!" Adam exclaimed, leaning the bat against the desk. "What the hell happened?"

Jonah rolled his eyes in embarrassment. "Still trying to piece that together, with Mina's help. Where is she?"

"She went out and asked me to come by." At the mention of her name, Adam went towards her bedroom, shutting the front door as he passed by. "Let me get you some clothes. You're getting too friendly with my sister's old blanket. I gave it to her for her tenth birthday, and she used to take it on sleepovers—thanks for ruining that memory for me."

"Yeah, sorry," Jonah said. "I didn't have it when I fell asleep, so I guess she threw it over me before she left."

Adam was hoping that Jonah had still been a husky when Mina covered him up, otherwise, she had gotten an eyeful of him. He harbored no illusions about his baby sister's innocence, but he didn't need any more reminders that she was a grown, experienced woman.

He returned to the living room with a sweatshirt and a pair of jogging pants. "These should fit you. I've been looking for them for years and had no idea that she had them all along."

Adam went to the kitchen to give Jonah a

moment of privacy to get dressed, and poured him a glass of cold water. As he handed Jonah the glass, he remembered his own cup of coffee that he had left by the door when he had arrived. As he stooped to get his cup, he heard footsteps and hushed voices through the closed door, approaching quickly. He stood and quickly threw the deadbolt, as he stepped back from the door.

"Something wrong?" Jonah asked, then scowled. "Is someone in the hallway?"

"Get somewhere out of sight," Adam said, handing him the bat.

"Fuck *that!*" Jonah snarled, swatting the bat away "If there's going to be a fight, our odds are better if we stay together."

"Nobody's looking for *me*, magic dog-boy," Adam said. "If they don't see you here, they won't waste their time or energy, needlessly."

"You don't know that!"

Their debate was cut short by the front door bursting open, tearing easily off its hinges like a page from a book. A swarm of thumb-sized wasps poured through the hole first, encircling Adam and Jonah in moments and stinging them just enough to force them back, as a quartet of white-hooded figures stepped nimbly through the ruined door.

The bat crumbled into sawdust in Adam's grip, the wasps vanished, and the lead figure of the quartet stepped forward to blow a fine powder into Adam and Jonah's faces before they could turn away. An overwhelming, stinging pain shot through Adam's eyes and nose, and he instinctively ducked to cover his face.

The momentary distraction provided the

intruders enough opportunity to throw something dark over Adam, like a blanket or tarp, obscuring his senses and restricting his movement, and he felt a claustrophobic panic as his arms were bound to his sides.

"I think I've changed my mind," a woman's voice said. "Leave the other one, and I'll have this one, instead." Adam felt something resting on his head, and he immediately jerked away from the unwelcome contact, causing a ripple of laughter. "They both have the potential and energy, but this one already has the sight."

Adam heard and felt Jonah's struggle next to him, sometimes sounding like a feral growl, then a confused shout as Jonah seemingly got himself loose, and Adam felt himself being guided forward, as the ties began to loosen from his arms.

"Imbeciles!" the first voice cried, and a fearsome, echoing roar sounded, from what Adam thought was the direction of the stairwell outside. "Stop them! Shoot them, if you must."

"Come on, this way," Jonah whispered hoarsely, leading Adam through the tattered front door, as Adam managed to pull the tarp off his head. They took a moment to assess the situation, as standing at the top of the stairs was Mina, with a massive, white-coated Tibetan mastiff literally hovering at her side. As it circled around her, the shadows of its luxuriant silver mane reflected as azure blue.

Mrs Krantz's door opened downstairs, as the old woman called out. "What's all the ruckus? Are you alright up there?"

"Fine, Missus Krantz," Mina said, with an

otherworldly, lulling quality to her voice. "Stay inside, and lock the door." The second floor apartment door closed and locked quietly.

"Mina Gideon," greeted the quartet, speaking as a single, layered voice, as they emerged from Mina's apartment. "One would expect your personal sanctum to be better guarded."

Mina didn't answer, and instead, the spectral dog bounded forward with a growl and plunged through the hole in her front door, dragging three of the figures back inside with its winding tail, with the fourth figure leaping out of the way at the last second. In the moment that the dog's serpentine tail cleared the doorway, the door restacked and repaired itself, cutting the fourth figure off from her support.

The last figure reached into the folds of her white robes, and Jonah lunged at her. Adam had only a moment to react, pushing Mina out of the way, just in time to hear the gunshot and feel the sharp, tearing pain at his side.

Mina screamed and caught him before he sank to the floor, as Jonah managed to wrest the gun from the shooter. He tried to grab the hooded figure, as well, but only managed to pull the white robe free before she leapt over the railing, plummeting down the stairwell, but Adam got the feeling that they hadn't seen the last of her. *If I stay around that long.*

His vision darkened, and he thought he caught glimpses of familiar faces and heard additional voices, from both the living and dead, but he wasn't sure if it was just his overactive imagination, or if he was really close to dying, for the second time that month. Jonah appeared next to Mina, and Adam was glad that at least she wouldn't be alone...

"No," Mina sobbed, cradling his head. "You can't leave me like this."

"Hey, *mei-mei*," he said, grasping her hand. "I always said I'd protect you, so I'm not leaving anytime soon. Mom and Dad wouldn't allow it."

Xani and Morgan stood at Mina's apartment door, staring at the splinters and shards that littered the floor and wondered where they fit, given that the heavy oak door looked perfectly intact.

Their locksmith, Bob, hadn't mentioned anything, as he was still working on securing the front door and hadn't even gone upstairs. He mentioned that, when he arrived, he had seen a blond woman leave the building in a rush, but he hadn't seen or heard anything out of the ordinary.

Xani knocked once on Mina's door and took a deep breath, smelling bleach and industrial-strength cleaner in the air, tinged with eucalyptus and lavender. To Xani's surprise, a stranger opened Mina's door: a tall, attractive stranger with silver-streaked black hair and startling, wide-set gray-blue eyes, wearing a sweatshirt emblazoned with the logo of Adam's college alma mater.

"You must be Alexandra and Morgan," he greeted, standing aside to let them inside. "Thanks for coming so quickly."

Xani noticed her brother's discomfiture easily. He was a little jealous of the older man, with good reason. "Hi, I don't think we've met,"

Xani said, extending her hand as Morgan shut the door behind them. As in the hallway, there were splinters and wooden shards on the floor, plus a huge pile of sawdust, and Xani noticed for the first time that the stranger was holding a dustpan and brush, which he hastily moved to his left hand so that he could accept her handshake.

"Sorry," he said sheepishly. "I'm Jonah Gideon."

"*Jonah* Gideon," Xani said, with some surprise. "Any relation to Malcolm?"

"He was my first cousin," he said solemnly. It was plain from his sober expression that he knew that Malcolm was dead. "Hold on, let me get Mina."

"No, don't bother," Xani said, slipping off her shoes once she was safely away from the door. "Looks like you have some sweeping to do here. Morgan," she said, as she took a look around at the apartment, hastily straightened but clearly in need of more tidying, "maybe you can give Jonah a hand while I take the supplies back to Mina?"

Xani darted towards the bedroom before Morgan had even answered her, as she had too many questions to ask Mina, but she only had more questions once she entered the bedroom. Adam was sitting up in Mina's bed, with wads of gauze secured to his side with generous amounts of cloth tape, and an empty water cooler jug sat on the floor nearby, containing three frantically squeaking and scratching white mice.

Mina was sitting on the edge of her bed, typing away on her laptop next to her. A small-caliber handgun lay on a small dishcloth next to her laptop, as well. Mina glanced up at Xani and smiled. "Hey, thanks for coming so quickly." She held out her hand, and Xani handed her the bag of supplies.

"Yeah, no problem." She started to ask where the dog was, but then she thought of Jonah's blue eyes and graying hair... *No, that's just a weird coincidence.* "So, where's Arkady?"

Adam chuckled, then winced, holding his side, and Mina unpacked the new roll of gauze and large bottle of pain reliever pills. She opened the bottle and handed Adam three pills and a glass of water from her bedside table. "Gone, presently," Mina answered finally, "but he'll be back in a few hours."

Xani circled to the other side of Mina's bed. "What happened to you?" she asked Adam.

"I was shot," he said shortly, sipping his water slowly. "With that," he gestured to the gun.

"Why didn't you go to a hospital?" Xani exclaimed. "Whose gun is that?"

"Too much to explain to the doctors and the police," he said tiredly. "It's just a flesh wound, and I trust Mina more than the hospital doctors."

Jonah appeared in the doorway. "I'm going to look for the bullet in the hallway," he said. "You guys need anything?"

Mina glanced at her laptop. "The battery's getting low. Can you grab my charging cord from my desk, please?"

Xani didn't miss the anticipatory smile on Mina's face as Jonah left, or how it slipped a little when it was Morgan who returned with the cord. Morgan didn't notice Mina's underwhelmed reaction, as he was more focused on Adam's bandaged wound.

As Mina plugged the cable into her laptop, she glanced over. "Oh, be careful not to knock over the bottle, please. I haven't figured out yet what I want to do with them."

Morgan seemed to only notice the bottled white mice then, as he had been so stunned by the sight of Adam injured and taped, just as Xani had been. "So many questions," he muttered.

"I'm sorry, guys," Mina said, her eyes focused on her laptop. "I know you want some explanations, but there's just a lot going on." She looked in the doorway, over Morgan's shoulder and past him. "Ah, fuck."

Adam set his hand on Mina's shoulder. "You're doing fine, kiddo. The spirits are just here to check on you—they're not in any rush."

Xani looked to the empty doorway. "What spirits?"

"Ghosts," Mina said shortly. "This is so weird," she said to Adam, "that you can see them now, too."

"With this last brush with death, I can hear them now, too." Adam narrowed his eyes. "Malcolm doesn't seem too happy to see me, though. He wants me to stay alive for a good, long time, because if I die now, I am *so* going to beat the shit out of him."

Xani shook her head. "Wait, why can you see ghosts?"

Jonah returned and handed a wadded tissue to Mina. "It was in the wall, just nicked a beam. I wasn't sure if you wanted me to wash it, or..."

Mina took the tissue with a grateful nod. "No, it's better not to. I want to see what else was on it, since the gun is clean." She explained to

Xani, "A traumatic event can awaken the sight, which is what happened to Adam recently. You've been through a lot lately," she said to him, "but it takes a lot to make you pass out, so I suspect there was something else at work."

Jonah turned his head sharply. "No, you still don't get to go into her room," he said to some unseen presence. "You're not invited. Come on, guys, let's give them some privacy," he said, motioning as though he was herding someone back to the living room area.

"He looks better, but still acts like your husky," Adam muttered to Mina.

Mina stared after him with concern. "I may not be able to cure him until I can figure out what was used on him. He'll be in flux, but at least he'll be able to anticipate his transformation. Too bad, I actually enjoyed our walks," she said lightly.

"Hold up," Xani interjected. "So, Jonah is Arkady? And he can see the ghosts, too. When you said that he'd be 'back in a few hours,' you meant he's going to change back into a dog, soon?"

Mina nodded. "That reminds me, I need to talk to him before he transforms, and see what he still remembers," she said, still clutching the tissue in her hand.

"Go ahead," Adam said. "I'll be okay for a while."

Morgan watched Mina leave, and Xani felt bad for her brother. He had the misfortune of pining for someone who was unlikely to give him the attention he craved, unless he was in mortal danger or cursed.

92

"We might need a rain check on dinner tomorrow," Adam smiled weakly. "Depends on how I feel."

"If you didn't want to have dinner with me, you could've just texted," Xani said mockingly. "You didn't have to get yourself shot for it."

## Chapter 6

Jonah heard Mina's footsteps before he heard her voice or smelled her lavender and orange scent. After a month of being sheltered in her home, surrounded by her presence and her artifacts, her treasures as well as her ephemera, he was starting to get attached to Mina's apartment, and to her. The apartment was not as aromatically rich, but much cheerier and more colorful than it had appeared when he was a dog.

"You didn't have to clean up," she said, looking around the space where the intruders had done the most damage. "I would've gotten around to it, once everyone was gone and things had quieted down. Shit, you don't even have slippers," she said, looking down at Jonah's bare feet. "And you're walking around on splinters! I'm sorry, I'm such an ass!"

Jonah looked down at his feet, and they still looked a little odd to him, after having only seen furry paws for the past several weeks. "I'm alright, really. I've been bare-footed for the past month, already, and I've built up some callouses."

He emptied the full dustpan into the garbage can and stooped in front of her bookcase, where some pottery and frames had fallen and broken. "I wasn't sure what you wanted to try to save out of this."

Mina crouched and picked up a cracked frame, with a faded picture of the Xing family at a park somewhere, when Mina was probably kindergarten age, with Adam and Mina sitting on their parents' laps. "I'll reframe any pictures. The rest of it can be tossed." As she shook out the glass shards over the garbage, a tiny piece nicked her thumb. Caught by surprise, she cursed under her breath in Chinese, as she set the frame aside.

"Let me see," Jonah said, pulling a tissue from a box on her desk to blot the cut. Clinically, he pulled her hand closer to inspect it for anything remaining in the wound. "Does it hurt?"

"No," she said quietly. "I'll be okay."

"Yeah, you will," he assured lightly, giving her knuckles a quick peck before he released her hand, keeping the tissue pressed against her thumb. "So, save the photos, and toss the rest. Got it."

"Listen," she said soberly. "You probably only have a couple of hours before you transform back, so I don't want you to waste it cleaning up my crap. While we can communicate, you should tell me what you remember right before you changed last month. You can also use the time to take care of your personal hygiene, while you still have opposable thumbs, and less fur to get in the way," she suggested delicately.

Jonah laughed, and he was astounded at how good it felt to be able to do that again. "I will clean myself up," he promised. "It's the least I can do, after everything you've done for me." He sighed. "When I change back into a dog, how long will be it be before you can make me human again?"

"I don't know," Mina admitted. "The elixir will stay in your system for another day or so, so you'll probably shift back to human again tomorrow. I'm hoping to find you a permanent cure, though, instead of dosing you again."

Jonah was pleasantly surprised, as he had expected his return to human form to be a one-time event. "This isn't too bad, I guess," he said. "As long as I could be human for part of my day, I could live with this." He saw Mina ready to interject. "Just for a day or so. I know."

"Until you're cured, resuming your life in Boston would be a challenge," she said, taking the dustpan and brush in hand. "And I'm not sure yet, how long that process is going to take."

"It'll take as long as it takes," he shrugged. "My family's used to me being out of contact for extended periods, anyway, and Boston's cool, but New York's starting to grow on me."

"Really?" Mina asked dubiously, sweeping up the broken knick-knacks into the dustpan.

*There's no one in Boston like you*, he wanted to say, but he held his tongue. That was too close to flirting, and he was already wary of Morgan Crain's ambivalence about his presence. He didn't want to get in the middle of anything, whether real or imagined, especially where Mina was involved.

Jonah had already learned that lesson with Malcolm. He looked over to the couch, where Malcolm was lounging and watching their exchange, and noticed his cousin's watchful glare. If Mina had noticed it, she was deliberately ignoring his petulance.

If he were Morgan or any other regular guy, Jonah would have gone after Mina in a heartbeat, but having his dead cousin's ghost hanging around definitely put a damper on things.

Mina scooped some loose jasmine tea leaves into a warmed tea pot while she waited for the water to reach a low simmer. For what felt like the first time that afternoon, she had a moment of quiet and time to reflect. Adam was finally asleep in the bedroom, and Jonah was curled up on the couch, back in his husky form. Morgan and Xani had left some time ago, after refusing her reimbursement for the cost of the first aid supplies they had brought.

At Xani's prodding, Morgan had shown his wrists to Mina, and she saw the tiny cut that marked a dark bruise, confirming their earlier suspicion that some blood had been drawn from him. In light of her conversation that morning with Sophie, followed by the attack on her apartment, Mina had good reason to suspect that Morgan was in some kind of trouble, or at the least, in danger of being used.

Mina didn't want to alarm the Crains, but they were smart enough to already suspect that their new potential client was possibly more trouble than their paycheck was worth. Still, she advised them to consider accepting the deal with Garrison Brothers, anyway, despite the latter's unsavory practices, if only to have some view into what their sisterhood division was planning. As long they remained vigilant and honest about their association with Mina, the arrangement could work to everyone's benefit.

Mina was most concerned for Adam. She had never meant for her brother to be endangered on her behalf, and now that his spirit sight had been awakened, he was a target in his own right. She wasn't sure if he remembered the nightmares he had had when they were children, when he described seeing tortured ghosts. It could have been Adam's youthful imagination, or an early sign of his innate sensitivity to the spirit world. Either way, Mina recalled their mother setting a picture of *Zhong Kui,* the vanquisher of evil spirits, over his headboard, to finally restore his peaceful sleep.

Mina used one of the spent candles from the night before to smudge protective characters and symbols around her window frames in her bedroom and bathroom, to reinforce the barrier that she had erected to protect her sanctum. As she went to her living room window to do the same, Malcolm watched her from her desk chair.

*You did that when we moved into our place*, he recalled. *It's supposed to keep evil spirits at bay?*

It was the first time that Malcolm had ever expressed an interest in what she did. "It's a barrier to anything that threatens whomever is inside," Mina clarified. "Sometimes, it's a spirit. Sometimes, it's a person."

*Seems pretty useless,* Jack scoffed. *It didn't keep those bitches out of here earlier.*

"It kept you out this week when you tried to force your way in," Mina reminded. She opened the door and scowled at the smudged markings against her threshold. "But the barrier works best if it's unbroken," she said, repairing the characters and symbols with new wax where she saw breaks and smears.

*Did you do that?* Malcolm demanded, looking at Jack. *You broke the line. It's your fault those witches got in here!*

*How was I supposed to know what that was!* Jack said defensively.

"It's okay," she said, feeling like she was mediating a children's squabble. "It's fixed, and my *ruishi* caught most of them."

*Was that your giant snow dog-lion thing?* Malcolm asked.

"Tibetan snow lion," she said. "It prefers mountains, but this one hangs out near the midtown skyscrapers and helps me out now and then." Mina shut and locked the door and went to her simmering tea kettle to fill her teapot. She always associated the smell of jasmine black tea with her parents' pantry, along with dried mushrooms and desiccated shellfish, and preparing and drinking her mother's favorite tea was a meditative exercise for Mina.

*You usually drink that stuff when you need to concentrate on something*, Malcolm remarked. *What are you trying to figure out?*

"Stop," Mina said sharply. "You don't have to be nice. I'll help you regardless."

*Can't I be nice, just out of the goodness of my heart?* Malcolm asked.

*Your heart's in the morgue, being packed in cold storage for your trip home*, Jack said snidely. *You should've made it up to her when you were alive, when there was at least a chance of a thank-you fuck.*

"Yeah, there was zero chance of that, even when he was alive," Mina said, pouring her tea. As she swished the brew in her cup to let it cool, she looked at both Malcolm and Jack. "You were both driven to kill yourselves, not actually murdered, so whoever did that didn't want your deaths to be traced to her."

*You don't think Sophie did this to us?* Malcolm asked.

"She cursed you, but she didn't want or need either of you dead. She wanted you both to stop being assholes, not to send your business my way."

*Yeah, why do you want to help us?* Jack asked suspiciously. *I would've hired you to get rid of my visions, but I can't pay you anymore.*

"Everyone deserves peace, and a final chance to make amends," Mina said, taking a sip of her tea. "I don't mean amends to me. For all I know, you both hate my fucking guts, but you're both what the Chinese call *yuan gui*, or 'ghosts with grievances.' It means that you have unfinished business to resolve before moving on, so if you've come to me, then I should help you, whether you can pay me or not."

*What about him?* Malcolm asked, pointing his chin at Jonas's sleeping form. *Are you going to help him for free, too?*

"We haven't discussed it," Mina said, hearing Malcolm's pettiness. "I'd have to charge him for room and board for the past month, too, if we need to itemize the expenses."

*Expenses,* Jack echoed. *That reminds me. When Sophie and I were out, she insisted on keeping all the receipts and said she was going to*

100

*expense it all, anyway.*

*She did the same with me*, Malcolm said.

Mina set her cup down. "I think I've been looking at this all wrong," she murmured. "I thought this was a personal concern, but maybe it's more than that. Especially in light of the visit earlier, and Garrison Brothers engaging the Crains for their building security, this may be bigger than just a vengeance ploy."

*The break-in wasn't just Sophie's friends coming to help straighten out her mess?* Malcolm asked.

"I had considered that, but then their plans changed," Mina said. "They were coming for Jonah but tried to grab Adam instead. Sophie has no interest in my brother, or any grudge against him. And if this was her problem, she would've been here herself; she's not senior enough in the sisterhood to send others to do her will."

*The leader seemed to be in charge of the whole operation,* Malcolm said. *And she said that Adam had the sight? Assuming that she wasn't just crazy, that is.*

"Let's see what my little guests have to say," she said, returning to the living room to look in on the water cooler bottle. She hadn't looked in on the trio of white mice since moving the bottle from the bedroom, but she had noticed that they had quieted down gradually, once they realized the futility of their escape efforts.

Mina was dismayed to see that two of the mice were stiff and unmoving, with white foam around their half-open mouths. The third mouse was cowering, trying to keep a distance from the other two.

"Shit," she muttered. "Malcolm, can you please check on Adam for me and stop in on Missus Krantz downstairs, and make sure she's okay?"

Malcolm vanished without comment. Working quickly, Mina unrolled her bamboo mat onto her living room floor, recited a containment incantation and carefully tilted the water cooler bottle over the mat, letting the last mouse scamper free from its prison while keeping the dead mice inside.

Once the mouse landed on the mat, it darted for the edge and tried to find a way off but was thwarted by Mina's incantation. Mina placed the bottle out of view, behind the sofa, and recited the words to undo her surviving prisoner's transformation. She perched on the arm of her sofa to watch her spell take effect.

As she changed from the small rodent back into a person again, the young, dark-haired woman screeched in terror, her mind still in its panicky, prey-like state. Only when she realized that she was full-sized again, dressed in her white robes once more, did she relax, a little, but she still despaired at being contained within the borders of the bamboo mat.

"You have no right to keep me here!" the young woman screamed, and Mina could tell from her voice that she was even younger than she appeared. "This is kidnapping!"

"You participated in a home invasion, destruction of property, assault and attempted kidnapping," Mina replied coolly. "You don't get to act so aggrieved and self-righteous here."

"Well...my sisters are dead because of you,"

102

she shot back, less certain now of her moral superiority.

"I never touched any of you," Mina shrugged. "And my *ruishi* does what it wants with trespassers without my direction, but it never kills. What happened to your colleagues was unfortunate, but not caused by me."

The brunette laughed harshly. "Isn't that convenient! Miranda was right; you think you're so much better than us, that you're blameless for everything that happens to the people around you."

Mina didn't acknowledge the false assumption, or that she had heard the leader's name: Miranda. It wasn't an uncommon name, but Mina personally knew of few who were practicing witches, even fewer who wielded such notable influence and power.

"So, why did you come here, then? To teach me a lesson about the importance of teamwork and sticking together?" she goaded. "How's that working for you?"

"You fucking bitch!" the girl railed. "They were my friends, my sisters. You should've let me die in there with them," she said miserably.

"That can still be arranged," Mina offered. "Would you like me to dispatch you, or would you like to try the poison that the sisterhood provided to them?" At the girl's frown, Mina clarified: "That foaming at their mouths was due to ingested poison, probably provided as a water-soluble tattoo that they could lick to self-administer."

"Miranda wouldn't order us to do that," the girl sniffed. This time, she realized that she had let the name slip but tried to control her reaction.

"Well, then, there's nothing for you to worry about," Mina said lightly. "Off you pop, out of my home. You can let Miranda know the others died honorably, rather than betray the sisterhood."

"You're just letting me go?" the girl asked, bewildered.

"Sure. Do you need cab fare, or want some tea before you go?" Mina ignored Jack's apoplectic shouts, beyond the girl's range of senses. "I can also pack your colleagues for you in a shoebox, if you'd like to take them back with you."

"How can you be so cruel, to mock their deaths?"

"Cruel?" Mina's faint, polite smile vanished entirely. "You and your sisters broke into my home and nearly killed my brother, so I'm not feeling too fucking charitable," she growled. "You can either accept the mercy I've offered and get the fuck out, or I can flush three dead mice down the toilet instead of two. I don't give a shit, either way."

"I'll go," the girl said, resigned.

"Fine." Mina dispelled the enchantment that kept the girl contained on the mat and led the way to the door. "Do you want to take your sisters?" she offered quietly.

The girl shook her head and rushed to the door.

Mina held out a five-dollar bill. "The subway's faster and cheaper than a cab. You can catch the southbound 6th Avenue train at 47th Street, and get off at West 4th."

As Mina closed and locked the door behind

the girl, Malcolm reappeared in the apartment and looked around in confusion. Mina crossed her arms and looked at the disapproving spirits in her living room. "What? She was hostile because she was disoriented and scared. So were both of you, when you showed up at my house, except that she's just a kid, and you were both grown-ass men."

*You released her?* Malcolm asked. *What if she decided to attack you?*

"I wasn't going to hold her against her will," Mina said. "That would be wrong, and illegal. The protective border's been restored, so she couldn't attack me. Anything she tried would've bounced back onto her."

She returned to her desk and opened up her laptop. "There's only one 'Miranda' I know with the resources or possible interest to encroach into my territory like this, and she does operate mostly out of Boston. We've never met, but maybe this is her way of introducing herself."

Malcolm looked over her shoulder. *That's not a typical web browser.*

Mina navigated the multiple text-heavy windows with ease. "No, it's not. It would be hard to stay hidden and private if we witches plastered ourselves all over the Internet." She found few images of purported sightings of Garrison Brothers' management team or Sophie's mysterious sisterhood, but even fewer of the mysterious Miranda. Mina had recognized most of images from past research efforts, and for the majority of them, Miranda was an elderly woman, wizened and walking with a stick.

*She doesn't look spry enough to command an*

*army of witches,* Malcolm said.

"No, she doesn't, does she," Mina mumbled, looking at the background figures. As she scanned the faces that were not obscured by cowls or scarves, she noticed a young woman with long, dark brown hair, who seemed to stare into the cameras, almost defiantly.

*Hold on*, Jack said, pointing to the girl.

"Sneaky, conniving witch," Mina snarled. It was the same girl that she had freed from the bottle and turned human again. "I'm such a tool," she berated herself, pushing away from the desk to look inside the water bottle at the two dead mice. "What's the only way to ensure that three people can keep a secret?"

Malcolm replied without hesitation: *If two of them are dead.*

Mina looked inside at the bottle, more carefully this time, and saw the prominence of the ribs and hip bones, the thinness of the fur, the yellowing of the claws and overlong teeth. "They weren't just poisoned, they actually died of old age."

*How can that be?* Jack asked. *They certainly didn't tear up your place like old ladies, or act like old mice when they were in the bottle.*

"They weren't," Mina said. "They were all young when they were captured. The last one sucked the life force out of the other two and killed them, or forced them to kill themselves." She shook her head despondently. "And I let her out."

*You didn't know. She didn't try to attack you when she got loose,* Malcolm said.

"She watched me go around the apartment

reinforcing protection circles," Mina said. "She knew she couldn't try anything in here once the protection was in place, so she probably killed the others while I was in the other rooms. And now Miranda knows what protection spells I use, so I'm going to need something new to keep them out."

Jack was a little slower to follow the conversation, but he finally caught on. *So, the old lady in the pictures isn't Miranda. It's actually the chick with the long dark hair?*

Mina nodded. "Yes, and I just set her free and gave her five bucks to get home."

"Son of a *bitch!* Black peppercorn..."

Adam crept along the hallway until he was able to peer into the kitchen area, where Mina seemed to immersing different objects and materials into small glass jars of some kind of liquid, while a burning white candle sat in its holder on the bamboo mat. She was seemingly too intent on watching for chemical reactions to notice Adam, but Jonah's husky-form raised his head and gave him a throaty, yawning greeting that almost sounded like: "Yo."

"Digitalis, nepeta and black peppercorn," Mina said, sprinkling a white powder into a jar that contained a light blue liquid, and the bullet that had pierced his side. "There was foxglove, catnip and pepper on the bullet, along with a few other, more standard additives. It was meant to knock you out—umm, knock *me* out—not cause any permanent damage, but of course, it hit you harder because you have no immunities."

"Immunities?" he asked.

"I've been dosing myself over the past few years to build up a resistance to some of these," she confessed. On her desk, her laptop was open, with several windows open displaying photographs of a young woman with long dark hair.

Adam listened to Mina with as much enthusiasm as he could muster, but really, all he wanted was some water. He did smell some jasmine tea in the air, too, and he spotted the teapot on the counter. He gestured to it silently, and Mina got him a cup.

"Anyway, I also found what Miranda had used to hide the enchantment on the boys, so that they couldn't remember everything, and to make it harder for me to detect what had happened to Jonah," she said, pouring Adam a full cup of tea. "It's a little tepid, now, but there's hot water in the kettle."

"This is fine," he said, taking the cup gratefully. "That's Miranda, I presume," he said, gesturing to the woman in the photographs on-screen.

"Yes." Mina knelt in front of the white candle with a bowl of fragrant, aromatic herbs and oils. To Adam, it looked and smelled like some kind of vinaigrette, then he remembered that it was his hunger that had driven him from bed. He distracted himself by watching her drizzle a teaspoonful of the mixture into the flame of the candle. White smoke to billow, like an incense cloud.

"So, this Miranda person, is she the leader of the group that's been plaguing us?" he asked.

"As far as I can tell," Mina said. "I'm just

purifying the apartment, in case she or the others left anything noxious behind for me. I also asked Malcolm and Jack to go down to MacDougal Street and scout out the Garrison Brothers brownstone, and see if they spot her."

Mina retrieved a can of mixed nuts and a box of sesame crackers from her pantry cabinet. "Sorry, I haven't had a chance to grocery shopping. There may be a jar of kimchi in the fridge, too?"

"This is fine, thanks," Adam said, grabbing a handful of nuts. "So, with Malcolm and Jack, do you trust them to do a competent job?"

"I don't really have a choice," Mina shrugged. "It's in their best interest to do as I ask, if they want to move on from their former lives. I can't help them, unless they're being totally honest with me."

"What about this one?" Adam asked, looking at Jonah askance. "Has he been honest, during the times that he's been human?"

Jonah's pale blue eyes shifted back and forth, as he could understand them but couldn't add to the discussion.

"Jonah would have the most to lose, if he tries to deceive me," Mina said. "He still has a life to complete, while Malcolm and Jack are done with theirs. Miranda made a mistake by using the same concealment spell to trick me this time, as she had before, so I was able to piece together what she did."

"Before? So, it wasn't Sophie behind all this?" Adam asked.

It took a second for Mina to remember that Adam hadn't been present for any earlier conversations. "Sophie started the process, but it was Miranda's involvement to push things further. Now, I have what I need to mitigate the damage, as much as I can."

"Okay, well, I don't want to add to your chores," Adam said. "I feel fine to go back to my apartment, so you can have your bedroom back."

Mina looked fretful. "I'd rather have you stay where I can keep an eye on you."

"I live in a building with a doorman," he reminded. "I think I'll be fine."

"A building which is practically just on the opposite side of Washington Square Park from where this sisterhood resides," Mina pointed out. "And I love Doorman Dave, but you and I both know he's more decorative than functional. I'll be fine out here with Jonah."

"I don't know if I feel comfortable having you sleep out here with Jonah," Adam said protectively.

"Oh, for God's sake!" Mina exclaimed. "I'm not sleeping *with* him. I mean, just look at him. He's going to remain a dog through the night and well past my wake-up time, so nothing's going to happen."

Adam was unconvinced, recognizing the early signs of Mina's attachment. She had been that flustered when she had first started hanging out with Malcolm, too. "Are you saying that, if he weren't a dog, you'd consider it?"

Mina threw up her hands. "I have so many balls in the air right now that I can't spare any brain cells to contemplate whether I should fuck my dead ex's cousin, okay?" She gave Jonah a joking pout. "Sorry, it's just not a priority."

Jonah blinked and seemed to shrug his haunches before setting his muzzle on the couch arm cushion.

"Okay," Adam said mildly. "I just wanted to make sure."

"Really, *ge-ge*," Mina said, shaking her head. "Only you would even bring up that notion."

"I'm the only one who would say it to your face," Adam corrected, sipping his tea, "but I'm sure I'm not the only one who's thinking it."

# Chapter 7

Cindy McManus was born a little over twenty-eight years ago as Cyril James, to Amity James, of Sunset Park, Brooklyn, who had recently emigrated from the West Indies. Cyril's young mother waitressed during the day and got her GED and took night classes in hopes of finding better work, and to show her only child someday, when he was old enough to understand, that the only limits to his success would be his imagination.

When Cyril was a little over one, Amity met Dan McManus, a handsome, hard-working and traditional man of Irish descent who saw past Amity's modest resources and cared for Cyril as his own, despite their obvious physical differences. The courtship was brief and affectionate, and it seemed as though Amity James McManus and her baby boy Cyril had realized their American dream.

Life changed dramatically when Cyril was approaching his third birthday, when Amity noticed an odd angularity to the contours of her son's shoulder blades during a bath. Cyril seemed untroubled and unhindered, but as the days went on, the skin of his back became thinner by his scapulae, and fine, pale bones like fingernails pushed through, until the bones formed into black nubs, sprouting overnight into diaphanous wings.

Cyril's wings reminded Amity of the life she had left in the Caymans. She, herself, was part-fae, but when she didn't sprout wings, she had hoped that her son would be spared, as well. Even when she had seen the tell-tale signs of his emerging wings, she had hoped that they would stop growing on their own. Dan had been horrified and furious that Amity had neglected to mention her own history, and he felt like a fool for being tricked into harboring faeries, but he loved his family and was determined to make the best of the situation.

Whenever Cyril went out, his mother had bound his wings and dressed him in baggy clothes to obscure his fae nature. Given his young age, however, he hadn't started school yet, so he spent most of his days indoors, under his mother's supervision.

One evening, while Cyril was playing rambunctiously with his dinosaur toys, as children often do, he was so overexcited that his wings began to beat wildly, and he actually hovered, like a bumblebee. For Dan McManus, it was too much to handle, and in a drunken rage, he took a knife to Cyril's wings and severed them.

Had Cyril cried out or screamed, Dan might have come to his senses and stopped, but Cyril thought of his mother, out grocery shopping with the money that came mostly from Dan's hard work, and the boy stayed silent. Even at his young age, Cyril understood that sacrifices were necessary to achieve and maintain happiness, and above all, he wanted his mother to be happy, so he shut his eyes tightly and refused to cry.

Cyril was actually surprised when it was over, as it hadn't hurt nearly as much as he had expected. By the time he felt the soreness in his back, the cuts had already stopped bleeding. As his drunken father stumbled back to the kitchen to wash the bloodied knife, Cyril saw his wings up close for the first and last time. Lying on the floor next to him, they looked scary—black and veiny like dragonfly wings—and Cyril considered that maybe his father was right to get rid of them before other people saw them.

In the years to come, Cyril wouldn't remember very much of the rest of that evening, as it was a memory best left buried or forgotten. He recalled that there was lot of crying that night, from both Amity and Dan, over the irreparable mutilation that Dan had inflicted on their son, all because he had been acting like a child and playing too joyfully.

Despite what he had suffered, Cyril considered his childhood a good one, once he forgave his father for what he had done. Dan, for his part, stopped drinking and focused his attention on being the best husband and father possible. While both his parents supported his ambitions and decisions through his school years, it had actually been Dan who first recognized that Cyril was unhappy and disconnected from his body and needed more than his loving relationship with Xani Crain could provide.

Cyril and Xani never stopped caring for each other, but their relationship became increasingly sexless, as their physical connection dwindled.

Xani liked men, exclusively, while Cyril—now beginning to live as Cindy—enjoyed and appreciated the charms of all genders. Over time, they separated as a couple but remained close as friends and business partners.

Since opening night of the Red Lotus over three years earlier, Cindy had overseen the business end of running the lounge, everything from its construction and décor, to payroll and finances. She was also in the bar most nights, usually working behind the counter, to satisfy her innate fae compulsion to charm and socialize.

Saturday evenings were usually the busiest, but Micah was an astute and effective bouncer, diligently screening customers at the door even when faced with an endless line of impatient guests. In his days of servitude, centuries ago, Micah had reportedly stood his ground against hordes of scimitar-wielding guards and assassins, so he could handle New York clubgoers with no problem. With his shaved head and smooth, tanned skin, it was impossible to guess his age, but with his looks and physique, it didn't matter.

No matter how busy the Red Lotus looked on any given night, there was always enough room for more, without feeling stifling or overcrowded. It was one of the reasons for the lounge's popularity with the locals, including Mina, who also liked its close proximity to her building.

Still, Mina didn't drink habitually, so she didn't typically visit the Lotus unless there was a specific reason, whether personal or business. Tonight, it was business, but Mina dressed the part of a club regular, with just enough makeup and shine on her clothes to blend in with the

Saturday crowd.

"You'd let me know, if I was hurting your profit margin, right?" Mina asked Cindy, as the latter mixed up her cranberry and seltzer, sans vodka.

Cindy clicked her tongue. "What you eat and drink gets covered by what the bar makes in tips in an hour. Don't worry your pretty little head about it. Besides, I still owe you a recruitment fee for finding us Micah," she said, setting Mina's drink on a coaster in front of her. "He never takes a day off, and I think some of our customers come just to ogle him."

"Let's call it even," Mina said. "Not many places in the city would have hired a jinn without references or decree of emancipation."

"Your word is good enough for me. Besides, we supernatural beings have to stick together," Cindy said, glancing at the red and white occupancy limit sign, which had just quietly changed the capacity limit from two hundred to three hundred. The walls pulled back a foot or so on all sides, and an extra door appeared in the back corridor, leading to an additional private room. It was a subtle, gradual change, which the owners of the Red Lotus also owed to Mina's witchy ingenuity.

"You look tired, honey," Cindy said. "I mean, you look gorgeous, as usual, but I hear your apartment was overrun with uninvited guests today, and Adam got shot—"

"Which of the twins told you?" Mina asked.

"—and that your ex's hot cousin is your personal 'Big Bad Wolf' for the foreseeable future? Not metaphorically, I take it."

*Xani.* "Damn it," Mina sighed under her breath. "It's complicated."

"That's what makes it fun," Cindy smiled. "You should've brought him tonight."

"I thought the Lotus had a 'no pets' policy," Mina said.

"He doesn't sound like a pet, from what I've heard," Cindy returned. "But if you want to keep him to yourself, I understand."

"It's not like that, Cin," Mina said. "He has people waiting for him at home, back in Boston, so he doesn't need any ties or distractions here."

Cindy shook her head. "If that were the case, then he wouldn't still be here. He would've found a way to get home, with or without your help. I'm sure he could've found a local Bostonian witch to help him." She noticed Mina's unconscious frown. "I knew it! You *do* like him!"

"No, it's not that!" Mina said. "I suspect that it was a local witch that forced the change onto Jonah in the first place, so until that threat is managed, he's not safe. My place isn't a fortress, but it's safer than almost anywhere else."

"It's not safer than here, honey," Cindy countered. "You should consider it. You need to remain objective, for yourself and your clients."

Mina finished her drink. "I need to find a place for Adam, too. Or I need to fortify his apartment before I can let him go home."

Cindy leaned over the counter. "Bring them both here. I'm serious."

"That's too generous, Cindy," Mina said. "I don't want you getting on the wrong side of this group, until I understand their weaknesses a little better."

"While I'd certainly enjoy extra time with Adam, this is not an entirely selfless offer," Cindy said. "I have a favor to ask."

Mina straightened on her stool. "I'm listening."

"I hear your downstairs tenants just vacated the duplex," Cindy said. "I have visitors from out of town who need a place to stay, for a couple of weeks or so."

Mina read between the lines and understood that the visitors were not of the human sort or needed special attention, otherwise, Cindy would've set them up in one of the hundreds of hotels in the New York area. "There isn't much furniture left in the place. The beds are there, but I can't vouch for the condition of the mattresses. How many guests are we talking about?"

"Three or four. Six, tops," Cindy said. "I can't offer you the going New York rate for the apartment, but enough to cover the utilities and taxes for this month and next. They're expected to arrive next week, and they just need some privacy and security until the end of the month, at the latest."

"The unit's sitting empty for now, anyway," Mina said. "Let me know when you need it ready, and I'll have it cleaned and purified ahead of time."

"Thank you," Cindy said, relieved that her offer was acceptable. Her relief was brief, however, as a handsome, well-dressed, blond-haired gentleman passed Micah at the entrance. Tall, blond with blue eyes and a perfect physique, almost glowing despite the dim lighting inside the lounge. *Fuck.* She affixed a winning smile to her face and greeted her regular customer, thankful for the Saturday evening throng to divert his focus from herself and Mina.

The customer stepped up to the counter and stood near Mina but did not sit. "Business looks good tonight, sweet Cin," the gentleman said, his voice clear and audible despite the noise of the crowd.

"I'd never be able to cover the exorbitant rent, otherwise, darling," Cindy said lightly. "Vodka or tequila, tonight?"

"One of each, I think," he said, turning his attention to Mina. "Can I buy you another drink?"

"You're funny. No, thank you," Mina smiled, setting her empty glass back on Cindy's side of the counter. "I'm sure you have enough drinks to buy for your marks tonight, Lucifer, without wasting one on me."

"It wouldn't be a waste," the handsome devil grinned. "And I'm hurt, that you would call my potential clients 'marks'. I don't make deals with unwilling or unwitting partners, you know that."

"The nuances of how you conduct your business, escape my tiny mortal brain," Mina said, "but I do believe that I may have encountered some of your human associates, and I will need to deal with them harshly, if they continue to meddle in my life."

Lucifer furrowed his brow, which added broodiness to his list of charms. "Oh, dear. They've upset you, in some way. Would you like me to—"

"No," Mina said shortly, knowing better than to voice any request to the devil. "Thank you,

Luci, but I'll handle them. I just thought that you might want to know."

Lucifer alternated between sips of the tequila and vodka shots. "I have noticed an uptick in the number of souls in my waiting room. Two more girls, just this afternoon. Sniveling, mousy little things—they had been much bolder and more audacious when they pledged themselves to me last year." He sighed with disappointment. "They misrepresented themselves."

Mina shrugged half-heartedly. "They can't all be winners. So, Garrison Brothers is one of your organizations?"

"Its management is pledged to me, yes," he answered readily. "Most of its sisterhood division and underlings, but not all; corporate HR diversity practices must be followed, you understand. I should thank you for uncovering their ambitions, as they're acting without my express authority. On that point, you also have my sympathies on the passing of your former spouse," he said softly. "He was not expected to come up for review quite so soon."

Mina's wary side-glance indicated that she picked up on some additional subtext. "Malcolm and Jack are no longer yours to claim, are they? If they had continued to live as they did, they would've been, more than likely, but as *yuan gui*, they have a last chance to redeem themselves."

Lucifer's blue eyes turned icy. "Technicalities, and you can see the unfairness of it, I'm sure; why should they have a chance to be absolved of a lifetime of evils, by a simple change of heart at the end of their lives? It's like a bullshit act of contrition during last rites."

120

Mina shrugged. "What happens to Christian souls during judgment is not my purview; my services are non-denominational, as am I."

"I can respect that. You know, my offer still stands, Miss Xing," Lucifer said. "I could use a woman of your talents on my staff."

Cindy cleared the empty glasses, with a reproving glare at Lucifer. "That just sounds sleazy, especially coming from you, Luci."

"Mina knows what I mean, but the other arrangement is always open, also." Lucifer smiled handsomely. "No conditions or temporal constraints, and your satisfaction is guaranteed." He leaned a little closer but did not touch Mina. "When was your last, really good fuck, Miss Xing? The last time you came so hard that you almost blacked out?"

"Since you asked so nicely, it's been a while," Mina said evenly, "but I think I'll pass. Thanks for the pity fuck offer, anyway. I'm sure someone here will take you up on it." She glanced at Cindy. "I'll see you later."

Cindy nodded. "I'll be here past closing. Come by, whenever."

Lucifer watched the brief, meaningful exchange between the women and Mina's quick, direct exit. "She used to crush on you pretty hard, when you were a boy, but there's still a little ember burning there, I think. Have the two of you ever…"

Cindy narrowed her dark brown eyes reprimandingly. "Don't insert yourself where you don't belong, Luci, and I mean that in every sense." She gestured to the teeming crowd of beautiful and eligible clubgoers filling the Lotus.

"Look, there is much easier prey about tonight. If you flash your smile now and again, you'll be swimming in free tequila and vodka all evening, and have your pick of any flavor of flesh you crave."

Lucifer snorted. "I leave the drunken and weak ones to Astaroth. I prefer my quarry to be stealthier and more cunning." He returned his beguiling blue eyes to Cindy. "What were you and Mina discussing before I intruded?"

"Nothing that requires your attention," Cindy said plainly, setting another two shots in front of him. "These are from the satyr at the end of the bar." She nodded her head towards the goat-man working his way through a bottle of ouzo, who raised his glass when he finally caught Lucifer's attention.

Lucifer raised his vodka with a lukewarm smile of thanks to the satyr. "As a prospect, he's neither stealthy, nor cunning," he said under his breath.

"Maybe not, but you're not the only one who's on the hunt on Saturday nights," Cindy reminded. "You may be just the kind of quarry *he's* looking for."

Mina returned to her apartment and found her four guests seated in a circle around her living room area, apparently in the middle of an intense discussion or debate of some sort, judging by their serious faces. She was happy to see that Adam's color was better, and surprised to see Malcolm and Jack more engaged and less peevish than they had been when they had first manifested the day before.

She set an order of roast chicken, lemon potatoes and grilled pita on her counter. "I already had some snacks at the Lotus, so that's for those of you who still eat."

"Perhaps you can weigh in, *mei-mei*," Adam said.

"Okay?" she asked tentatively.

"Who would win in a fight: Ripley or Buffy?"

*Nerds never die, they just enter nerd-vana*, Mina thought to herself, as she tugged off her boots. "I'm going to guess that you mean Ellen Ripley from *Alien*. She's got experience, but Buffy the Vampire Slayer's got supernatural healing and strength, plus special training. They both died, but Buffy was actually resurrected, while Ripley was cloned, so technically, Buffy has the edge on actually surviving after the fight."

Jonah woofed victoriously, slapping his tail against the couch cushion.

"But I have to side with Ripley," Mina said quietly, tossing her keys on the shelf by the door, next to the abandoned leash.

*Why?* Jack scoffed. *You just said Buffy would win*.

"In a theoretical match, probably," Mina said. "But as a mostly-human being, I'd like to believe that someone like me would stand a chance of beating someone with real supernatural advantages." She sniffed her sleeve and picked up a subtle smoked-paprika scent that reminded her of Lucifer. "My clothes reek like the devil, so I'm going to go change."

With Adam and Jonah temporarily preoccupied by the food she had brought back, Mina had a moment's privacy to change out of her clothes. Reminding herself that she needed to go back out later, she reached into her closet without switching on the light and grabbed a simple top and a clean pair of jeans. She heard a quiet knock on her door. "What?"

"You okay?" Adam called.

Mina yanked open the door, with her wrinkled shirt, undershirt and socks in hand. "You took the bandage and splint off your finger!" she scolded, noticing immediately.

"My finger's fine," he insisted. "Ever try eating bone-in chicken with one hand? It's a mess. Anyway, how did it go at the Lotus? Was Lucifer there?"

"Yeah, we talked briefly," she said, edging past him to return to the kitchen area, tossing her undershirt into the tub under the bathroom window on the way. "He was still at the Lotus when I left, but the place was packed with his usual type, so I'm sure he'll be gone by the time we go over later."

"If he's not?" Adam asked warily.

"The Red Lotus is still more secure than here," Mina said to the group, dropping her shirt by the window sill. "There are more eyes and fewer exits, and it's known as a safe haven." She looked at Malcolm and Jack. "How did it go downtown? Did you find anything at the Garrison Brothers building?"

*The doors and windows were blocked, so we couldn't get inside,* Malcolm said, *but they apparently don't believe in using drapes, so we were able to peek into some of the rooms.*

*We saw nine different women,* Jack said, *including Sophie, but not Miranda, or whoever that girl was, who was here earlier.*

"Thirteen or some multiple of three is the standard for a coven," Mina said, discarding her socks by the door. "Presuming that they're following convention, they'll want to replace the two who died, so we may have some time before they have a full complement again."

"And you're sure that those two were actual members of the sisterhood," Adam confirmed, "and not just...I don't know, assistants or trainees?"

Mina had to recall the earlier conversation with Luci, which she did with some unease. "Lucifer said they pledged themselves to him last year, and he's already taken possession of their souls, so I would say it's a safe bet they were full members."

*Lucifer?* Malcolm scowled. *You've spoken to the devil?*

"Technically, he's *a* devil," Mina qualified. "One of several. Hundred... Okay, several tens of thousands," she revealed, "if you count all the minions and demonic forces, too, but that's not important now," she said dismissively. "The point is: Garrison, or some portion of it, is acting without Lucifer's direct authority."

"Guys," Adam said, noting the stony expressions in the room, "I know it sounds a little off, for Mina to be talking with Lucifer, but she doesn't actually serve him. You get that, right? Not all witches are devil-worshippers, or even follow Judeo-Christian doctrine."

"Thank you!" she said to Adam, with great relief. "I'm glad *someone* is seeing the bigger, pantheistic picture with me. So, guys," Mina said to Malcolm and Jack, "focus, please, and tell me what else you saw."

*There was a lot of activity in and out of a room on the first floor*, Malcolm said. *It's one of the inner rooms, without windows, so we couldn't see inside.*

*But we saw a lot of candles*, Jack said. *We looked through the door when it was opened for a few seconds. Definitely candles, maybe some statues.* He exchanged a look with Malcolm. *We saw Morgan Crain go inside the building, too.*

*We couldn't see or hear where he was going, or who he was meeting*, Malcolm said, *but it was definitely Crain.*

On the one hand, Crain Private Security was negotiating with Garrison, so there was nothing unseemly about Morgan being on-site, but on the other hand, Morgan didn't typically work on weekends, especially not Saturday afternoons. Moreover, with his blood recently stolen by Sophie Lyons during their meeting, his presence at the brownstone seemed even more ominous.

Mina grabbed her phone and began sending a text. "Did you see him leave?"

*No, we waited for an hour or so,* Jack said, *but we didn't see anyone leave.*

Mina didn't have long to wait for Xani's reply to her text about Morgan's whereabouts. "Xani says he left their apartment a couple of hours ago, to take a walk and clear his head, but he hasn't come home yet. He did check in with her, though, to say that he would head over to the Lotus tonight."

Mina quickly glanced at Adam's crisp, buttoned-down shirt. She remembered its dark, jewel-toned pattern of stripes and smiled sheepishly. "You found that in my closet, too?"

"Yeah," he said staidly. "I thought I lost this in Tokyo two years ago."

"Oops, sorry," she winced. "Hey, on the plus side, it still fits you!" She looked at Malcolm and Jack, as she took the leash from next to the door. "You're welcome to come along, but I'll be back soon."

"You're coming back here?" Adam frowned.

Mina nodded, as she fastened the collar around Jonah's furry scruff. "I'll go over with you to make sure you're settled at the Lotus, but all my work materials and supplies are here. This is my sanctum."

It was Adam's third visit to the Red Lotus in as many nights, and each evening was more surprising than the previous. Thursday night had been subdued and relaxed at the lounge, and Friday night was busy, but mostly with business types looking to unwind at the end of their stressful weeks. Saturday night saw the lounge packed and pulsing with energy and excitement.

As he followed Mina closely past Micah's post, with Jonah close at her hip like a service dog, Adam noticed a dreamlike aura to the Lotus that he hadn't noticed before. Glancing at the faces of some of the other customers, he saw glimmers and edges of their façades, as though they wore human masks and costumes. He then recalled what Mina had said, that the Red Lotus was "a safe haven."

"Try not stare, *ge-ge*," Mina cautioned. "Some of these guys are sensitive enough as it is, before they start drinking."

Despite the long bar area being crowded two and three deep, Mina and Adam managed to reach the counter's edge with minimal shoving. That was partially Jonah's doing, as his surprising and imposing lupine appearance ensured that the customers gave him plenty of room, and the fact that he had passed Micah's security check meant that he had every right to be there.

Cindy sidled her way to their end, and Adam was bewitched by her beauty. Her lean curves were cinched in a crushed red velvet corset, and her dark curls were streaked with scarlet and bronze, accenting her shimmering, warm brown skin. Even without the golden jewels in her hair and draped around her long, slender neck, Cindy's demeanor established her as the Queen Boss of the Red Lotus, with dominion over everyone in the room, if not the island of Manhattan.

"Why don't you come on back, where it's a little quieter?" Cindy invited, nodding her head to the side rooms. Signaling her team of bartenders that she was taking a break, she led Adam, Mina and Jonah to the locked back office, and Adam noticed the drape of red velvet that covered Cindy's back and shoulder blades completely, like a capelet.

"Have Morgan and Xani shown up yet?" Mina asked, unbuckling Jonah's leash once they were inside the office.

"Not that I've seen," Cindy said, shutting the door behind them. She looked at Adam and Jonah briefly. "You're both so pretty, it's almost a shame to hide you back here. You don't shed much, I hope," she said to Jonah, who answered with a low rumble. "Good."

"You understand him?" Mina asked. "I can't, when he's in this form."

"I can see why," Cindy said, leaning over to peer into Jonah's eyes. "Someone went through additional steps to hide his true nature. I can see that you've started undoing the enchantment, but you need a stronger magic to counteract this kind of curse."

Mina watched, as Jonah sat quietly for Cindy. "He was with me for a month, and I never got any kind of enchantment vibe off him. I'm usually pretty good at picking up on that stuff."

"Nobody's perfect, honey," Cindy said, going to the safe behind her desk. "You didn't know to look for anything out of the ordinary, and you're working against some powerful forces. He's lucky that you got to him first; left untreated for a few more days, he'd be stuck in this form forever." She turned around with a tiny glass vial in hand, the type that perfumeries and cosmetics shops used for cologne samples, filled with a silver-gray powder.

"What is that?" Adam asked.

"This will cure him of the curse and get him back to normal," Cindy said, locking the safe. "Just a little bit should do the trick. I'll leave the rest with Mina to use as she needs. Okay, hold still, handsome," Cindy said, kneeling in front of Jonah.

Mina shook her head, almost in despair. "Cin, you don't have to do that."

"I know. I *want* to do this," Cindy said

resolutely. "What do you say, handsome?"

Jonah cocked his head and ears, looking at the vial, then back at Cindy, then tapped his paw against her hand with a low grumble.

"You're going to feel ill for a few minutes," Cindy warned, uncapping the vial. "But once that clears up, you'll have your life back. Close your eyes, and take deep, slow breaths." She emptied the vial partially into her palm and softly blew the glittery silver dust over Jonah's head and muzzle, letting it disappear into his fur and nostrils.

At the sound of Mina's snapping fingers, Adam looked over at her, in time to catch an oversized black trench coat that she had pulled off the office coat rack. By the time he straightened it out and realized that it was yet *another* garment that Mina had "borrowed" from him, Jonah had transformed back.

Adam rushed to throw the coat over Jonah, who was naked and shivering uncontrollably, either from what Cindy had done, or the abrupt loss of fur, or both.

"Thank you," Jonah said quietly, to both Cindy and Adam. "If you'll excuse me, I feel really nauseous."

"Bathroom's that way," Cindy said, pointing to a black wooden door, as Adam offered his hand to help her back to her feet. Jonah rushed towards the bathroom, as Mina stared worriedly after him. "Thanks, honey," Cindy prompted after a moment, tugging her hand back.

"Oh, sorry," Adam said, finally releasing Cindy's hand. "Is he going to be okay?"

"He'll feel better in a few hours," she said.

"You may want to warn him: if he falls asleep, he may have some intense, vivid dreams...but he's a grown man, so it won't be anything he hasn't experienced before." She replaced the cap on the partially-filled glass vial, which she held out to Mina. Adam couldn't help noticing the fine silver dust that still speckled her hands.

Adam still had a trace of it on his own palm, however, from when he had helped her to her feet. It shimmered with a faint iridescence but felt like ash or soot.

"It's fae dust, honey," Cindy smiled. "You're welcome."

"One of the rarest substances in the world," Mina said quietly, taking the vial and giving Cindy a prolonged, heartfelt hug. "Thank you, Cin."

"You're welcome," Cindy said, patting Mina's hand and giving her a peck on the cheek. "Let me get back to the front, see if our red-headed Crains have shown up," she said playfully, putting her somberness behind her. "You can check the closet for clothes for your boy, but if he wants to stay in just the trench coat, that's fine by me, too," she said with a wink, as she breezed out of the office.

"Fae dust," Adam mused, seeing the light glinting off his palm where the dust clung. "Why does Cindy have it?"

"It's her own," Mina said. "Cindy is part-fae, and her wings were severed when she was a child, so her mother burned them and saved the dust. It's like a mystical cure-all, and Cindy keeps some on hand for emergencies, usually life and death situations."

"That was incredibly generous of her," Adam

said humbly. "Shit, I'm glad you told me. I was considering washing my hands, but now that seems really rude."

"Yeah, just a little," Mina smiled. "Just... don't worry about it. Rub it into your hair, or something. It'll look perfect for days."

# Chapter 8

Xani Crain was born three minutes before Morgan, but she was older in other ways, too. She was more aware, intuitive and outgoing, and her skills complemented Morgan's introspective, logical, and methodical inclinations very well. While Morgan considered their exclusivity to offer Mina's services an odd, quirky bonus to draw their more eccentric security clients, Xani had seen enough in her adult life—especially during her years with Cindy—to appreciate Mina's talents more fully.

Together, Xani and Cindy had dreamed up the idea for the lounge, but even after they separated, they believed in its concept and purpose enough to rope Morgan into their scheme to make it a reality. They had designed every aspect of the Lotus to feel blissful and harmonious, if not necessarily tranquil on the busier nights, and Mina's blessings helped to maintain its peaceful atmosphere.

From the watchful presence of Micah by the door, to the surreal elegance of the posh lounge spaces, Xani felt transported whenever she entered the Red Lotus, away from the bustle and noise of the city. Even when it was filled to near-capacity, the upholstered surfaces and ceilings helped to muffle the din, and whatever charms and protections Mina had provided, imbued the lounge with a kind of Zen-like calm that moved even belligerent, hostile entities to conduct themselves with more restraint and respect than per their usual habits.

Making an effort to blend in with the clientele, Xani had gone back to her apartment to change into her standby little black dress, a draping silk sheath that dipped in front and back and ended halfway to her knees. She left her red curls loose, not wanting to bother with the effort of putting it up for the few hours that remained of the evening.

As Xani scanned the crowd to look for Morgan, her attention was instead drawn to a tall, handsome blond man in a bespoke black suit. As she approached the bar, she noticed him cleaning dark red stains from his hands and nails with a cocktail napkin.

"Miss Crain," Lucifer greeted. "A pleasure to see you, as always."

"Is it really, though?" she returned. Lucifer had been visiting regularly since the Lotus's opening, yet he had never tried to charm or seduce her as he did the others. "I'm starting to think you don't like redheads."

"On the contrary, I love redheads," he gushed. "But you would require a special kind of effort, personally, and I'm still trying to puzzle it out. Besides, I don't think I'm allowed to proposition you on the premises."

"No business allowed, but sincere and unconditional overtures are fine." Cindy had emerged from the back room and seemed surprised to see Lucifer. "I thought you had left for the night."

"I hope you don't mind, dear Cin, that I came back for another round," he said, his blue eyes still focused on Xani. "I'll have whatever Alexandra's having."

"Pineapple and seltzer, it is," Cindy said, preparing two glasses, and garnishing them with orange peel twists. Xani smiled a little at Lucifer's look of puzzlement. "Miss Crain doesn't drink when she's working," Cindy explained. "But I can add something to yours—"

"No, that's fine," Lucifer said shortly. "It's good to cleanse the palate." As he clinked his glass with Xani's and took a tentative sip, he followed her wandering eyes. "Where is your counterpart tonight?"

"He should be here," she said. "I hope he's okay."

"I'm sure he's fine," Lucifer said lightly. "He's a grown man, fully capable of taking care of himself, isn't he?"

Xani felt herself lulled into a false of security by Lucifer's voice. He had a soft, seductive cadence that invited her to share her confidences, and even though she knew that he was seated a full arm's length from her, it sounded as though he had whispered against her ear.

"Hey, honey," Cindy's voice snapped her out of her lull, as well as the touch of her fingers on the back of her hand. "Would you mind checking to see if any messages came in on my phone? I'll keep an eye out for Morgan for you."

Xani nodded, knowing that the devil was listening. "Yeah, no problem."

She realized once she arrived at the office that Cindy had sent her away from the bar for her own protection, as Mina was just leaving the room. "Cindy asked me to check her phone," Xani said wryly. "I guess she doesn't trust me around Lucifer?"

Mina smiled. "She doesn't trust him around you; there's a difference. I'm glad Luci's here, actually; I should have a word with him. If you can keep an eye out in there for me, that'd be great!"

Mina looked dressed for a night out, in a silky cherry-red halter top and skin-tight jeans, with her black hair loose and lustrous and her golden skin almost glowing. Mina noticed Xani's inquisitive stare and looked down at her bare shoulders and arms. "Damn fae dust," she muttered, trying futilely to wipe off the shine. "Well, whatever. I'll be back."

Xani entered the office cautiously, hearing voices that were suddenly hushed. She saw Adam first, lounging on the leather couch. She began to say something, then heard the scraping noise of hangers and realized that someone was inside the open closet. It wasn't Morgan, otherwise Cindy would've mentioned it.

"Just pick one!" Adam said impatiently. "We'll find something else for you, later. For now, you just have to be dressed." He met Xani's eyes and shook his head with an exasperated eye roll.

Xani snickered, remembering the assortment of clothes that Morgan kept in the closet in case of accidental spillage. They were discards from his closet, received as well-intended gifts over time, from relatives and old girlfriends, and now kept as spares that he wouldn't miss if they were ruined or torn.

"Fine," came Jonah's terse response from the closet. He appeared a moment later in a pair of faded jeans and a maroon-hued dress shirt. Morgan had disliked the shirt for its trim cut and the way that the red wine shade accented his darker freckles, but it worked for Jonah.

*Hot damn.* Dressed in something more fitted than gym attire, Jonah's lean-muscled form was on prominent display. The shirt's burgundy color drew attention to the subtle dark flecks in Jonah's blue eyes, and he was broader in the shoulders and chest than Morgan, which just meant that the top buttons stayed undone. As with Mina, his skin had a subtle glow to it, but more silver than gold.

"Hi, Xani," Jonah said, sheepishly, tucking the tail of his shirt into the Morgan's frayed jeans. "I hope your brother doesn't mind my borrowing his clothes for a while."

Xani shook her head. "He probably won't care." *I certainly don't mind.*

Adam straightened in his seat. "Is Morgan outside?"

"Not yet. I'm starting to get worried; this isn't like him, at all. I'd wait by the bar, but Lucifer's lurking about, again."

"Mina's out there, with Lucifer?" Jonah remarked distastefully, and said to Adam: "Stay here and rest, and I'll check on her."

As Jonah left, Xani noticed that he had socks and slides on—not the best look, but better than being barefoot. She turned back to Adam when she heard his sharp breath, as he was trying to adjust his position without aggravating his side. He had been hiding his discomfort, but it was clear from his scowl that he was still in pain. It had only been a few hours since he had been shot, after all.

He looked up and caught her worried gaze. "I'm okay."

"Bullshit," she scoffed. "When was the last time you took something for the pain?"

"I don't know, an hour ago?" he answered tersely, but his hand went to his side subtly, as though he was testing the bandage. "You don't have to babysit me. I promise I won't burn the place down."

"I'm not here to babysit," she said. "Apparently, I've been sent back here for my own good, too." With a tired sigh, she took a seat on the couch next to Adam.

"I see," he said. "So, this is like a time-out corner, to keep us from causing more trouble for the real adults?"

"I guess it's something like that," Xani smiled. "But I can tell Mina just wants you to be safe. She misses you and talks about you a lot."

"I've missed her, too," Adam said, holding back a wince, as he moved a little to give Xani more room. "I can do without the gunshots, though," he chuckled, then regretted it, as he grimaced and held his side. "Ow."

"Let me make sure you're not bleeding through," Xani said, reaching for Adam's shirt, as he tried to tug the tail free. She shook her head. "No, you're going to have to unbutton that," she said, trying to stay detached, even as she brushed her fingertips against the edges where the bandages met his tender skin. The dressing was still pristine, and there wasn't even any noticeable discoloration.

"I told you I was okay," Adam whispered, which reminded her of how close she had gotten to him. "Was this just a ploy to get my shirt off?" he teased.

For someone who had spent most of his work career desk-bound and in front of a computer, Adam was surprisingly fit, with the unbandaged parts of his torso taut and lean. Noticing her stare, he sat straighter and started to button his shirt.

*When am I going to get this chance again?* With her heart pounding, she stayed his hands with hers. Before she could hesitate, she leaned over, closed her eyes and kissed him.

She panicked for a second, as he seemed to freeze at her boldness, but then she felt his fingers through her hair, and his other hand at the small of her back, pulling her closer. It had been so long since she had kissed anyone, and she was so excited by the opportunity to be with Adam, that she was a little too enthusiastic, and he gave a startled grunt of pain, as she accidentally pressed into his side. "Sorry!"

"It doesn't matter," he whispered, stopping her from pulling away by kissing her again. "I can barely feel it, now," he said, sliding his hand under the drape of her dress and spreading his warm fingers across the span of her back. "You. I just feel you."

Back in Boston, Jonah Gideon had been a self-made man, who had the good luck and better business acumen to make a series of lucrative investments with the money he had earned from years of working different jobs. He kept to himself and spent little of his hard-earned savings, preferring to use it as seed money for his family's various ventures. He drove a used pickup and kept a wardrobe of mostly jeans and t-shirts.

Before Jonah had turned thirty, he had seen his younger cousin Malcolm develop, build and sell a design prototype and patent that made them millionaires overnight. As Malcolm's drinking had worsened, Jonah had helped to manage the finances for his cousin's fledgling enterprise and handled the negotiations for the buy-out. Months after the deal was finalized, Malcolm and Mina's divorce was, too, with little animosity from either party. It was Malcolm who had insisted that Mina be given "a fair share," which totaled in the millions.

That was years ago, before Jonah had any clue about the kind of relationship that Malcolm and Mina had. In the intervening years, he noticed Malcolm's creativity and focus gradually waning, and he realized that Mina had been a greater muse and inspiration than Malcolm had let on.

Anyway, that was back in Boston. Here in New York, Jonah wasn't anybody of significance, just one of hundreds enjoying the festive ambiance of the Red Lotus on a Saturday night. Undetected in the crowd, he watched Mina from a hidden corner, as the smarmy, black-suited devil tried to charm his way past her defenses, inching closer as the minutes ticked by.

Jonah had always imagined the devil as a

swarthy, urbane figure with sleek black hair and an impeccable moustache, but the man sitting next to Mina, with his graceful fingers just inches from hers, seemed to have a disposition as sunny as his beach-tan glow and bright blond waves. Jonah reminded himself that Lucifer was purportedly a fallen angel, who would have possessed the cherubic, affable qualities of his former celestial host, and he did have a generic, model-handsome look that struck Jonah as familiar and commonplace.

When Lucifer was nearly elbow to elbow with Mina, Jonah couldn't stand to watch any longer, and he joined them at the counter. Cindy gave him a quelling glance and set a glass of ice water in front of him, then moved down the bar to other customers.

Lucifer gave him a quick visual assessment and smiled at the socks and athletic slides that Jonah had found in the office closet. "I don't believe we've ever had the pleasure. Mister Gideon, is it?"

"He's not bothering you, is he?" Jonah asked Mina quietly, glancing at Lucifer's shoes: finely-tooled, thin-soled Oxfords, polished to a patent-leather shine.

"No, we're just having a chat," Mina said. Her body language was relaxed, but Jonah sensed that she was guarded, like a chess player anticipating her opponent's next moves.

Lucifer laughed, his blue eyes sparkling. "I assure you, I have no desire to cause Miss Xing any discomfort or grief... I'm sorry, *Missus Malcolm Gideon*," he corrected himself with an ironic smirk. "I must concede: my ladies did choose the perfect species for your shapeshift, Mister Gideon. You are as stalwart and loyal a companion as any natural-born dog; are you sure you wouldn't like to return to that guise?"

Mina set her warm hand on Jonah's and shifted her stance against his, partially blocking him, as if to keep him from Lucifer's reach. "I think we're done for tonight, Luci," she said quietly. "Thank you for your time."

"Just one more thing." Lucifer was undeterred, as he looked over Mina's head, directly at Jonah. "Mina is such a winsome and wily mistress, isn't she? Resourceful, too, when it comes to avoiding tickets."

Jonah finally recognized his features as those of the police officer who had almost written her up for his missing dog tag the evening before, and Jonah felt the familiar, protective indignation rising from his gut. Mina turned sharply, dropping any attempt at subtlety to make herself a barrier between the men.

"I need to speak with you in private, *now*," she said, laying her hand firmly on Jonah's chest.

"Until next time, then," Lucifer said casually, giving Jonah a mocking wave behind Mina's back.

Jonah followed Mina towards the office, wary of the covetous stares and side glances that followed Mina, as they left the main lounge. Cindy intercepted them in the hallway, shaking her head, as she tossed Mina's jacket to her.

"Not the office. *Está ocupado, mis amigos.*"

"Why, Cin?" Mina asked. "What's going on?"

Cindy waited until she led them to an empty private room before she answered. "Xani and

Adam are spending some grown-up time together, and I accidentally walked in on them."

"Oops," Mina murmured, following Cindy into the chamber with Jonah.

"It's all good," Cindy replied. "I must confess, though: I've never wanted to be part of a threesome more in my life. Just do me a favor, and lock the door, if you want privacy?" She retreated from the small room, closing the door behind her.

The snug chamber was decorated like a boudoir, with velvet and silk drapes along the walls and even from the ceiling, amidst the ubiquitous scarlet pumpkin lanterns. As he wondered about the cleaning necessary for keeping such rooms ready for customers, Jonah noticed the photo frames and personal effects, like hairstyling brushes and a full makeup caddy, on a nearby dressing table.

"This looks like someone's actual bedroom," he remarked.

"Cindy stays here overnight sometimes," Mina said, tossing her jacket over the back of the tufted velvet couch. "If she has to close later than usual, or if the weather's bad. There's actually a Murphy bed behind that paneling," she pointed to a cherry-stained wall segment.

As Mina went to lock the door, Jonah admired her silhouette, from the fall of her silky hair partway down her bare back, to the curve of her waist flaring slightly to her hips, to her long, lean legs. For the first time in years, he was able to see her through a man's eyes, without having to endure the glower of his jealous cousin. *Missus Malcolm Gideon.*

"I always wondered: why did you keep your married name?" Jonah asked. "As I recall, you had even offered an annulment, instead of going through divorce proceedings, so it seemed like you were ready to leave the name behind."

"I offered an annulment in case Malcolm ever wanted to remarry in a church someday," she said. "And it also would've let him keep most of his money, but he wanted to give me half, on the condition that I keep his name until I remarry. A few million dollars, *and* I didn't have to change all my legal documents? That was a no-brainer."

"It's been four years," Jonah said, sinking into the tufted couch. "Never found 'Husband Two'?"

She laughed tiredly, settling into the opposite end of the sofa. "Why bother looking? I'm busy enough with work and friends, without someone else making demands on my time."

"Is that how you saw your marriage to Malcolm: a demand on your time?"

"No, never," she said, leaning her head on the back cushion. "But he made me feel like I was one on his." She paused thoughtfully. "I don't want to talk about the past anymore. Since you're here, I want to help you get home and resume your normal life."

"And then you can return to socializing with...whomever."

Mina smiled. "Like cops and devils?" He held his tongue, as it wasn't his place to comment on her choices. "You've lived with me for a month, so you know my habits: I don't date, and I don't hook up."

"I wasn't keeping track," he said, not entirely

truthfully. He knew that she never brought anyone home with her, she never came home smelling like anyone else, and she didn't go out often at night unless it was for work. "I just wanted to know that you were happy. Or, at least content."

She lolled her head to look at him, and he was reminded of long evenings parked next to her on her couch, studying her with his canine senses. His brain was different then, and his affection and devotion towards her were simple and familial. Being next to her in his human form, his emotions were more complicated and conflicted.

"*You* wanted to know," she asked, "or were you finding out for Malcolm? What would you have told him, if things had gone according to plan?"

"I wouldn't have been able to give him a definitive answer," Jonah said. "You wouldn't have let me into your home as readily, if I had met you like this. You wouldn't have confided in me the same way, had you recognized me. I would've returned to Boston without knowing you at all."

She closed her eyes with a pained scowl, and he worried that she regretted opening her home and feelings to him. "But to answer your first question, I wanted to know for myself. Malcolm was never quite the same after you left, and I wanted to see how you had fared without him."

"Now you know, so you're free to go home with a clear conscience," Mina said. "Lucifer said that you weren't changed on his order, but he told me how it would've been done. Now all that's left is to recover your memories of that night, and for those, I just need to mix up a restorative draught for you."

"You actually take Lucifer at his word?"

"Not always, but in this case, he has no reason to lie," she said, getting to her feet. "I'll be back later tonight, as soon as I can get the draught ready for you."

Jonah had forgotten that Mina had only intended to stay a little while. "Is the apartment safe? What if the sisterhood returns?"

"I don't know if you noticed, when I returned to the apartment before," she said. "I took the clothes I wore and spread them around the main entrances. Luci had gotten a little cozy with me earlier in the evening, so my clothes were marked. If the sisterhood suspects that he's claimed my place, they won't trespass."

Jonah hadn't smelled anything pronounced on her clothes, beyond a sweet smokiness. "Cozy, in what way?"

Mina met his eyes, as he got to his feet. "Relax. He never touches me," she assured. "He's not allowed to, so he just gets very close into my space, but his proximity is enough to transfer his protection to me."

"If you say so," he said, holding her jacket open for her. As she turned her bare back to him to slip her smooth arms into the sleeves, he caught a trace of her perfume. He released his hold on her jacket when he felt her gentle tug. "Be careful."

"I'm always careful," she said blithely, turning around, and she flicked her hair out from under her collar. "I still have to find out what's happened to Morgan."

*Oh, yeah, him.* "Morgan, right," he said, taking a step back. "I hope he's okay."

Mina was peering into his face. "You really do, don't you?"

"Well, I don't want to see anything bad happen to him," Jonah said gruffly. "He seems like a good guy, and you need more of those in your life, to balance out all the assholes."

"Thanks," Mina chuckled. "That's actually, really sweet. I guess you're one of the good ones, too."

"Maybe, or just an asshole trying to reform," he said sheepishly, moving to the door to open it for her. As much as he wanted her to stay there with him, he had to let her go. She was needed elsewhere, and she didn't need him getting in her way.

To his surprise, she stood on her toes and gave him a lingering kiss on the cheek. "Don't reform too much," she smiled. "I kind of like you the way you are, already." While he was figuring out how to respond to that, she laughed and slipped past him, out the door. "I'll be back as soon as I can, but in case the draught recipe takes a while to finish, don't wait up."

# Chapter 9

By the time Mina was halfway back to her building, there was still no sign of Morgan at the Red Lotus, or at least she hadn't gotten any texts from anyone telling her otherwise. She felt better knowing that Adam and Jonah were safe within the protective confines of the lounge, and Xani and Cindy with them, but Morgan's situation was problematic.

Jack's ghost appeared next to Mina as she was waiting for the light at the crosswalk on her corner. *Morgan's waiting for you outside your apartment*, he warned. *He looks unwell.*

Mina popped one of her earbuds into her ear to pretend that she was on a phone call, instead of appearing to talk to herself. "Unwell, how?"

*His complexion looks like mine*, Jack said, holding up his bluish-white hands. *Excuse me a second.* He vanished from her side, and Mina glanced around quickly. She spotted a crying young woman across the street in very high heels and a very short, tight skirt, trying to outpace a brutish lout who was staggering and shouting obscenities after her.

A sudden gust of wind blew a full sheet of soiled newsprint out of a nearby recycling bin and plastered it against the face of the lumbering brute, interrupting his pursuit long enough for the girl to dart into a waiting cab and get away safely.

Jack reappeared next to Mina, with a satisfied smile.

"Did you do that? That was pretty cool," Mina said.

Jack shrugged. *She reminded me of a cousin of mine. If I'm stuck here, anyway, I may as well try to do some good, right? I really wanted to throw the whole motherfucking trashcan at the shithead, but I could only manage a sheet of paper.*

"No, it's better to be subtle," Mina said, crossing with the light. "Tell me what's waiting for me inside. What's Morgan been doing?"

*Muttering to himself and pacing. At least, he's quiet about it, so Missus Krantz isn't freaked out. He's not armed, that Malcolm or I could see.*

Mina let herself into the building quietly to avoid disturbing Mrs Krantz, rather than sparing Morgan. She suspected that Morgan was listening for her return, and sure enough, he was waiting for her at the top of the landing.

"Where have you been?" he asked worriedly.

"At the Lotus, mostly," she said, skirting him to reach her apartment. "We were waiting for you to come by."

"'We,'" he echoed, furrowing his brow.

"Yes, Cindy and Xani, especially, but we were all there." Mina played with her keys, hesitating to unlock her door. Jack was right, there was definitely something different about Morgan tonight.

"I had planned to stop in, but I wasn't feeling

up to dealing with the noise and crowds," Morgan said. "So, was Jonah there with you tonight, too?"

*Be careful,* Jack said, seeing Morgan over her shoulder. *I know a jealous rage brewing when I hear it.*

"Noted," Mina whispered under her breath.

"What?" Morgan asked.

"No," she replied, facing him directly. "He came out to the bar briefly, but he stayed mostly in the back. Lucifer was there, though," she said, watching for Morgan's reaction, but there was none. "You should text Xani and let her know you're okay."

Morgan leaned against the doorjamb. "Actually, do you mind if I come in and sit down for a few minutes?" When she didn't agree right away, he added, "I'll stay out of your way. I'm just feeling a little light-headed, all of a sudden."

She nodded and unlocked the door, looking first to the windows and the hallway to make sure the apartment was as protected as she had left it, before she felt comfortable enough to take off her boots and shut the door. Without a thought, she gathered up the fur-covered blanket from the sofa and tossed it into her bedroom, before she even took off her jacket.

Morgan noticed. "Is Jonah not coming back, or is he not a dog anymore?"

"Perhaps both," Mina said, sending a quick text, copying both Cindy and Xani, to let them know that Morgan was there, before she finally took off her jacket and tossed it over the back of the sofa.

"He doesn't love you, you know," he said. "He doesn't know you, like I do."

"You mean Jonah?" Mina walked around him and took a seat at her desk, opening her laptop. "Whatever feelings you think I have for him, they have no bearing on our friendship."

"I don't believe you," he said, standing behind her swiveling chair. "I see how you look at him."

"Jonah and I—"

He spun her seat around and loomed over her, inches from her face. "I hate the way his name sounds, coming from your lips," he seethed.

She was confident in her apartment's defenses, as she saw her *ruishi* appear and sniff around Morgan's hair and shoulders silently and curiously, without his notice. The celestial lion-dog shook its silver and azure mane playfully, as it darted away and paced at a distance. It sensed that Morgan wouldn't intentionally threaten or harm her.

Perhaps that was true, but accidents could happen... "You're not in your right mind," Mina said, rooting herself in place. "You need to take a step back."

"I'm not a fucking kid!" he snapped, trying to shove her chair away.

"Then stop acting like one," she returned coolly, shutting her laptop again. *So much for him staying out of my way.* "If you have something on your mind, Morgan, just come out with it." She stood from her seat, lifting her chin to look into his glassy green eyes. "Let's not waste each other's time."

He took her arms roughly and kissed her. It was a hard, demanding kiss—not necessarily unpleasant or violent, but it wasn't what she

151

would've expected from Morgan, who was always gentle and amenable with her. *"Was"—past tense.*

As he pulled her closer and held his hands against her bare back, deepening the kiss, she kept her arms folded and wedged between them. She let her eyes drift closed for a moment to forget what was happening, as kissing Morgan felt almost as dirty and taboo as the idea of kissing Adam.

"I've waited for so long to do that," he murmured against her lips. "You feel something, too, don't you?"

*Probably not the same thing you're feeling, buddy.* She rested her hand over his heart, as she was trying to let him down easy. "We've known each other a long time, haven't we?"

He nodded. "I still remember the first time I saw you, ten years ago, like it was yesterday. When you came back, after being gone so long, it felt like I could breathe again."

*Shit.* It wasn't just some weird enchantment that had Morgan in its grip. She could hear in his hushed, halting voice and feel in his heartbeat that he was sincere with her, which made it that much harder for her to spurn him.

"You and Xani are like family to me," she said, as a not-so-subtle hint.

"Your feelings will catch up to mine, eventually," he said, undeterred. "I'll wait," he said, leaning in for another kiss.

*God, no!* "Please, don't," she said, more gently, trying to twist free of his grip without hurting him. "Don't wait for me. I'm not worth it."

"Shh," he said. "Of course, you're worth the

wait. Don't be so hard on yourself." His hands were surprisingly strong, and she found his hold tightening. "Is that why you're trying so hard to help everyone? They're not worth your time. They don't care about you."

"If you really care about me, then let me go," she said, trying to step back. "Let me do my job."

"No!" he said, almost desperately, his fingers pinching her arms painfully now. "Don't you see that they're just using you? I won't let them take advantage of you like that!"

"Morgan, let me go, *now!*" she demanded, and the *ruishi* swept between them to shove Morgan back. Before it could do anything to subdue him, Malcolm's spirit appeared and knocked Morgan onto his back, anchoring him to the floor. Malcolm's handsome face contorted into an expression of mad fury that was intimately familiar to Mina.

"Stop!" she ordered with a resonant, room-shaking voice, commanding order and stillness instantly. "We're wasting time, and I already don't have enough of it."

Returning to her laptop, she checked a couple of windows that she had left open on the screen, then pulled some jars and bottles to start mixing the recipes she had retrieved. As she started the stove burner to bring her tea kettle to a simmer, she started collecting ingredients into her granite mortar.

"What is it, Jack?" she asked, noticing his intent stare from the other side of the counter. He was staying far out of her way, as was Morgan, who was on the couch with his head buried in his hands, and Malcolm, who guarded

Morgan with a menacing focus.

*I have to tell you something, but you might change your mind about wanting to help me, if I do.*

"I already thought you were a dick when you were alive, so helping you now just means I get you out of my life for good," she whispered, out of Morgan's hearing. She noticed Jack's continued hesitation.

*Maybe you can stop for a second, so you can hear—*

"Jack, I can multi-task just fine." She had learned how to manage multiple burners and dishes over years of working in hot take-out restaurant kitchens in her teenage years, so this was nothing. "Just start talking."

*Do you remember turning down my friend who asked you out, back in high school?*

*Shit. Why does it keep coming back to those years?* "Yes, I remember. It was towards the end of sophomore year. He couldn't even keep a straight face when he was talking to me, so I knew that you had put him up to it."

*We kept trying to catch you off-guard.*

"You were making bets on which one of you would get to fuck me first," she said bluntly. She had been so scared of encountering Jack and his friends in school after hours that she curtailed her extra-curricular activities and made few friends during her time there. "You guys didn't even like me; I was just a challenge, and you called me something behind my back every time I ignored you. What was it? Oh, yeah, 'retarded cock-sucking cunt.'"

As Jack was abashedly silent, Mina added a

few dashes of powdered cardamom to the mixture in the mortar and lowered the burner to a simmer.

*You knew about that?* he asked finally, avoiding Malcolm's glare.

"I was a witch, Jack," Mina said lightly. "I heard everything, and the more I knew, the less I wanted to do with you. When you turned Harmon on me in junior year, I had the feeling that my days were numbered there, one way or another."

*We wanted to punish you, and Harmon was into young girls*, Jack confessed. *Especially the ones that kept to themselves, like you did. He said he tried, but someone walked in on you.*

"He tried to make a move, and I blew a dust in his face that made him feel like I had kicked him in the nuts," Mina said, taking her kettle off the burner and adding a splash of the simmering water to her mortar. "I found out after I transferred, that he had been into little boys for a while, too."

Mina stirred the mixture slowly, ensuring that everything was well-incorporated, until it had the consistency of a thick, clumping paste, almost a dry dough. "He had been your little league coach when you were in grammar school, and you quit the team, but then you saw Harmon again when you got to high school. Not even you could escape your past."

Jack looked stricken. *I didn't want anyone to know what we had done, so I gave him leads, to ensure that he wouldn't say anything.*

Mina shook her head. "Harmon took advantage of you when you were a little kid." When she had finally found out about his abuse, she had forgiven Jack for his inability to speak out, but not for his own actions against others. "But that doesn't excuse your own conduct. You set up other people to become victims, and you became a bully and a predator yourself. I don't even know how many people you hurt, and you probably don't, either."

*I never went after kids*, he said staunchly.

"I was fourteen when you and your friends started taking bets on whose cock I'd suck," Mina said matter-of-factly. "You code-named me 'the chink ho' and didn't make much of an effort to hide it from me. I'm sure you got more creative with nicknaming your other targets and victims, as you got older."

*Come on, we were all young—*

"I'm not your judge, so I don't need to hear your shit excuses," Mina snapped. "If you've said what you needed to get off your chest, and your conscience is clear now, let me do my job, and you can go to your review." She used the pestle to break up some of the dry chunks in the mortar into a powder.

*Review?*

"Yes, the final judgment on your soul," she said, tossing some of the loosened powder into the air, watching it pass through Jack's spirit like particles of starlight and form images, symbols and scenes from his perspective. "There she is," Mina muttered, seeing the guise of the sisterhood's leader, Miranda, as the old woman, shoving against Jack as she passed him on the crowded street.

*I remember. I couldn't sleep that night, so I took some sleeping pills. I had a dream that I was being chased and tortured by demons, and the dreams kept getting worse as the days went on.* He started pacing anxiously, as though he was reliving his dreams, and Mina had to track him back and forth to see the images around him. *Eventually, I got a text from an unknown number, that listed your name, number and address as someone who could help me. You didn't answer my calls, and I couldn't sleep…*

Jack stopped pacing, and the images dissipated. *I don't even know what I took that last night. I took everything I could find, just to get the visions to stop.*

She could hear the pain still lingering in his voice, but she couldn't muster much sympathy. He had treated others appallingly when he was alive, and had shown little remorse, even in death. "In hindsight, I can see why your messages sounded so disturbed and tortured," Mina said, "but can you also understand why I wanted nothing to do with you?"

*Over shit that happened over ten years ago?* Jack asked. *Seriously?*

Mina set aside the mortar and crossed her arms, frustrated at his denseness. "I got death threats and people saying that I deserved to be raped, while you and your buddies were getting ready for junior prom and college tours. Why the fuck would I want to be reminded of that shitshow, hmm?" She saw a trace of chagrin on his face, but more of being put on the spot, rather than actual regret. "Did you think we'd get a beer and have a laugh over it? Maybe you could finally get that hand job you wanted; no hard feelings, right?"

157

She looked over to the couch and saw both Malcolm and Morgan staring at her: Malcolm nearly foaming with outrage, and Morgan looking confused and horrified.

"Who are you talking to?" Morgan asked.

Mina shrugged. "Visitors, clients, whatever you want to call them. It's better if you forget what you heard; it's a private matter." She glanced at Jack and pointed him to a place on the couch, cuing him to wait.

"Fuck that!" Morgan said, leaping to his feet then listing from light-headedness. "What you said about what happened to you..."

"Is my history, and none of your business," she warned, shooting a glance at Malcolm, as well. "And has nothing to do with the current situation. Malcolm, you're up," she said, gesturing to him.

"Malcolm is here, too?" Morgan asked, looking around futilely.

*You deserve better than him*, Malcolm scoffed, passing by Morgan. *He knows shit about you. Does he even understand what you're doing?*

"Shh," Mina said quietly, taking a palmful of the revealing powder and pointing Malcolm to stand where Jack had been. "Adam's known me my whole life, and even he doesn't know everything about me, so shut up."

She tossed a sprinkle of the dust over Malcolm and watched the patterns emerge. Again, the images and scenes appeared as through Malcolm's eyes, and they started— curiously enough—with Sophie.

The silent images weren't clear enough for Mina to read lips, but she saw Sophie's nod, and an exchange of money. "What in God's name did you do, Malcolm?"

Malcolm struggled for a second. *I don't… Sophie said she could ensure that you wouldn't recognize Jonah, and that he wouldn't fall in love with you.*

"He was your cousin," she said incredulously. "You didn't think to ask for details on what she intended to do?"

*She said no one would be hurt by it*, Malcolm said. *I might have also been drunk when I agreed to it.*

"Malcolm's the reason that his cousin's a dog?" Morgan surmised from what he could hear of the conversation.

*Stay out of this, carrot-top*, Malcolm glared, then flinched as he was doused with another pinch of Mina's concoction. He didn't feel it, of course, but he reacted automatically to her aggressive flick at his head. *Maybe I should've said something earlier, but I barely remembered that it had even happened.*

Mina was hardly listening, as nothing he said added anything she didn't already see from the images emerging through his apparition. "Miranda passed by you one night in Boston Common. It happened quickly, so you didn't see her face."

Malcolm struggled to recall the evening. *It was a bunch of girls, teenagers cutting through the park after hanging out at the Frog Pond or something. I was going to meet some friends for dinner in Chinatown. The girls kind of flowed around me, and one of them bumped me with her backpack.*

159

Mina saw the long-haired brunette amongst the images, jostling Malcolm without the slightest regard, as she sailed past him in the company of the other girls. "Were you plagued by demonic visions after that, also?"

*Not right away. At first, it was an angel, promising a way that you and I would reconcile. The demons came later, to warn me that you were in danger.* The eerie, sinister figures stalked into Malcolm's playback, with cryptic symbols flashing intermittently between the visions. *I thought if I could save you, we could try again.*

"God, Malcolm," Mina said, dropping her eyes. "How did you even think there could be another chance for us?"

*It's clear to me now that there never was, but in the moment, everything was possible. When we were together, there wasn't anything that was beyond our reach*, he said, and Mina heard the hopefulness in his voice. *Do you remember?*

"I remember everything," Mina said grimly. "And I swore to never let myself go through that again." She squared her shoulders and faced Malcolm again. "On a whim, you asked Jonah to come to New York, perhaps not really expecting him to agree. Once he did, you panicked and shared your concerns with Sophie, and she promised you that she would keep Jonah from me.

"But you didn't know that Sophie had her own plans for him," Mina said. "Maybe you didn't care. You might have even thought that your visions were warnings about Jonah himself being the source of danger. Whatever the reason, you got worried when weeks went by and he was still gone, and you decided to come here yourself."

"That's why Malcolm was in New York?" Morgan said. "He was checking on you?"

Malcolm glowered at Morgan's interjection, but Mina didn't bother chastising him, since Morgan couldn't see him anyway. "What's your grievance, Malcolm?" she mused, noting a milky, cloudy blur to the rest of the images. "What is it that you want to resolve before moving on?"

Malcolm seemed to give her question some thought. *Now that I'm free of my dependencies, I have real clarity. I guess there is something that I want to say.*

Mina crossed her arms expectantly, but Malcolm shook his head. *But not to you. At least, not yet.*

Adam felt like he was floating on a cloud, even as his limbs felt leaden at his sides. Xani was draped over him, semi-conscious as he was, and while she lay pressed against his bandaged side, he barely felt any pressure, and no discomfort at all. He reached over Xani to pull down the oversized trench coat to cover her, although it was far too late for either of them to feign modesty.

When Cindy had walked in on them earlier in the evening, he and Xani had both frozen in shocked embarrassment, but only for a second, as they were both well past the point of stopping, even if they had wanted to. Something about that scandalous moment heightened Xani's excitement further, and she shuddered and moaned, as she continued to ride him, not caring who saw or heard them. Cindy had discreetly shut and locked the door behind herself, and Adam and Xani resumed their lovemaking without further interruption.

It did feel like lovemaking, too, as opposed to just a basic, meaningless hookup. Adam felt connected to Xani on a deep, primal level, as though she had always been present in his life, despite the fact that before that week, they hadn't seen each other in nearly a decade. It wasn't just her beauty, but something about her energy and positivity that illuminated everything around her, and made him feel whole, in a way he hadn't been in years.

Xani rested her riot of flame-colored curls against his shoulder, as she picked up his left hand and studied his fingers, one at a time. She stopped at his left ring finger. "This was the one that was broken two weeks ago? You can hardly tell."

He crooked it easily. "I know. I can barely remember how it happened."

Xani tilted her face towards him and gazed at him with her wide green eyes—the color of jade, or the mountains of Guilin covered in morning mist. She brushed her fingers lightly over his forehead. "Didn't you have a cut here? I can't even see where your scab was."

"I'm sorry, would more scars make me more appealing?" he grinned.

She laughed and kissed his smooth jawline. "No, it's not that. I've just never met someone who healed so quickly. It's kind of miraculous, and a little eerie."

"Oh, you've been hanging out with my sister, and you think *I'm* the eerie one!"

"I think it's sexy," Xani purred. "It makes you a little more mysterious, like a superhero."

She seemed a little mysterious to him, too, with how easily she accepted the weirdness all around them without questioning. "I don't usually do this kind of thing," he confessed. "I usually make more of an initial effort to know who I'm…um…"

"Fucking?" she smiled. "It's okay, this isn't normal for me, either." She curled against him and gave a languid, satisfied sigh. "Don't get me wrong—I've always liked you, and I still do, but I don't typically go for guys like you."

He raised an eyebrow. "Asians?" he joked.

"I meant friends, you jerk!" she exclaimed, laughingly, as she punched him in the arm. "Cindy was the probably the last partner whom I genuinely loved and liked as a person," she said, more seriously, then she sat up. "Sorry, that came out wrong. I didn't mean to imply that I *don't* like you, or anything, but if you want to keep this a one-time thing—"

Adam sat up and interrupted her with a deep kiss. "Let's discuss it in the morning, okay?" he suggested, brushing his fingers behind her ears and along the back of her graceful neck. "There's no need to rush," he whispered against her lips. "We have the whole night to figure it out."

Jonah awoke panting for breath, his body tensed and restless, but his dream hadn't been awful. In fact, it had been so amazingly hot and intense that it was almost infuriating when he woke up and realized that he had just been dreaming. As he eased himself up to sit on the couch in Cindy's boudoir, waiting for his body to settle back down, he tried to forget Mina's face and body as he had imagined her.

The fact that he hadn't purposefully fantasized about her didn't alleviate his guilt or frustration. He was a grown man, for God's sake, with plenty of willing and available partners back home, just a text or phone call away, so he had no business thinking about Mina that way. He could at least divert his conscious thoughts, but he never had control over his dreams: if his subconscious wanted to fuck, then damn it, it was going to make him do it while he slept, whether he wanted to or not, however and with whomever it wanted.

Except that he did want to, very much. If he didn't want to, he would've felt a queasiness or revulsion when he woke up, as he did after nightmares or other disturbing dreams. He would've tried to forget the dream, instead of replaying it in his head.

Jonah heard a quiet knock on the door. *Please, anyone but Mina,* he hoped.

"Jonah? I'm sorry it got so late," came Mina's voice through the door.

*Fuck!* He scrambled to find a throw blanket or something to toss over his lap, where the evidence of his arousing dream refused to subside and had now, in fact, found new reason to stick around. "Just a second," he called, recoiling at how raspy and strangled his voice sounded.

"Are you alright?" she asked with concern, trying the doorknob.

"Yeah, I just woke up, that's all," he covered. He found his discarded shirt, which he had shed when the room had started feeling too warm, and had pulled it on just in time, as Mina opened the door. He drew his knees up and kept shirt tail loose. "Hi."

"Hi?" she said, looking at him quizzically, as she dropped her jacket on the tufted seat by the dressing table.

She was still in her jeans and red halter top, which showed off her golden shoulders and back, but her hair was cinched up, which he had learned she often did while she was mixing, brewing or cooking. As she sat down at the far end of the couch, clutching a wine tote, Jonah caught a whiff of a man's cologne, an odd combination of seaspray and evergreen.

When he first smelled it earlier that day on Morgan, he had envisioned the young man as a seafaring lumberjack, in a flannel shirt and rubber waders. "That's Morgan's cologne, isn't it? It's certainly a distinctive scent," Jonah commented.

"I have too many odors on me to notice," she said, then sniffed her arm and nodded. "Yes, probably. I think it's called 'Sequoia' or something." She reached into the wine tote and pulled out a tall, insulated coffee cup.

"As in the botanical relative of the mighty, towering, awe-inspiring 'red...wood'?" he joked, taking a jab at Morgan's fiery hair color. "That's not very subtle."

Mina shook her head, fighting a smile. "Don't be a dick, Jonah," she said, passing him the cup. "Drink."

"No, I think he's a sweetheart," Jonah grinned. "I just question his choice of men's fragrance." As he took a first tentative sip of the bittersweet herbal brew, he noticed Mina's pensiveness. "Are you okay?"

Mina peered at him uncertainly, then said, "Yeah, just a little tired. It's been a long and busy day. I was hoping to take a quick shower to wake up, but Morgan was waiting for me at my apartment."

"I didn't know that," Jonah frowned. "I thought you met him here. What did he want?"

"Nothing," she said, too quickly, as she got to her feet. "I shouldn't have mentioned it. Finish your draught, before it gets cold."

"That's bullshit!" he said, then gulped half the cup's mystery contents to appease her. "God, that's vile," he muttered. "Anyway, you should know by now, not to stay quiet when something happens to you."

"Oh, fuck off!" she snarled. "Morgan's not Malcolm, okay? He's not like that! He would never try to hurt me. He thinks he loves me, and he wants to protect me."

Jonah's heart sank, and he finished the rest of the draught in the cup. "Yes, it usually starts that way," he said quietly. He retrieved the wine tote from the floor and slipped the empty cup inside it.

"What usually starts that way?" she questioned.

"Has he told you yet, that he's the only one who knows and cares about you like you deserve?" Jonah asked, returning the tote to the floor. "That everyone else is trying to use you? That no one else can possibly love you as much as he does?"

From Mina's averted eyes, he knew he had hit a nerve. "I'm sorry to be unkind, but those words sound familiar to you, don't they?"

They had been Malcolm's words, once, now spoken by another, and Mina's stricken expression conveyed that she recognized the signs and patterns emerging, too. "But that's not Morgan," she said. "None of that even sounds like anything he would ever say, especially to me."

Mina's eyes widened and brightened, as if a light bulb turned on inside her head. She had hit on something, and her look of mischievous determination made Jonah smile. *She's figured out something—there's my brilliant Mina!*

"You're totally wrong about Morgan, but for all the right reasons," she grinned. "Or, right about Morgan, for all the wrong reasons!" In her excitement, she leaned over and kissed him on the forehead. "I'll be right back. You may want to stay on the couch, in the meantime. That draught is going to hit you like a semi in about three minutes."

Jonah sank back in his seat and watched Mina dart out the door. Whatever was in the drink didn't do a thing to alleviate his turgid state, but at least Mina hadn't noticed it. He looked down at the part of himself that was straining for release. *Settle down, or you're going to get me in a shitload of trouble.*

# Chapter 10

Cindy leaned on the bar counter to rest a moment, now that the lounge was quieting down. She straightened a little when she saw Mina emerging from the back rooms. "How's it looking back there?"

"I don't know. I completely avoided the office. Adam and Xani will come out when they're ready. As for Jonah, I gave him the draught and will check on him in a few minutes."

"Still worried about Morgan?" Cindy asked.

"A little. He seemed okay when I left him, but I'll feel better when he checks in that he's gotten home," Mina said. "Jonah gave me an idea."

"That man gives me *lots* of ideas," Cindy simpered with a raised eyebrow.

"About what's happened to Morgan," Mina clarified, ignoring Cindy's saucy tone. "I don't think the sisterhood means to harm him. I think they're using him to get to me."

"Isn't that the case with all the boys hanging around you right now, living and dead?" Cindy asked.

"Malcolm and Jack were sent to distract and test me, but Morgan is meant to push me towards the sisterhood," Mina said. "The way he's been acting and talking to me, is not his usual behavior. He's more aggressive, the way that Malcolm used to be, but the sisterhood knows I wouldn't risk hurting him. They expect that I would need their help to restore him back to normal."

"And do you need their help?" Cindy frowned. "They don't seem the altruistic type of organization, to help a fellow witch out without demanding something in return."

"I don't intend to ask for their help," Mina said. "I already know what kind of blood magic they used on him, and how I need to fix it."

"Good," Cindy said with a nod of relief. "What about Jonah?"

"His condition is due to personal reasons."

"He's not here because of the sisterhood?" Cindy asked.

Mina shook her head. "Jonah's here and got changed into a dog, because his asshole cousin didn't trust him to keep his pants zipped," she summarized. "The sisterhood might have been involved in hiding the truth from me, but Sophie changed him for her own reasons."

"Sophie," Cindy echoed. "The name doesn't sound familiar. Is she local?"

"I doubt she's been in here. She was with Garrison Brothers in Boston until recently. She used to be Mary Sophia Leone, back in school, but goes by 'Sophie Lyons' now. Miranda's the actual leader, the one who holds the power."

"We get other customers from Garrison," Cindy said, "but I've never seen either of them in here. I remember Mary Sophia, though; she was a sweet girl, came to a few of the school's pep

169

rallies but didn't socialize much."

"Of course," Mina smiled. "You never forget a face."

"It's a blessing and a curse, especially when it comes to true faces," Cindy said, looking past Mina's shoulder.

Mina followed Cindy's pointed gaze to the door, where Micah was checking IDs for a trio of women who took an empty booth. Between the protection circle that Mina had erected, and the security system that the Crains had installed, the grotesque, demonic nature of the alluring women was plainly visible to Micah, Mina and Cindy, but to the mortals in the lounge, they looked like young, fresh-faced co-eds out for a night of partying.

"Margaritas all around, my lovelies?" Cindy called over to the table.

A festive whoop erupted from the booth. "And a round of daiquiris, too, Queen Cin!" one of the trio said. "Our sister Gorgo is settling down, with a mortal man!" One of the other women hid her face shyly beneath her crown of chestnut curls.

"Congratulations!" Cindy returned warmly. "You ladies deserve true love as much as anyone!" She added as an aside to Mina: "If succubi are so inclined."

Cindy and Mina deigned not to attempt conversation over the noise of the blender, and Mina offered to deliver the tray of drinks over to the table of succubi.

"Little Mina, you're out past your bedtime, aren't you?" asked Isolde, an angelic-looking blond.

"Working late, that's all," Mina replied,

setting down the glasses.

"You're wearing fae dust!" pouted one of the others, who wore her jet-black hair in a coiled braid, with licorice-like tendrils curled along her cheeks. "That's not fair; you're already prettier than most human girls."

"Says the succubus who's claimed a thousand souls," Mina returned. "The dusting was unintentional, Hester. You know I'm not looking for company nowadays."

"Good for you," Isolde rejoined. "Males are only necessary for their seed. A tongue and a phallus are enough to satisfy any other needs."

"It's the promise of exclusivity that's special, sister," Gorgo remarked, twirling a dark brown curl around her diamond-adorned finger. "Otherwise, they all start feeling the same after the seventieth or eightieth. Isn't that right, Mina?"

"Our baby witch isn't like that, you stupid twat!" Isolde laughed. "I hear she's only coupled with one man: her husband."

"What, the dead one?" Hester asked, scrunching up her nose, a black curl bouncing off her perfect cheekbone. "Hasn't he started decomposing, already?"

"Not recently!" Isolde snapped. "When they were still married..."

"Malcolm was having hallucinations until he was killed," Mina interrupted, "with these symbols appearing intermittently." She dipped her finger into a pool of condensation and, on the table, drew out the symbols that she had seen when sprinkled Malcolm and the others with the revealing powder, back in the apartment. "Do these look familiar to you?"

Hester traced her slender fingers over Mina's marks. "You know what they are, little one. They are marks of the sisterhood operating under Garrison Brothers, pledged and beholden to Lucifer."

"But Lucifer's involvement in Malcolm's death would jeopardize his claim on his soul," Mina said. "That's not Luci's style, anyway."

"Then someone at Garrison is overstepping her authority," Gorgo commented, stirring her drink daintily. "But there are few of Lucifer's minions who would dare to act without his authority, so he is aware, regardless of what he says, even if he didn't issue an order."

Before Mina could continue her questions, the succubi's collective attention was diverted to the scrumptious eye candy that approached Cindy at the bar. The glamorous succubus trio looked past Mina with appreciative and flirtatious smiles at the handsome young man.

"Cindy, is this in-house entertainment, or is he here for a private show?" Hester called, biting her lip.

"He's a guest, girls," Cindy called back, giving him a reassuring wink. "So, control yourselves."

Isolde looked undeterred. "We won't hurt him—that would be against house rules. He's much too pretty for rough play, anyway. Gorgo, I believe he has less hair on his face and body than you do!"

Mina turned around, probably expecting to see Jonah, and seemed shocked and dismayed to see Adam at the bar, on display like a tray of

sweets for the tantalizing succubi. For his part,
Adam looked flattered but bemused by the
sudden female attention. Cindy saw Mina's panic
and gestured to her subtly to relax.

"Oh, is he yours, little one?" Gorgo asked
Mina, noticing her stunned expression. "My
sisters can back off, then."

"He's not *mine*, per se," Mina answered,
adding under her breath, *"Ta shi wo-de ge-ge."*

The succubi understood her clearly, judging
by their synchronized nods. "Older brother,
interesting," Hester said, intrigued. "I'm with
humans all the time who prefer me to look like
their sisters, or mothers—"

"Hey, we're close, but not like that," Mina cut
in. "Can we get you ladies anything else?"

Isolde asked easily: "Do you have another
brother that you're less protective of?"

Mina retreated from the table to a chorus of
giggles, which sounded to most humans like
flirty, girlish laughter. To more experienced ears,
it was like a mash-up of cockroach hisses,
twisting metal and shattering glass.

Cindy noticed Adam's involuntary shiver at
the noise. "Are you alright?"

Adam looked hastily dressed, with his shirt
carelessly buttoned and the creases on his
trousers slightly skewed, but his hair was
immaculately disheveled, as though a stylist had
gone to great lengths to make it look wind-
tousled. "My dust looks good on you," Cindy
smiled.

Adam smiled shyly. "Thanks. I just came to
get some water for Xani, since she was thirsty,"
he said, blushing a little towards the end of the

statement. "Some of your late-night customers are lively," he remarked. "They're not really human, are they?"

"Don't mind them," Cindy said, setting two glasses of ice water on the counter for Adam. "Succubi like to prey on the weak-minded and desperately horny." She garnished each glass with a generous twist of lemon and extra wedges of pineapple. "Let Xani have your pineapple."

"How did you know…?" His voice trailed, and his blush deepened. "Okay, I think I should go back now."

"Go get her, tiger," Cindy teased, feigning a playful, flirtatious whip crack.

"Come on, Cin," Mina chided, once Adam had gone. "Be nice. He doesn't need reminders that you and Xani used to be a couple, and that you remember her favorite post-coital snacks."

"He'll get used to it," Cindy said unapologetically. She really hadn't been thinking about it from the perspective of Xani's former lover, but more as a friend who happened to know Xani's habits and quirks. "I guess I shouldn't tell him about the spot on her lower back that she likes stroked during lovemaking."

Mina shook her head fervently. "*I* don't need to know about it, either."

Cindy clicked her tongue. "Humans are so hung up about sex. Considering how preoccupied some of you get over it, you should be discussing it more openly. Not you, of course: you hardly think about it at all."

"Preach, Queen Cin!" shouted Isolde, raising her margarita in a toast. The customers who still lingered in the lounge paid little attention to the succubi's repartee and accounts of memorable conquests, now openly and unabashedly ribald.

"Shit, I forgot," Mina muttered, noticing the time. "I told Jonah I'd be right back. He's probably asleep again."

"Then let him sleep," Cindy said. "The draught will stay in effect for hours still, and he won't be of any use to you while he's only half-awake."

Isolde took a deep breath and turned towards the rooms in the back. "Do you mean the other one? Oh, he's awake, trust me," she said hungrily. "He hasn't been claimed yet, tonight, but he's more than ready. If you don't want him, we could take him off your hands."

Cindy waved Mina off silently. "Quickly, before the girls get to him," she warned. "Another round of margaritas, my lovelies, on the house," Cindy offered to entice them to stay where they were. "Two, if you behave."

Mina knocked gently on the door to Cindy's boudoir before she eased the door open, just in case Jonah was... well, after what Isolde said, she wasn't sure what to expect. "Are you awake, Jonah?" she ventured.

"Yes," he replied, his voice steady and calm. "You can come in."

Mina slipped inside and shut the door. "Sorry that I was gone so long. I got distracted by succubi."

"Succubi," he echoed, with clear interest. "Really?"

"You're safe here, otherwise, they'd eat you alive. Literally, if you don't meet their expectations." Mina went closer to the couch to check Jonah's eyes and pulse.

"You weren't kidding about the draught packing a wallop," he said, sitting still for Mina's brief exam. "I felt like I was drop-kicked onto concrete, then dragged across it for a mile. My mind felt like it was scrubbed clean afterwards, though, and my memories from the night have been restored."

"That's what the draught was supposed to do," she said, holding Jonah's wrist between her sensitive fingers. His pulse was a little elevated, and his pupils slightly dilated. She glimpsed fleetingly that he was "more than ready," as Isolde had called it, and avoided looking below his waist again. *Definitely better that he stays in here.*

"Your phone went off a couple of times while you were gone," he said.

"Messages? From whom?"

His pale eyes were curious and questioning, the way they often were when he had been a dog. "I didn't look. It's your phone."

"Thanks for respecting that," she said, retrieving her jacket from where she left it, by the dressing table. She perched on the arm of the couch next to Jonah as she pulled out her phone. "One from Morgan to the group, that he's home, safe."

"That's a relief," Jonah said. "And the other one?"

"Sophie Lyons," Mina said. It was surprising to see Sophie's number show up, but more so to read the text message.

"What does Sophie want?" Jonah frowned.

*We need to meet...* Mina locked her phone and slipped it back in her jacket pocket. "It's not important right now. Let's go over what you remember."

"Can you sit, please?" he asked, watching her precarious perch on the arm of the couch. "You look like you're about to fall over."

"I'm fine," she said, fighting a yawn. It did feel good to close her eyes, but she figured it was just the cold, dry air or seasonal allergies. "I'll ask Cindy to brew me a double espresso or something."

"Sit," Jonah said, waving her down. "I swear, I'll stay on my end of the couch and keep my pants zipped."

Mina's eyes inadvertently flicked down for an instant at his mention of his jeans, which looked uncomfortably constraining. "Sometimes, being a dog and not needing clothes is easier, isn't it?"

"Much easier," he said tiredly, shifting into his corner to give her space. "I won't touch you, I promise, but don't look at it," he warned lightly, "or you'll encourage it."

"It could be worse," she said, sliding into the opposite end of the couch. "Malcolm could be here, sitting between us, playing chaperon."

She smiled sympathetically at Jonah's clear discomfort. "Relax. I live in New York City, a stone's throw from Times Square. I've seen my share of dicks...and their sad little wieners. I can stay professional, if you can."

Jonah laughed, despite himself. "Thanks. I swear, this usually doesn't happen to me."

"Well, that's a relief." She angled herself to look at his face more directly. "Let's get to it.

What do you remember, from the day you left Boston?"

Jonah closed his eyes to better concentrate. "It was an overcast night, but balmy, so I didn't take a jacket. I got to South Station after the evening rush hour, to catch the last scheduled southbound train."

"You were alone?" Mina asked.

"Yes," he said shortly. "I wasn't here to sightsee or vacation, and I wasn't planning on staying long, so I packed lightly and didn't invite anyone to join me. That's why it was a surprise to see Sophie on board, once we were underway."

Mina focused on his face, watching his micro-expressions and listening to his inflections, which told her just as much as his words. "You invited her to sit with you, and you started talking."

"Sure," he said. "We chatted about some of our mutual acquaintances, and we ordered a few drinks to pass the time. I got up when we got close to New Haven, to stretch and use the bathroom. In hindsight, it was stupid to get up and leave my drink unattended, but I've known Sophie for years and didn't think anything of it. My drink was still on the napkin the way I left it, when I got back to my seat."

"You fell asleep at some point."

"Yes," he said. "When I woke up, I saw Sophie standing over me, undressing me. At first, I thought she was pranking me or something, but then I realized that *I* was different. My senses and my body had already shifted, and she was stripping me while she had the chance. I didn't fight her, as it was harder to move my legs when they were stuck inside the clothes, anyway."

178

"Did you try to communicate with her?"

Jonah shook his head. "I didn't have to. She was doing all the talking. She said that she was just doing a favor for Malcolm, and she wasn't going to hurt me. In fact, she said she wanted to take care of me."

Mina could understand that. "You're probably nicer than most guys Sophie's dealt with."

"Should I feel lucky that she didn't do something worse?" Jonah scowled. "I didn't stick around to find out. As soon as she got my clothes off, she pulled out a leash and told me that it would only be for a couple of weeks. The idea of staying chained up like a beast for that long was intolerable, so I bolted and hid until we got to Penn Station."

"Instead, you were stuck that way for a *month* because you ended up with me," Mina said apologetically.

"Something tells me that I wasn't going to be freed, no matter what Sophie promised," Jonah said, shaking his head. "My instincts told me that I needed to find you, while I still had enough of my wits to seek you out. I followed the crowds out to the street, and remembered that your address was north, so I went towards the marquee signs while I could still understand words and letters. When I picked up your scent, I tried to track you, but only got as far as your block."

Mina recalled the rest after that. "I found you sniffing around the garbage and recycling and invited you into my building." She wrinkled her nose. "My scent, huh? I didn't realize I was that pungent."

"You weren't. I mean, you're not, but it was the mix of tea, incense and your soap that I remembered from years ago, that reminded me of you." He paused with a grimace. "Sorry, that sounds creepy, doesn't it?"

"Not creepy. I'm flattered, actually," she said, closing her eyes. "Considering how rarely we saw each other when Malcolm and I were together, I didn't think I'd be very memorable at all." Mina lay her head against the back of the sofa, intending to rest her eyes for only a moment.

Jonah watched her fall asleep, and he smiled at her peaceful, unconcerned stillness. After the craziness that had filled her day, she deserved her moment of rest, and he cherished his private, stolen view of Mina Gideon, unguarded and vulnerable.

Over the prior weeks, as her dog, he had seen her fall asleep on her couch from time to time, but this was different. The softness of her closed eyes, the gentle flow of her breath and the enticing slackness of her full cherry lips touched him more profoundly, as a man.

*Shit, I am falling for her*, he thought with dismay. He hadn't meant to, and he had denied it vehemently whenever Malcolm suggested it, even in jest, but he had always felt a bond with her. From the first time they met, when Malcolm introduced her as his fiancée at a Gideon family barbecue, Jonah had found her smart, funny and beautiful, of course, but what had struck Jonah most was her confidence, self-assured and serene, even as she was mobbed by a back yard full of boisterous, well-meaning Gideons.

Mina shifted her position slightly, and Jonah spied a long, fine gold chain that she always wore, that he had never seen her remove. With the deep décolletage of her top, he finally saw what she wore on the chain: her wedding band and engagement ring. Jonah was reminded of the arrival of Malcolm's ghost in her apartment that first night, when he had perused Mina's bedroom in search of her rings, wondering if she still had them.

*She hasn't forgotten him*, Jonah realized with consternation. Despite her coolness and distance with Malcolm, she continued to wear the tokens of their marriage on a daily basis. "Do you still love him, Mina?" he whispered.

"No," she whispered back, readily. She opened her eyes a sliver and saw that her rings had slipped into view, and closed her eyes again. "I don't wear them for that. I wear them as reminders of my weaknesses."

"You're not weak," he said quietly. "You were in love. There's a big difference."

"Love," she scoffed. "It's a luxury for the worthy and the lucky. There's still hope for you, but—"

"You'd better not say 'not for me' because that's bullshit," he cut in sharply. "You're not even giving anyone a chance to get close to you, anymore. You're too young to be that jaded."

She sat up, chin raised. "Not jaded. Realistic. I'm a menace to the men around me: Malcolm kills himself in traffic, Adam gets shot, Morgan gets enchanted, you get shapeshifted…"

He leaned forward in his seat, ready to debate her. "You're not responsible for those around you, or what others do to us to get to you. You may be a witch, or shaman, or whatever, but you don't have enough power to protect us all."

"Well," she said, throwing up her hands, "then I guess you're fucked, some of you more than others."

"I guess so," he shrugged, tracking easily with her dry gallows humor. "I think I'm pretty lucky, though, all things considered. I could've ended up at a kill shelter, or hit by a car, or stayed Sophie's captive, indefinitely. Instead, I was taken in by you. Even if I never make it back to Boston, I'd say I had a pretty good run."

"I was lucky, too," she said. "I liked having someone waiting at home who was always glad to see me, who would listen to me without judgment. Okay, there were a couple of times when it looked like you were judging me," she recalled with a smirk.

"It was sometimes a bit concerning, especially when you would come home with your clothes smelling of blood or other effluvium," he said, closing his eyes. "When you were gone, I worried about you and missed you, more than I had any right to."

He opened his eyes at the feel of Mina's hand on his cheek, slightly bristly from going days without shaving. She had slid a little closer to him and brushed his hair back, to get a clear look at his face. "You kind of miss the fur, don't you?" he teased, staying still for her exploration.

"I didn't find you as scary or as intimidating, when you had it," she said.

"Even with the bone-crushing teeth and claws?"

"I've learned that the worst monsters wear human faces," she said quietly.

She started to pull her hand away, and he held it against his cheek, turning his face briefly to kiss her palm. "Whatever happens, I would never hurt you. Come here," he said tugging at her hand. When she balked, he shook his head. "I'm not going to start anything, I swear. You just look like you need a hug."

Mina was as skittish and suspicious, as he expected her to be. She was probably unused to being alone with men who didn't have ulterior motives, and she edged closer cautiously. Recalling the etiquette he had mastered as a dog, he remained perfectly still and let her approach him at her own pace. After a moment, she relaxed enough to rest her head on his shoulder and drape her arm across his midriff for a slight squeeze, and he brought his arm around her shoulders for a gentle, protective embrace.

"I'm going to miss this," she murmured, as her eyes drifted closed again, and she fell back asleep.

He kissed her forehead and tucked her a little closer against him. "Yeah," he whispered. "Me, too."

# Chapter 11

Mina looked out the window next to her small café table, watching the misty rainfall accumulate into rivulets. She found it peculiar and a little disconcerting that the downward flows automatically reminded her of blood. *That's too macabre for a Sunday morning, even for me.*

She took a sip of her coffee: black, with a teaspoon of sugar and a pinch of salt. She glanced at her phone and noted the time and looked over to the door, where Sophie Lyons was arriving for their nine o'clock meeting, right on time. Sophie's golden curls were perfect, despite the inclement weather.

Mina stood to greet Sophie and waited for her to sit across from her and noticed that Sophie slung a large, weathered canvas messenger bag on the back of her seat. Sophie shot a brief, cautious look around the near-empty café, watching for familiar or suspicious faces.

"You can relax," Mina said. "There are protective measures in place, that will keep us from harming one another, if things get heated."

Sophie managed a tight smile. "If I were staying longer, I'd ask if you had a guide or map to these kinds of places in New York."

"You're welcome to stay as long as you'd

like," Mina said, sipping her coffee. "The city is big enough for both of us, as long as we don't step over each other."

"Maybe someday, but right now, I think I need to leave, while I can," Sophie said, tucking a loose blond curl behind her ear nervously as the aproned server approached. "I'm sorry, I wasn't planning on staying long."

"Take a breath, Sophie," Mina soothed, modeling the gesture. "Nadim and his family import and roast the beans in-house. The Turkish coffee is awesome, but they also make a beautiful latte. Please, take your time and have something. I'm sure you wouldn't have texted me, if it wasn't important."

Mina found herself in the unique position of being Sophie's confidante, after thinking of her as the possible enemy, but she held her comments, to let Sophie take the lead on their conversation.

Sophie waited until the server was out of earshot before she spoke. "I owe you an apology, Mina," she said with difficulty. "You were right about the sisterhood."

That seemed secondary, at the moment. "Are you okay? Did something happen?"

Sophie dropped her gaze. "I started thinking about what you said yesterday morning. I didn't want to consider that I was being used, you know, but what happened to Malcolm and Jack wasn't my plan. I didn't want them dead."

"I know, you told me that," Mina said.

"I wasn't sure that you believed me, to be honest. I don't know that I would've believed you, if our places were switched," Sophie said. "Anyway, I started thinking about who *would* want them dead. The only one I had told about my plans for them was Miranda, who was a mentor to me. She taught me most of the spells I used and asked me about what I was doing—I was flattered by her attention, honestly."

"I knew you weren't involved, when your sisters invaded my sanctum without you," Mina said. "I met Miranda, and I saw how easily she could manipulate others. She took the lifeforce from the others."

Sophie bowed her head, almost shamefully. "When I got your text yesterday morning asking to meet, I was so happy and told Miranda, and she encouraged me to go. When I got back to the brownstone after our meeting, and the others told me that Miranda had gone out on an errand, I thought the timing was odd, but didn't think anything of it. Then, our sister returned smelling of gunpowder, and later Miranda came back, extolling our fallen sisters for sacrificing themselves…"

It was clear from Sophie's reddened face that she had known nothing of the plan. "It's not your fault," Mina said. "She fooled me for a little while, too. I had her, and I let her escape."

"I guess I always knew she could be dangerous," Sophie said, "but the power was such a draw, you know? I learned so much from her, more than I could've managed on my own." She paused for a moment, as the server returned with her latte, the foam festooned with a rosette and heart design. The sweet detail made her smile, which gladdened Mina, too.

"Jonah was a different case, wasn't he," Mina said. "You didn't curse him like the others, and your consideration might have spared his life."

Sophie continued to stare at her coffee, not wanting to ruin the beautiful pattern. "Jonah's different. I liked him. He was nice to me, and he didn't deserve to be hurt. Malcolm hired me, but just to keep Jonah out of the picture, so I was just going to shift him temporarily to keep him safe. If he's still in his dog form, I'll be happy to take care of him for you."

Mina shook her head. "You can't keep him like a pet. He has to go home at some point."

"I wasn't planning to leave him like that," Sophie said. "I figured Malcolm would find his way to you, and once you guys patched things up or whatever, I could return Jonah back to normal. He might forget about Ellie, or she may move on from him, and he could get a fresh start."

*Ellie.* That was a new name for Mina, but then again, she hadn't been in touch with the Gideons in years. For some reason, she had thought that Jonah wasn't involved with anyone, but... *Why should I even care?*

Sophie was unaware of Mina's inner monologue and was onto her next point. "I didn't realize that Miranda might want to use him, too. I found out afterwards that the shifting curse that she had taught me was meant to be permanent. I never meant for *that* to happen, I swear. I posted flyers and looked in shelters everywhere for him; I didn't know until you mentioned it yesterday that he had already found his way to you, and that you could find a way to cure him. I'm glad he found you."

"It sounds like Miranda really has it in for

me," Mina said, steering the conversation away from Jonah. "What the hell does she care about what I do? We don't even travel in the same circles."

"I think she finds you to be a threat to her philosophy," Sophie said easily. "I've thought a little about it, too. You're solitary, you don't adhere to a hierarchy, and you are too attached to your men. If they're gone, then you're more vulnerable."

"My men?" Mina smiled dubiously. "I hadn't seen Malcolm or Jonah in years, and I couldn't even tolerate Jack."

"But you're helping them anyway," Sophie noted. "Morgan is just another example of the same. I didn't know why Miranda wanted his blood; I just figured that she was using it for securing the headquarters. I didn't realize that she would use him as leverage over you."

"It's just blood magic, and Morgan's stronger than he looks, so he'll be fine," Mina said. "So, is your decision final? You still want to run?"

"I don't have it in me to stand against my sisters, after everything they've done for me," Sophie said with some regret. "I can't fight. I'm not a warrior, like you."

"I'm not a warrior, just a witch," Mina snorted, "and a pretty half-assed one at that. But I understand your position, and I appreciate you telling me all this in person."

"There's also this," Sophie said, picking up the oversized, frayed messenger bag from the back of her chair. "This is Jonah's. I figured he'd want his things back. I kept everything together: his clothes, his shoes, his phone… I didn't want his family to worry, so I texted them from his phone every few days to check in."

Mina shook her head but saw Sophie's red-faced shame. "That was a big risk, Sophie. If he had been hurt or killed—"

"I know," Sophie said, her eyes watering. "It was stupid, but I was desperate and didn't know what else to do. Please tell him I'm sorry."

Mina took the bag—it was heavier than it looked. "You assume he's still with me?"

"My sisters said he was still with you as of yesterday," Sophie said, wiping her eyes and finally taking a sip of her latte. "And if I were him, living with you, I wouldn't be eager to leave, either."

Sophie got to her feet. "I should go before my sisters start looking for me. You'll forgive me, if I don't tell you which way I'm headed, but I think it's better for both of us if we maintain a healthy distance."

"That's probably for the best." Mina agreed, finishing her coffee. "Your timing sucks for your sisterhood," she said, rising from her seat and pulling out her wallet. They're already short a few members and would need time to return to their full strength."

"That's the idea," Sophie said with a wink. "'Have fun stormin' the castle!'" she quipped in a caricatured voice, and Mina laughed at the Miracle Max reference. "It may not be your religion, Mina, but 'Godspeed,' anyway."

As Mina opened her wallet, she found the scrap of notepad paper that she had gotten from the police officer on Friday night who had asked about Jonah, with just the name and number.

Mina held out the paper to Sophie. "Does this mean anything to you?"

Sophie's blue eyes widened, but she didn't take the paper. "'D.Alighieri'… Where did you get that?"

"Better that you not know," Mina said, recalling that Lucifer had effectively admitted to impersonating the officer in question. "What is it?"

"It's the password and the ten-digit security code to get into the lobby," Sophie said. "If you're planning on visiting my sisters, that's your ticket into the brownstone."

As much as Cindy enjoyed having her friends around and was always happy to help when there was a need, she also didn't sleep well when others were under her roof, whether it was her own apartment, or the Red Lotus. She felt an obligation to watch over her loved ones, to ensure their rest, even at the cost of her own.

As a result, while Adam and Xani occupied the office, and Jonah and Mina slept in the spare bedroom, Cindy had curled up on one of the couches in the lounge, after she had seen her last customers out, said good-night to Micah, locked the doors and shut everything down for the night.

She had only slept a few hours when she heard the spare room door open, and saw Mina tiptoe out, alert and fully dressed in the clothes she had worn the night before.

"That's the most underwhelming walk of shame I've ever witnessed," Cindy had called over, as Mina entered the lounge.

Mina had whipped around, shushing her to

keep her voice down. "Nothing happened between Jonah and me!"

Cindy had hung her head exhaustedly. "Well, that's just sad. That beautiful man is very into you, and you just left him hanging? Did you make out, at least?" she had asked, assuming the minimum, but Mina shook her head. "You don't deserve that face and body, if they're just going to waste like that!"

"I was thinking of more important things than sex!" Mina had shot back.

"The problem is that you *never* think about sex," Cindy had chastised, getting to her feet. "Mina, honey, you know I wouldn't say anything if I didn't care, but you're going to regret it, if you let Jonah go home without letting him how you really feel about him."

Mina had given her a pat reassurance and rushed off with the excuse of an early morning meeting, and Cindy watched her go with an almost-maternal level of concern. Mina had a tendency to lose herself in her work, and Cindy could see the signs of that familiar, obsessive spiral starting to form again.

Fully awakened by her brief exchange with Mina, Cindy continued cleaning up the lounge, picking up where she had left off the night before. She had worked in enough bars and restaurants after school in high school and college to know what details needed more attention than others, and there were always more forgotten valuables dropped between cushions or under tables on Saturday nights than the rest of the week.

She had just crawled underneath a booth to retrieve a fallen champagne flute and a shot glass when she heard a voice by the bar, remarking: "Yeah, this is much better than the pool bar on Beacon Hill."

"The drinks are better," rejoined another male voice.

Cindy stood with the recovered barware and looked at Jonah and Adam, both grinning innocently. "The bartender's much prettier, certainly," Adam smiled.

Cindy gave him a wink for his casual compliment. "You need to tell Mina to loosen up a little," she advised Adam, as she returned to the bar to set down the dirty glasses. "Or she's going to become a shriveled old crone before she gets to enjoy herself with tasty morsels like this one," she said, nodding at Jonah.

"I'm a little conflicted, when you phrase it that way," Adam said.

"I don't think I've ever been called a morsel," Jonah muttered.

"Mina needs an intervention," Cindy said. "There's no reason she should've been alone with you all night, with nothing to show for it."

"She was alone with you, all night?" Adam asked Jonah. "And nothing happened?"

"I swear," Jonah said solemnly. "Our clothes stayed on, and our lips never touched."

"*Dios Mio!*" Cindy exclaimed. "That's nothing to be proud of! You're both healthy young humans who obviously care about each other," she said to Jonah. "*You* know what I'm talking about," she said to Adam, then shook her head. "No, you don't. She's your little sister, so you don't want to even think about her having sex."

"I'll talk to her," Adam promised, probably

just to silence her. "But I'm sure she's fine. Where did she go, anyway? It's barely eight o'clock, on a Sunday morning."

"She said she got a message from a Sophie Lyons last night," Jonah recalled. "Did she say if she was coming back?"

Cindy shrugged. "You know more than I do. She left about an hour ago and just said she had a meeting. She probably went back to her place to freshen up and change."

"She'll probably head back to her apartment afterwards, if she hasn't already. It's better if I actually look in on her than to just text her," Adam said, noting Cindy's look of concern. "It's fine. It's only a few blocks away, and this was very generous of you, but I can't stay here."

"I'll go with you," Jonah offered, and Adam nodded. "I'm done hiding, too, and I don't like the idea of Mina out there by herself."

Cindy sighed, hoping the guys weren't in over their heads. "Well, I can't stop you from leaving, but I understand your worry." She was heartened, actually, that Adam and Jonah cared enough about Mina to go out after her, despite the lack of guarantee of their own safety. "Have some breakfast before you go, at least. The elves are prepping for today's menu, so they can whip up whatever you like."

"Elves?" Jonah asked uncertainly.

"They're small but industrious and have a highly-developed sense of taste and palate. Just don't stare at their ears. Some of them are sensitive about those."

Having received no response from his text to

Mina, Adam knocked on her apartment door before he unlocked it with his spare keys, with Jonah keeping an eye on the quiet stairwell, just in case.

Mina was out, but signs pointed to her being there recently. In addition to Jack and Malcolm's ghosts pacing the living room, there was a glass mason jar on the counter filled with something that resembled fine potting soil, and an oversized canvas messenger bag on the seat cushion of the desk chair. The apartment was warm and filled with a smoky, peppery smell.

"Hey, my bag!" Jonah said, slipping off his slides by the door as he went to retrieve his luggage. "I guess Mina did meet Sophie this morning."

Adam looked on the kitchen counter, where the tea kettle was still warm and Mina's cup of green tea was half-finished. He turned to the mason jar of dirt, which seemed to exude its own warmth.

*She says not to touch it, or to even open the jar*, Jack said. *In case you were thinking about it.*

"What is it?" Adam asked.

*She said it was demon ash*, Malcolm said. *She pulled something that looked like a blackened hand out of a plastic bag and threw it in one of her cast iron pots and cooked it down while she went to change.* He caught Adam and Jonah's sharp glances. *I didn't peep on her, guys. Jesus! Anyway, she went out to meet Sophie and by the time she came back, there was nothing left in the pot but that stuff. She packed most of it in there and took a salt shaker with the rest of it.*

"Should I be concerned that my baby sister is

194

using demon parts?" Adam frowned.

"I've seen her bring home worse things than a hand," Jonah said. "Did she say where she was going?"

*No, but she emptied out her bag when she took the demon hand out,* Jack said, pointing to a piled assortment on the couch, *and repacked it with different jars and bottles when she left.*

As Jonah took inventory of his own bag, Adam looked over what Mina had left behind: half a box of zippered plastic bags, soiled black gloves, a handful of ponytail holders and a sleek, sheathed dagger of Japanese design. He pulled out the blade to make sure it was still clean and well-maintained. The blade had a highly-polished gleam but Adam saw a little staining in the *shinogi*, the ridge that ran the length of the blade.

*I'm pretty sure that's illegal to carry around*, Jack commented.

Adam remembered the *kaiken* as something he had given Mina as a wedding gift, as it was a traditional Japanese gift to new brides, but he had never expected or hoped that she would ever need to use it. "It's meant for self-defense in close quarters. From the look of it, it's seen some use over the years."

*I'm glad she left it*, Malcolm said. *She could seriously hurt herself with that thing.*

"She knows how to use it," Adam affirmed, wondering if Mina had ever contemplated using it for self-defense against Malcolm. Adam used a paper towel to thoroughly clean the blade and its crevices, thinking of what Mina had fought with it, for the dagger to accumulate such a variety of different substances in its grooves. "I taught her everything I knew, and then she learned some more on her own."

He resheathed the dagger and played with it on his fingertips, testing its balance and weight with a nimble touch. It had felt heavier to him when he had it as a boy, years before he gave it to Mina.

"I'm going to go change," Jonah said, his arms laden with clean clothes, as he dropped his shoes by the door. "Maybe we can figure out where she is."

As Jonah ducked into the bathroom, Adam finally got a reply from Mina, to his text from an hour earlier: *In the middle of something. Where r u?*

He wrote back: *Your place. U?*

She texted back: *Your place*, followed by a smiley-face emoji.

He replied: *Come home. Don't do anything stupid.*

He waited for almost a minute, watching the message screen, wondering what she was thinking. Finally, she wrote: *Gotta go. Change your bandage. Talk later*—and a heart emoji.

"You're such a pain in the ass!" Adam screamed futilely at her, shaking his phone, before he dropped it on the counter. He was, however, grateful for the reminder to check his gunshot wound, as he had forgotten all about it.

He pulled up his shirt and examined the gauze and tape, which looked perfectly clean. Peeling back the dressing off his side, he was stunned to see that his skin was whole and unmarked, aside from some fading bruising and a scabbed-over scar where the bullet had grazed him.

"Shit, is that it?" Jonah asked, astonished. "From the gunshot you got yesterday?" He balled up the clothes he had borrowed from Morgan and threw them on the desk chair on top of his bag. "Do you mind if I take a look?" he asked Adam.

Adam shrugged and threw the barely-soiled gauze aside.

"That is...definitely unexpected," Jonah said, peering at Adam's side. "I can barely tell where it was, aside from the scab. Wow."

Adam pulled down his shirt. "I'm going to let you in on something, but you can't say anything, not even to Mina." He looked over at Jack and Malcolm, who were also listening raptly. "Don't fuck this up, I mean it," he warned.

*What could you do to us anyway?* Jack sneered.

Adam waved his hand, as if delivering a back-handed blow, and Jack reeled. Malcolm and Jonah both turned to Adam in shock.

*What the fuck?* Malcolm cried. *You can touch us now? Since when?*

"Probably for a while now," Jonah realized. "You're more involved in this stuff than you've told Mina. She thinks this is all new to you."

"Some of this definitely is," Adam said, taking a deep breath now that he could confide in someone. "I've had cuts and broken bones my whole life, but recovery only started speeding up like this after my accident in Singapore. I saw ghosts as a kid, mostly in my dreams, but I grew out of that, and it started up again a few months ago."

"Did something happen around that time?" Jonah asked.

"Not that I remember," Adam said. "But honestly, I was so consumed at work that I barely paid attention to anything going on around me at the time. Whenever I had a moment of peace and quiet, I'd hear little whispers or catch a flicker out of the corner of my eye, but I'd ignore them and go back to work."

"When are you going to tell Mina?" Jonah prompted.

"Soon, when this stuff with the sisterhood is done," Adam said. "Until then, I have to figure out what it is that I'm supposed to do. Mina said there's no such thing as coincidences, so, if I'm here, there has to be a reason."

By noon, Xani was back at the Red Lotus, helping set up before the doors opened. She had gone home to change and had hoped to find Morgan sleeping in, or some other indication of his presence, but aside from his rumpled bedsheets and discarded clothes at the foot of his bed, there was no sign of him. For lack of anything better to do, and in need of company, Xani headed back to the Red Lotus to hang out with Cindy and do her share of upkeep for the business.

The chores of cleaning and sweeping helped distract her from her concerns, but Xani allowed herself brief moments to savor the memories of the hours she had spent with Adam in the office the night before. She was aware of Cindy's keen, inquisitive eyes on her, but Xani was too giddy to keep the smile off her face.

"It's nice to see you happy," Cindy said. "It's been too long."

"I don't want to say too much and jinx it," Xani said, wiping some lint off her jeans. Just the thought of Adam's smile or voice was enough to make her grin. "It feels too good to be real."

"I get it," Cindy said. "Enjoy it. You deserve to have some fun, and I'm glad for you."

At the sound of the opening door, Xani was immediately on her guard. It was barely after noon, and Micah hadn't arrived yet, but they had a customer. The silhouette was of a tall, slender man, and Xani glanced at Cindy. "Should I send him away?"

"No, honey," Cindy said warmly. "This is one of those exceptions."

Xani watched the customer approach the bar in a serpentine pattern, as he seemed to study the décor and layout with leisurely interest before he actually stepped up to the bar counter. The man was striking, with a crown of dark curls over a flawless olive complexion and wide, doe-like eyes. While his tailored clothes were as dark-hued as he was, he possessed a wholesome glow about him.

Cindy set a napkin on the bar in front of her new customer. "We don't see your type in here too often."

"We don't get much free time," the man said, his voice clear despite its deep timbre. "Usually, just Sabbath and Sundays, but I thought I should make an effort, to see what my ilk have been up to, as of late."

Cindy smiled. "What can I get you?" The man wrinkled his brow uncertainly, but Xani couldn't quite call the gesture a frown or a scowl. He seemed incapable of having any expression that was unflattering or unbecoming. "If you have a fair tolerance, I would recommend a vintage Amarone that your brethren seem to favor. They say it's reminiscent of the wine that was served at the Last Supper."

The man nodded. "Very well. I'll give it a try." As he waited for his drink, he looked around the lounge with a sense of wonder. "I had imagined it to be less cheerful, influenced by darker elements."

Xani returned the broom and dustpan to its closet behind the bar. "It's all a matter of perspective. We're not all whom we appear to be."

"That is quite true," the man said amiably. "Miss Crain, is it?"

"Yes," she said, surprised that he knew her, then she noticed Cindy's knowing smile. "And you are?"

"I'm known to most as Gabriel," he said with a slight bow of his head, and Xani noticed a pin in the shape of a shofar on his lapel.

"The angel? *The* Gabriel?" Xani said.

"*A* Gabriel?" he returned lightly. "The name isn't that rare here, is it?"

"But you are a real angel?" she asked, fascinated. She had seen all sorts of supernatural beings in the Red Lotus, but this was her first angel sighting. "I'm sorry. I've never seen angels in here before."

"That's a shame," he replied. "It's in places like these where we are most needed."

Cindy returned with Gabriel's glass of red wine. "I think you would be surprised. Most of our customers are just here for some peace and some reprieve from prejudice and persecution, not to drown their sorrows and troubles in drink or seek salvation."

"I stand corrected," Gabriel said. "I'm speaking generally of bars, of course, not this place in particular. Your establishment has developed something of a reputation since its opening."

"What kind of reputation?" Cindy asked. "Should we be worried? I shouldn't expect catastrophic fire or floods, I hope."

"Not at all, Miss McManus," Gabriel smiled amiably. "Some consider this place Eden-like—a sanctuary for all of our Master's creations." He noted Cindy's corrective simper. "I said 'some.' I recognize that not everyone believes in God's omnipotence and dominion over all."

Gabriel took a sip of the red wine. "This is lovely, Miss McManus. Thank you for an excellent recommendation. What do I owe you for this?"

Cindy smiled graciously. "We don't list prices, as everyone's currency is different. Some customers offer money, others jewels or a blessing. From you, Gabriel, I would only ask for a civil tongue and an open mind."

Gabriel took another sip, as he considered the price. "I can do that."

"Thank you," Cindy said. "Because our second customer just arrived, and I think you know him."

Xani hadn't even heard the door, but Cindy had a clear line of sight, so she saw Lucifer's arrival and hadn't said a thing. As he was previously, the devil was dressed impeccably, in a pristine black suit. His golden blond curls and arched, groomed brows were so perfectly placed that he bore almost a molded, plastic kind of flawlessness.

"Sweet Cin, a double espresso with a Fireball shot, to go, for Bubbe, and a vodka for me, for here," he called before he stepped to the bar. "Well, well, look who dropped out of the sky," he remarked, shooting Gabriel a sideways glance.

"Russian or domestic?" Cindy asked, ignoring the chill between the angel and devil.

"Russian today, my fae beauty," he replied, with a charming grin that curved his handsome, thin lips. "A fresh bottle, if you please. Good afternoon, Miss Crain," he greeted. "I didn't see you hiding back there."

Xani hadn't meant to lurk or hide, but she was fascinated by the presence of the two supernatural beings and wanted just to listen or observe like a fly on the wall.

"Let me get a new bottle from the back," Cindy said diffidently. "Xani, would you mind keeping an eye out?"

Xani slipped behind the bar and watched the casual, low-key interaction between the immortals without openly staring. "The kitchen staff is nearly done with their preparations, if you'd like something from the menu."

"Thank you, Miss Crain, but we generally don't partake of food or drink," Gabriel said.

"Gabriel considers an extra piece of matzoh gluttonous," Lucifer said, almost affectionately. "It makes it all the more surprising to see you here."

Gabriel took another sip of his wine. "I am curious about your habits, that is all. It is my understanding that you visit here on a regular basis, and I wanted to see its appeal for myself, besides its most obvious charms," he said, turning his eyes to Xani and Cindy, who had returned with a new bottle.

Xani recognized it as one of the most expensive vodkas that they served. "Will this work for you?" Cindy asked, showing the label to Lucifer.

"That would be splendid, thank you," Lucifer nodded. "As you can imagine, Gabe, someone like me is not welcomed in most respectable establishments, especially where alcohol is served, so there are few places where I can be myself."

"Are you allowed to be yourself here?" Gabriel asked with a questioning glance at Cindy and Xani. "Truly?"

"Within these walls, I can socialize, but business dealing is verboten," Lucifer sniffed. "As you recall, I don't typically mix business with pleasure anyway, so I am willing to make an effort not to piss where I drink, so to speak."

Lucifer took the icy-cold glass that Cindy set in front of him and clinked it with Gabriel's wine glass in a silent toast, his well-manicured fingers untroubled by the frost forming on the glass.

The front door opened, and Micah came inside, dressed in only a black t-shirt and dark jeans, despite the damp chill outside. "Sorry, bosses. Am I late?" he asked, looking warily at the figures seated at the bar.

"No, sweetie," Cindy said, "some VIPs just

decided to come early. I'm firing up the espresso machine for Luci, so I'll brew you one, too."

"Oh, the kitchen's making *lokma* for tonight's special dessert later," Xani said, "so tell them to set some aside for you."

"Oh, you ladies are the best," Micah laughed, giving them a beaming smile, as he ducked towards the kitchen.

Gabriel watched Micah as he passed through the lounge. "He's jinn."

"And we have elves and salamanders in the kitchen," Xani said, as Cindy started to prepare the rest of Lucifer's order, setting up two shots of espresso, as she poured an ounce and a half of Fireball into a small cup.

"Salamanders," Gabriel echoed uncertainly.

"They're fire elementals," Lucifer said patronizingly.

"I know what salamanders are," Gabriel answered in kind. "You have quite a diverse crew here."

"We have a diverse clientele," Xani replied. "God's image takes on many different forms, none superior to the rest."

"You are a believer," Gabriel realized, "yet you consort with pagans and otherworldly creatures." Xani and Cindy's shared expression hinted at their disapproval of his phrasing. "Perhaps 'consort' is not the proper word— socialize or associate? I am keeping an open mind, just trying to understand the finer points of this culture." He shot a look at Lucifer. "You're enjoying my discomfiture."

"I'm just here on a quick smoke break," Lucifer said innocently. "I told Beelzebub that I'd bring him back some coffee," he said, as Cindy set the to-go cup of spiked coffee in front of him. He gestured to it flamboyantly, as evidence of his veracity.

Xani fought a smile, as Lucifer was very charming and charismatic, despite his sinister reputation and devious nature.

"What do I owe you, ladies?" Lucifer asked, his blue eyes sparkling.

"The usual," Cindy replied meaningfully, waving him off.

"Of course," he said with a bow of his head, the coffee cup in hand. "Until next time, then." While it was spoken with a light, playful tone, there was an ominous undertone, given the speaker.

Once Lucifer left, Cindy took his emptied vodka glass and started another double espresso for Micah, and Xani asked, "That reminds me: do we have additional insurance or indemnity clauses in our policy, in case things get out of hand?"

"Just the standard stuff, everything short of 'acts of God,'" Cindy said lightly, flashing a smile at Gabriel. "So, yes, there is a chance that if a fight breaks out here, we may not be covered."

Gabriel savored the last of his wine with a smile. "As I see it, your Red Lotus sits outside of anyone's sole jurisdiction. It has no alignment, no affiliation, so it is a sanctuary for all. Is that correct?"

Cindy nodded. "That's the intent."

"Well, then," he said, passing the empty glass back across the bar, "if anything *were* to happen, I imagine that your regulars would have it rebuilt and operational before your insurance agent could even give you an estimate. And that's *if* anything could happen. When I passed through your door, I noticed that you have protection circles and magicks in place?"

"We'd be stupid not to install extra security measures," Cindy said, setting a fresh glass of Amarone in front of Gabriel. "Our friend Mina took care of the spellcraft and blessings, and she keeps it maintained on a scheduled basis."

"Mina," Gabriel said thoughtfully. "That would be Missus Gideon, correct? The former Miss Xing?"

Xani felt her phone buzz, as Cindy poured both finished espresso shots into a cup for Micah. Xani glanced at the incoming text and was relieved that it was Morgan but didn't understand the message.

"Excuse me," she said to Cindy and Gabriel, as she went towards the office for privacy. "I have to call Morgan and find out what's going on."

# Chapter 12

Cindy watched Xani duck into the office to make her call, and saw Gabriel's cognac-brown eyes focused intently on her when she returned her attention to him. "Yes, I still love and care about her. She's moved on from me, but she is still my best friend."

"I understand," Gabriel said. "You have exceptional friends, Miss McManus."

"Which you would know, because you've had your eyes on them," Cindy said easily, wiping the counter clean where Lucifer had set down his glass.

"Why would you assume that?" Gabriel asked.

"Timing," she said. "While Lucifer seems to visit the Red Lotus whenever he's bored, this is your first visit here. Your appearances are always more deliberate, more calculated. You are like a harbinger of impending conflict."

"Sometimes, if things don't go well," he said, "but I would prefer to be a sentinel, to keep watch and ensure that dealings are fair and equitable."

"All this that's happening around Mina," Cindy said, leveling her dark eyes at Gabriel, "hardly seems fair or equitable. What is Lucifer's role in this? What is his interest in her business?"

Gabriel smiled and took a sip. "If you were human, I wouldn't speak as freely, but you have a wider view, so I will be frank: Lucifer has his minions at Garrison, but he finds a number of them lacking. He sees Miss Xing's loyalty and commitment to her friends as his tool to help cull his followers." He paused. "Does she prefer 'Missus Gideon'? She is difficult to read sometimes."

"To me, she remains 'Miss Xing,'" Cindy said. "So, you're saying that Lucifer *wants* Mina to take down his sisterhood?"

"Not entirely, but its members tested, certainly," Gabriel said. "He's given his tainted, indirect blessing to the leadership, in the form of more virulent and malicious magicks that challenge Miss Xing's ingenuity and tenacity to overcome."

"And Sophie was just another tool, using the magicks that her leaders taught her without understanding how dangerous they were," Cindy said, shaking her head. "What if this is too much for Mina, and she fails to do what he wants? What if she can't stop the sisterhood?"

"Then Lucifer is gratified that his followers are stronger than he had estimated," Gabriel said. "And he would see that Mina is weaker than she lets others believe, and perhaps vulnerable to his maneuvers."

Gabriel noted Cindy's guarded stance. "You love Miss Xing, too."

"It's not a romantic love, Gabe," Cindy clarified. "But she is like a sister to me, and we have a history. She's weaker than she appears, because she refuses to share her burdens and carries them alone. What sets her apart from the sisterhood may be what threatens her the most."

Cindy was surprised that she divulged so much to Gabriel, as she wasn't one to gossip or unload her concerns on anyone. In fact, she was usually on the receiving end of spilled secrets and confessions.

Gabriel was raptly focused, with a warm, beseeching smile. "From my perspective, she does not appear to be alone," he whispered conspiratorially, "as long as her companions and friends are true."

"Is there something you're not sharing?" Cindy asked.

"It'll take more than a couple of glasses of wine to loosen my tongue," he smiled slyly. "Be patient, Miss McManus. Everything will be revealed soon enough."

Jonah watched the clock on Mina's microwave oven turn to one o'clock. He was physically more comfortable, dressed in his own clothes, with his phone and other personal effects back in his possession, but he was mentally unsettled. He watched Adam pacing from one room to the next, texting or calling Mina or waiting for her to respond to one of his earlier messages. Adam was checking his phone so obsessively that he and Jonah finally exchanged numbers, just for a momentary distraction, as he waited.

Jonah was looking at his own phone, too, and was a little surprised to see that it had been used regularly for texting in the weeks since he had left Boston. Sophie had apparently been pretending to be him to his family, text-wise, and the brief, terse messages sent from his phone were apparently short and impersonal enough to pass for his own texts.

"It's been over two hours since her last message," Adam said. "What could she be doing?"

Jonah could sympathize with him. For the better part of a month, he had spent day after day, locked in the apartment for hours at a time, waiting for Mina to return from her jobs or errands, without any way of knowing where she was or whether she was alright. Jonah thought of saying something, but then reconsidered; Adam was already leery of the fact that Jonah had lived with Mina for that long, and didn't need to be reminded that he didn't always have canine thoughts and feelings about her.

Adam's phone chimed, and he picked it up immediately.

"Mina?" Jonah asked.

Adam shook his head with a frown. "Xani, actually. She says she just had a long, rambling conversation with Morgan, and she didn't like the way he sounded."

Jonah recalled his conversation with Mina the night before about Morgan's strange behavior. "Where are they?"

Adam was already deep in the text exchange with Xani. "Xani's at the Lotus, with Cindy. According to Morgan's location app, he's around the Arch right now."

Jonah shook his head. "What Arch?"

"Washington Square Park, lower Manhattan, in the Village," Adam said. "The sisterhood's brownstone is near the southern edge, and my apartment building is almost directly across the park from it, on the north side, about two blocks away."

"Is Mina still at your apartment?" Jonah asked, alarmed.

Adam glanced at his phone. "Maybe. She didn't text me to say she left there."

*Yeah, she's still there*, Malcolm said, his spiritual form popping up from the couch next to Jonah.

Jonah jumped. "Fuck! You almost gave me a heart attack."

*Then we'd both be dead, and that would suck*, Malcolm said wryly.

Adam looked around. "Is Jack avoiding me, since he knows I can beat him up now?"

Malcolm chuckled. *Nah, he's keeping an eye on Mina. Not in a stalky way, he just wants to make himself useful.* At Adam's dubious look, he said, *Jack knows now that he was a shithead in life, and that this last chance for atonement may not be enough to wipe his slate clean before his review, but he wants to make the most of it.*

Adam was slow to drop his gaze, and Malcolm knew him well enough to pick up on his unspoken criticism. *I was a shithead, too. I'm sorry for how I treated Mina.*

"I know you're sorry, and I'm sorry we couldn't discuss this when you were alive," Adam said. "There's nothing I can do about it now but forgive you and move on. In the meantime, I have to get downtown," Adam said, sending another text, presumably to let Mina know he was going. "She's going to need some help."

Jonah moved to get up. "I'll go with you."

Adam shook his head. "I think it might be better if you stay, just in case Mina and I manage to miss each other. She'll most likely come back here to restock, maybe check in at the Lotus, before she pays a visit to the sisterhood."

*So, she'd leave downtown to come back up here, and go back down?* Malcolm asked doubtfully. *That sounds like a convoluted way to go.*

"Yeah, well, I know my sister." Adam pointed to the *kaiken* dagger. "She'd come back for *that*, if nothing else."

Jonah acceded with a nod. "That's true. She does love that knife." He tossed over Adam's keys, as Adam got his shoes on. "You have my number. Call me if something comes up." Before Adam could ask, he added: "Yes, I'll text you, if I see Mina first."

"Thank you," Adam said solemnly. "I'll see you soon."

Once Adam left, Malcolm snarked: *You seem pretty chummy. If Mina's not doing it for you, maybe Adam's more your type.*

"Wow, homophobic *and* petty," Jonah shot back, locking the door and returning to the kitchen area. "I'm trying not to take your crankiness personally, but you could try being less of a dick. Your attitude undermines the sincerity of your apologies."

*I meant it when I said I was sorry, but what's the point? There are no more do-overs. After I leave here, my soul's up for review. If I'm lucky, I get to wear a halo and play a harp. If not, then it's eternal damnation.*

"The point is to leave the world better than

when you arrived," Jonah said. "It doesn't mean a perfect world, or that *you* had to be perfect. Just better by the end: you and the world."

*Do you actually believe the shit you say, or do you just say it to make people like you?* Malcolm asked.

"I don't give a fuck, whether people like me," Jonah returned. "Lies are easier to keep straight if there are fewer to keep track of, so yeah, I believe in that shit."

*Yeah*, Malcolm said, watching Jonah's face. *Speaking of lies, I can see them more clearly now. What I can't tell is whether you're believing your own lies.*

Jonah went to the fridge to get himself a bottle of water. "What are you talking about?"

*Aha!* Malcolm exclaimed. *Like that! You deflect, you avoid eye contact, you try to walk away from being called out on it. Admit it: you're in love with Mina.*

Jonah rolled his eyes. *Shit, not this again!* "How many times do I have to tell you—"

*I never believed you, not once*, Malcolm said. *Now I can actually see it in your eyes. I saw it last night, too, when the two of you were at the Red Lotus*, he said, a little guiltily.

"What the fuck, Malcolm!" Jonah shouted. "You were spying on us?"

*I knew nothing would happen, but I was curious about how you were together, when I wasn't around*, he confessed. *Looking back now, I know that marrying her was a mistake. I thought I loved her, but what I loved was what she represented.*

Jonah looked at Malcolm. "What do you

mean?"

*We both wanted her, but I saw her first. I loved having something that I knew you wanted, and you didn't want to be the asshole who broke me and Mina up, but I could tell that you were falling in love with her.*

Jonah finally took a drink of water, to cool down, in more ways than one. "Why are you bringing this up, Mal?" he asked testily.

*I wanted to apologize, for messing up whatever chance you had with her.*

"I never had *any* chance with her," Jonah said. "You made sure of that. Mina and I barely spoke to each other except when you were around."

*I didn't trust you*, Malcolm said. *The few times you talked, I would always grill her about what you discussed. Even after we married, I was afraid that you'd steal her from me.*

Jonah realized that their marriage was doomed from the start, if Malcolm's jealousy had consumed him so profoundly. "You messed her up, you know that? She doesn't want to be with anyone, anymore, probably because she thinks everyone's going to turn out to be an asshole like you," Jonah said. "I hope you're happy."

*You know I'm not*, Malcolm scowled. *I made a lot of mistakes, and I want to try to fix them.*

"It's a bit late for that," Jonah sighed. "But for what it's worth, I hope you get to enjoy your afterlife. You weren't always a jerk when you were alive."

*Thanks. Will you take my advice?*

"Yeah, sure," Jonah said, resigned to hearing it, whether he agreed or not.

*Don't wait to go after what you want,*
Malcolm said solemnly. *As someone who's forcibly
moving on, I can tell you that it sucks, knowing
that I wasted the years and the opportunities that
I had. You already know what you want, and
now's your time to go after her.*

Adam had no messages waiting for him when
he got out of the subway, so he started his walk
back towards his apartment building, staying
alert for suspicious characters lurking along his
route. Unfortunately, it was Sunday afternoon in
Greenwich Village, so interesting characters were
everywhere he looked, but he had a native's sense
of what was normal and what was not.

As he reached the corner of his building, he
watched Morgan approaching from the building's
direction. Morgan's color was good, but his visage
was serious. "Is everything okay?" Adam asked.
"Xani said you sounded a little strange on the
phone."

"Fine," Morgan said, leading Adam towards
the landscaped shrubs to get out of the way of
pedestrian traffic. "Mina's finishing up with your
apartment and should be down shortly. Xani's
keeping an eye on the brownstone and waiting for
us to join her."

Adam glanced at his phone. "That's funny. I
didn't get any messages from anyone."

"Hmm," Morgan said. "I know the service can
be a little spotty in this area. Who's your
carrier?" he asked, peering over Adam's shoulder
down at his phone.

Adam felt like an idiot for falling for
Morgan's simple distraction, when he felt a pinch

on his back, between his shoulders, and realized he had been hit with a tranquilizer of some sort.

Morgan caught Adam's slumping weight easily against his shoulder, as a black sedan pulled up to the curb. Through his unfocused eyes, Adam saw the pavement swaying and tilting in front of him, like concrete waves, as Morgan guided him towards the waiting car.

Adam tried to push back but felt his arms turn rubbery and useless. "Where? What?" he managed.

"Just across the way, to the brownstone," Morgan said cheerily, even greeting concerned passersby who saw Adam's disoriented state. "No, we're good, thanks! Walking might be faster than driving around here," he said to Adam, "but we wouldn't want any mishaps, would we? Watch your step getting in!"

Adam felt himself pushed into the back of the sedan, upholstered black to match the exterior. The last thing he felt was the cool black leather of the seat against his cheek.

"See you around, Dave," Mina said brightly, saluting the doorman as she slung her bag over her shoulder diagonally.

"Anytime, Miss Xing. Enjoy the rest of your Sunday," the white-haired man nodded with a tip of his hat.

Outside the front door, Mina stopped short, as Jonah was just arriving, with her wine tote in hand. "What are you doing here?" she asked him. From his serious expression, it wasn't for anything good.

"We've been trying to text you," he said.

"Have you been upstairs this whole time?"

"Yeah, I told Adam I was here and that we'd talk later," she said, switching her phone back on. "I turned off my phone to save the battery. Why? What's happened?"

"Adam left your place about an hour ago, to meet you here," Jonah said. "You haven't seen him, have you?"

"No, I haven't," Mina swallowed, feeling the dread settle into her bones, as she saw Adam's last text come through.

"Fuck!" Jonah spat. "Xani told him that Morgan was in the neighborhood down here, so Adam came to check on you. When she didn't hear back from either of them, she came by your apartment." He pulled out his phone and put the speaker on.

"Hello?" Xani's voice came through clearly.

"I found her. She's here with me," he said.

Mina heard a familiar windchime in the background. "Are you still in my apartment?"

"Sure. I just needed a fast and secure internet connection to get to our server," Xani said. "Your computer's not the zippiest, but it'll do."

"How did you get onto my computer?" Mina demanded, giving Jonah a look of frustrated bewilderment, as Xani's mocking laughter echoed through the phone for nearly half a minute.

"Mina," she said when she finally stopped laughing, "you're a consultant for us, so of course, we have a back door into your laptop, for our clients' safety and for our security. Now, just give me a second. Talk amongst yourselves."

Mina faced the southern edge of the park,

focusing on MacDougal Street where the Garrison Brothers brownstone stood. "I'm going to take a wild guess that Morgan and Adam didn't go very far."

"His phone is still on," Xani said, "and it's at the brownstone, as we would expect. I know my limitations, and I can help you more from here, than in person; that's why you're there, and I'm sitting at your computer."

Mina turned at the touch of Jonah's hand on her elbow.

"You're not planning on going in empty-handed, are you?" Jonah asked.

She noticed that he had changed into his own clothes, which fit his personality and his physique better. "You found your bag, it looks like. You know what happened to you, and you're cured of it. Sophie's left town—she's sorry for what she did, and she's unlikely to try any more enchantments on you, if you cross paths again."

She lay her hand on his. "You need to go home, be with your family and bury your cousin. There's no reason for you to stay."

"I meant that you should have something to defend yourself," he said, holding out the wine tote, which held a towel-wrapped bundle. From its slender shape and metallic rigidity, Mina recognized it as her dagger. "But I'm going with you, anyway."

"I want you to stay somewhere safe," she said.

"I want you to be safe, too," he said.

"Hello?" Xani's voice cut in. "I'm not interrupting a moment, am I? I have the plans for the brownstone up on the screen, if you're interested in finding the quickest way in and out."

Adam startled awake at the feel of icy water and a sharp slap across his face. He tried to swat at whatever had struck him but realized with trepidation that his hands were bound behind the back of the chair where he was seated. Easing his eyes open, he recalled being ambushed near his apartment building...and meeting Morgan.

Adam looked around the dimly-lit room, its walls and ceilings covered with patterned foam that was typically used for soundproofing, and saw Morgan's silhouette, leaning against one wall. Standing more directly in front of him, looking into his face, was a woman with a long blond braid. A younger woman with long, loose brown hair stood close by, holding an empty water glass.

"Welcome back, Mister Xing," the blonde cooed, stroking her cool fingers against his cheek and jaw. "You recovered quickly. We're impressed."

He didn't recognize the blonde, but he recognized the brunette as Miranda, knowing her face from Mina's research photographs. "Do you actually want something, ladies, or are you just torturing me for fun?"

"This doesn't have to be torture at all," the blonde said easily, leaning over to nip his ear. "This could be a very easy and pleasurable experience for everyone," she said, brushing her fingers through his hair. "Fae dust. You must be very special, indeed."

"If you wanted me for my ability to see

spirits, you can let Morgan go now," Adam said, noticing his mannequin-like stillness. He tested his bindings and felt the bite of nylon rope against his skin.

"Mister Crain is useful for other things," Miranda spoke. "We're not very strong, so we need his muscle and stamina, to ensure your compliance, if we can't entice you to pledge yourself to our organization."

Adam started laughing at the ridiculousness of Miranda's proposal. "Do you want me to join Garrison, or to pledge myself to Lucifer? Neither is going to happen." He was resolute in his refusal, especially on the latter suggestion—he would never agree to serve Lucifer, or otherwise undermine or betray Mina willingly.

Miranda's smile slipped a little. "We'll see how you feel in an hour." She nodded to the blonde, who pulled a vial out of a pocket in her robes. "This may help ease your discomforts in the meantime."

The blonde tried to force Adam to drink, but he clenched his jaw tight and refused to turn his face towards her. In the next moment, he felt his head snap back, and a jarring pain in his jaw, as Morgan stepped back with his fist still clenched,

Adam spit out a mouthful of blood and spittle, relieved not to find a tooth in the mix. "Dude, I'm glad you throw a weak punch," he chuckled feebly, "but you're wasting your time and effort. You're not getting my cooperation this way."

"Just drink, and it'll be over," Miranda said. "It's sweet, a little like cherry or fruit punch."

"Oh, you want me to 'drink the Kool-Aid,'

literally," Adam quipped. "Not gonna happen."
He looked at Morgan and studied his impassive,
emotionless stance and visage. "Is that what you
did to him?"

"No, he's under a blood spell," the blonde said
lightly. "Personally, we don't care if you get
emotional or hurt too badly; it helps intensify
your sight, if you are."

"Enough," said Miranda, sharply, like a
warning. "Other matters await us."

"Fine," the blonde said. "This is boring to
watch, anyway." She looked at Morgan. "We'll
check on your progress in a few minutes. Don't
overexert yourself, in case he's more stubborn
than he looks. And make sure he remains
conscious, so we can extract his assent."

Adam waited until Miranda and her fellow
sister left the chamber before focusing again on
Morgan, who punched him in the gut, a little too
close to the recent gunshot wound. "Son of a
bitch, Morgan. I thought we were friends," he
said, glaring. No response from Morgan, aside
from a little twitch of a frown by his lips. *It's
something.*

"What would Mina say, if she saw you right
now?"

Morgan blinked, and Adam realized that his
emotions were the key. The witches' control was
easier to maintain if they didn't have to manage
or override Morgan's pre-existing or instinctual
feelings, but what if his anger got the better of
him?

"I don't know about your past girlfriends, but
my sister's not into getting beaten up." He tried
something that he hated to even joke about:

221

"What about Xani? Does she like getting slapped around—"

Adam's head snapped to the side, and he felt the blow against his eye socket where Morgan's fist connected. Morgan was clutching his hand in pain, and he was seething, showing a crack in his mask of calm. *Touchy. Now, we're getting somewhere.*

"Don't take anything I say now too personally," Adam warned. "I'm going to make some highly inappropriate remarks about Xani, but it's for your own good. They stay in this room, okay?" Adam steeled himself. *Here we go.* "She and I had sex last night. Let me tell you all about it."

# Chapter 13

Jonah looked around the empty corridor, aware of Mina's presence a step behind him. "Xani's good at this. Everything is exactly where she said it would be."

Mina peeked around a corner. "She majored in engineering and architecture in college," she said, "so schematics and blueprints are child's play for her."

"We don't know if Morgan had started doing anything to secure the building for the sisterhood, right?" Jonah asked. He had acted as Mina's lookout when she inputted the alphanumeric codes to get through the front door and was surprised that she had the information without having to ask Xani.

"No, but if he did, it would be some electrical work. Cameras and heavier locks take a little longer to set up."

Jonah paused in his step, tugging Mina's elbow at the sound of approaching footsteps. "No security guards?" he whispered.

Mina shook her head, reaching into her sling bag. "The sisterhood opted out of using the local security personnel services. Whatever guards we encounter won't be human." She pulled out her dagger, still in its sheath. "They will try to kill us, though, so don't be shy about hitting them first."

"Okay," he replied, more tentatively then he intended.

"You don't have any special powers or healing abilities that I should know about, do you?" she asked casually, silently unsheathing the dagger.

"What? Me, no," he replied, thinking briefly of Adam's rapid recovery and ability to touch spirits, and Mina shot him a look. "Honest, I got nothing."

Mina spun away from him, around the corner, and a choked gurgle followed. He was just a step behind her, but still missed how she had slashed the throats of both guards so quickly that they were dead before they hit the floor. He had a moment to see their oozing, raw-fleshed faces and boar-like tusks before Mina crossed in front of him to wipe the dagger blade clean on the tail of one of their uniforms.

"There's a conference room up ahead, according to Xani," Mina said, reaching into her bag and pulling out a flip-capped salt shaker, filled with a black, sooty powder.

"Is that your demon ash?" Jonah asked.

"Yeah, stand still," she said, popping the lid open and sprinkling some of the ash on Jonah. "I'm sorry to mask the fae dust, but this will help diminish any curses that anyone tries to cast on you. It won't neutralize them entirely, but it'll minimize the effects."

Jonah grabbed a nightstick from one of the dead guards and stayed next to Mina, as she shoved open the doors. Inside the wood-paneled conference room were two young-looking women, caught by surprise. Young-*looking* because he recognized one of them immediately as Miranda, the leader of the sisterhood, and knew that she was much older and more powerful than she appeared.

"Find them," Miranda snarled to the other woman, who darted off through a side door. "Miss Xing, and you are?" she asked Jonah.

"Hello. My name is Jonah Gideon," he said evenly. "You killed my cousin. Prepare—"

Miranda vanished in a cloud of black, sulfurous smoke, and Mina started to choke, but when Jonah went to her aid, he realized that she was actually laughing.

"Did you just paraphrase Inigo Montoya?" she cried, wiping her eyes.

"I tried, but Miranda didn't let me finish," Jonah said with annoyance. "Too irreverent for the situation?"

"Are you kidding?" Mina chuckled, running towards the door through which Miranda's compatriot had escaped. "I'm sorry I didn't think of it first."

On the other side of the door was another elegant room, furnished like a study, and a different woman was in the middle of performing some kind of incantation, her eyes rolling back in her head as if in a trance.

"Hey!" Mina barked, trying to break her concentration, to no avail. Jonah grabbed the closest hard-bound volume within reach and hurled it at the woman's head, and that *did* get her attention.

The witch yelped and reeled with her hand to

her nose where the book had struck her, spine first. While she was distracted, Mina stepped behind her and knocked her out with a blow on the back of the head.

With his eyes on Mina, Jonah forgot to watch his back for a moment, until he saw the black cloud of smoke erupt around him, cutting him off from Mina. He heard her panicked shout, and felt something constricting around his neck like a serpent, forcing him to gasp for air. As he gulped for breath, he felt something drain past his tongue and down his throat that tasted all too familiar; it was just like his drink on the night he came down to New York from Boston, the night he became Mina's dog.

*Oh, fuck, not this again.* He choked and fell to the floor, losing his balance momentarily.

"Let's try this again, since Sophie fucked up the last time," Miranda hissed by his ear. "The master seems to prefer you the other way."

With a cruel snicker, Miranda vanished again, and the air cleared, as Mina knelt by him. He expected to fall unconscious as he had the first time when Sophie had changed him, or to start feeling his senses distort the way they had when he shifted the first time, but he just felt light-headed and cross-eyed.

"Go," he said. "I'll catch up. I'll find you."

"I can't leave you like this," Mina said. "Not until I know what she did."

As his visual and mental clarity returned, he understood what had happened. "I can feel exactly what she did. She tried to shift me, again, but between the fae dust and your demon ashes, the effect is almost nothing," he said, getting to his feet easily, although he had an overwhelming urge to stay on all fours. "I'm mostly human, with just a smidge of dog."

"Come on," he said, following his nose. "I know where Adam and Morgan are."

Morgan looked askance at Adam, for multiple reasons. While Morgan's hands and wrists were still sore, reddened and cut from the beating that he had given Adam in the basement interrogation room, Adam showed little sign of being injured at all, aside from a stray drop of blood or two on his exquisite cheekbones. It was a blow to Morgan's masculinity, in a way, to see that his strikes had so little lasting effect on the man who insulted and besmirched Xani to him.

Adam hadn't meant any of the awful things he said, of course, and he had, in fact, apologized profusely once Morgan had broken out of the witches' blood-fueled control. Morgan would have preferred not to hear any of it, but he appreciated Adam's willingness to rile him to such a level of rage that he was able to snap out of the enchantment, and also Adam's willingness to accept the beating for his benefit.

And Morgan was starting to get the sense that Adam had endured the torture longer than he needed to, just for the sake of liberating him from the witches' spell.

As they had left the interrogation chamber in the basement to get to the main control room upstairs, they had encountered some lumbering, masked guards, whom Adam managed to knock out with startling efficiency. Now that Adam was no longer tied to a chair, Morgan found him more than a little intimidating.

"What kind of research did you do for Global Pacific, again?" Morgan asked, as they stepped around another unconscious guard.

"New products and emerging markets, mainly," Adam said. "Why?"

Morgan shook his head. "You act like you've had combat training."

"Some of the regions are a little unstable. Self-defense training is required for all of our overseas personnel," Adam said. "Was. Not my company, anymore."

"I hear there are positions open at Garrison," Morgan joked.

"Funny," Adam said dryly. "Where are we headed, again?"

"The server room," Morgan said. "Up on the second floor. Sophie said Garrison wanted an internal master to monitor and control where everyone was in the building, in case of a physical breach, so I set up a workstation for a demo scheduled for this week." He paused. "Which probably won't happen now."

Adam grimaced. "Sorry to make you lose your potential clients."

Morgan shrugged. "Not worth the ROI," he said. "Money's not everything. In the meantime, we can take a look at the layout of this place and how we can get away without getting maimed."

At the plain oak door of the server room, Morgan typed a ten-character code into the keypad to unlock the door, and he opened the door tentatively. At the sound of buzzing, he eased the door closed but didn't lock it.

"Problem?" Adam asked, as he turned at a

sound in the stairwell behind them.

"There shouldn't be any buzzing in there," Morgan said. "Sounds like large, angry wasps."

"Had to deal with wasps the other day," Adam growled. "I hate those fuckers."

Morgan felt something trying to tug the door open from inside and saw tiny clawed hands scratching and working their way around the edge of the door. "Fuck. Not wasps."

The sound from the stairwell became louder and more discernable as footsteps, heavy and multiple. "More guards, the big ones," Adam guessed. "I have an idea. When I give the word, get as low as you can and get inside as fast and as quietly as you can."

He took over Morgan's place to hold the door securely, going back and forth between watching the claws scratching at the top of the door, and listening to the lumbering steps quickly approaching.

Morgan had an idea of what Adam had in mind. "What if this doesn't work?" he said in a hushed voice.

"Then hopefully Mina will hear our dying screams and come to avenge us."

"Not funny!" Morgan hissed. "This is a shitty way to go—"

"Now!" Adam snapped, yelling and banging on the door loudly to agitate the creatures inside and draw the guards clambering out of the stairwell. He immediately fell silent, lowered himself to a crouch next to Morgan and released the door, unleashing the flying beasts into the corridor.

All enraged and excited by the commotion,

the lumbering guards and the flying imps engaged each other, as equally belligerent aggressors. In their instinct to defend themselves in the confusion, the guards and the imps ignored Adam and Morgan sneaking into the server room around them, until it was too late, and Morgan slammed the door shut and locked it.

"Holy shit, I can't believe that worked," Morgan gasped, dropping into the seat.

"Don't get too comfortable," Adam cautioned. "We're going to need to fight our way out when we're done. They're not the smartest, but they outnumber us."

"Oh, shit, you're right," Morgan muttered, turning his attention to the equipment. With his nose wrinkled in disgust, he picked up the keyboard from the desk, speckled with food and whatever else the imps had deposited, and shook the surface clear before he started looking at the building layout.

While the screens updated, he glanced at his phone quickly for missed messages. There was a single line, from Xani: *Cavalry in the house.*

"Xani says we've got support. The perimeter alarms haven't been triggered," Morgan said. "So, if our friends are in the building, they probably haven't been detected. If I know Xani, she would've pulled up the plans for this place and let them know how to get in and out without being seen."

"Any alarms triggered for escapees like us?" Adam asked, listening to the battle still raging outside.

"No internal alerts, yet," Morgan said, "but all the main exits have been locked. Someone knows we're loose and doesn't want us to escape, but they're staying quiet, for now. Actually, I can check the motion detectors, while we're here," he remembered. "I didn't have time to set up cameras, but I did set up some basic sensors in the stairwells and main areas—we can try to get a peek at where the action is right now."

Activity was concentrated in two key areas: one main conference room, in the finished basement area at the other end of the building from where they had come; and in the stairwell outside the server room, where they were now sitting ducks.

The noises outside dwindled to mostly feral snarling and the occasional thud against the door or wall. After a moment of stillness, Morgan jumped at a sudden knock, and he saw from the screens that the motion outside was minimal.

The knock repeated, and Jonah's low voice called: "You guys okay in there?"

Adam grabbed a small fire extinguisher by the door as a makeshift weapon, in case it was a trick. "What's the password?"

Jonah's tired laugh filtered through the door. "How about 'my cousin was a dickwad'? Does that work for you?"

Adam opened the door, and Jonah's wolfish, blood-spattered form filled the doorway. A few spots of blood even marked his thin, grinning lips and dripped from his fingertips. A number of unmoving bodies littered the corridor, and Morgan knew logically that some of them had fallen before Jonah's arrival, but it was still a disconcerting sight to see them as his backdrop.

"Mina is someplace safe?" Morgan asked,

setting the keyboard back on the desk. "Did she come with you, or..."

"We came in together, but I have no idea where Mina is now," Jonah said impatiently, offering Adam a nightstick to arm himself. "One second, she's right behind me as we're following your scent trail through the rooms, and the next thing I know, she's gone off in her own direction."

Morgan looked back at the screens, at the concentration of movement by the conference room in the basement. He recalled its bare stone walls and floors, which had reminded him of a medieval dungeon. "I think I know which way she went."

Mina sheathed her dagger, tucking it back into her sling bag, as she picked her way towards the stone chamber in the basement. She had been diverted from following Jonah through the rooms, to the upper floor, and was instead drawn down to the basement by the lure of concentrated energy, which felt like a raging bonfire on a cold wintry day. She had considered letting Jonah know that she was going in a different direction but decided not to interrupt his tracking; it was more important to her that he rejoin the others and help keep them safe.

She knew that Jonah could protect himself. After Miranda's misfired shifting spell, Jonah had started acting and looking more beastlike: detecting different odors and scents, moving more stealthily and quickly, and ripping the winged imps and demons out of the air with nimble pounces, dispatching them with well-placed bites and pinches from his sharpened teeth and nails, which he almost seemed to call forth at will, like a cat's hinged claws. He was still human, but he could tap into a more feral nature without losing his mental acuity or focus. It was unlikely that Miranda had intended her enchantment to affect him like that, but all the dustings and elixirs that Mina and Cindy had layered on Jonah over the past days had shielded him from the worst effects and left him with the better ones.

The granite and bedrock-lined chamber was cavernous, larger than the footprint of the brownstone's foundation. Xani had initially thought there was a mistake on the building plans when she had read off the dimensions to her and Jonah, but Mina saw that the measurements were correct: square, fifty feet along each wall. Xani had even mentioned a four-square-foot alcove near one of the back corners, that was barred and padlocked.

The center of the chamber was marked off by thinner, polished stone tiles set into the floor in a circular pattern, which was where Miranda and the remaining sisterhood members were congregated, white-robed and hooded, with their hands joined and their voices melding in an ominous, droning chant. Their heavy cowls obscured their view, and their concentrated chanting drowned out the sounds of Mina's approach, allowing her to steal into chamber silently and look around undisturbed.

The chamber smelled of candle wax and was decorated by clichéd symbols: inverted crosses, horned statuettes and pentagrams, among other tired examples of anti-Christian iconography.

Mina skirted the edge of the room, waiting

for someone to confront her, but the robed sisters remained focused on their chant, and stooping to peek, she saw their eyes were closed in their concentration on whatever summoning ritual they were performing. From the containment circle they had marked off, they were expecting something the size of a rhinoceros or hippopotamus.

Mina thought to interrupt them with a shout, but figured they would continue their droning chant over her, so she tried something she had learned from pet-sitting her one-time next-door neighbor's cats. Dashing towards the circle, Mina pulled a spray bottle from her bag and began spritzing the sisters and their joined hands, dousing them with a fragrant mist that made them recoil from her and each other, screeching as they struggled to wipe themselves dry.

"You've defiled our ceremony!" one of them cried. "What is that—holy water?"

"Nope," Mina said, spraying the air around her without concern. "This is lavender and geranium, with a splash of catmint." She tucked the spray back in her bag, satisfied that she finally had their attention and stood near the chamber entrance, where she could see or hear anyone else coming. "I didn't desecrate anything. You sense no divinity or profanity about me because I don't share your doctrines; your deities and saints don't guide my actions."

Miranda swayed, as if in a trance. "It doesn't matter that you don't believe in them. Our master believes in you."

Mina wiped off a streak of dust that covered the cloven hoofs of one of the Satanic idols. "I didn't say that I doubted their existence," she said. "I just don't answer to them."

Mina snapped her fingers. "Oh, I almost forgot. I have something of yours." She reached into her bag and pulled out a gauze bundle containing two tiny desiccated skeletons, covered in tattered, discolored white fur. She unwrapped the gauze and slid the whole packet across the polished tiles into the circle, landing them perfectly in the center like a demonic game of shuffleboard. Within the magic circle, the dead mice transformed back into their original human form, and some of the witches in the circle gasped, recognizing the aged, wasted faces of their sisters.

"You forgot to take them with you," Mina said to Miranda, "so I thought you might want them back."

"Are those…" exclaimed one of the sisters. "Miranda told us you slaughtered them!"

"You didn't find it suspicious that Miranda came back looking younger than when she left?" Mina challenged.

"Their faith is absolute," Miranda laughed mirthfully. "They've seen the power our master has gifted me, and nothing you say will sway them." She looked at the bodies the circle. "Thank you, Mina. You don't even realize how much easier you've made this for us. Sisters, now!" she commanded, and the circle returned to its unbroken formation, hands joined, with Miranda leading the chant.

Before Mina could charge through and break the circle, an invisible force shoved her back, and she could only watch as Miranda shouted a summoning prayer to call forth a demon.

The creature appeared within the circle, absorbing the dried corpses into its mass as a sacrifice, as it snarled and clawed at the floor. Sure enough, it filled the rhino-sized circle, even before it stood on its hind legs. It looked like a mass of burning coals given a misshapen humanoid form, and it sensed Mina outside the circle, flaring its nostrils at her before turning its burning eyes on the one that summoned it.

"Destroy our foe," Miranda commanded. "Tear her apart!"

The demon slowly faced Mina, baring its blackened teeth, and Mina took a few steps forward to hold up her empty hands in supplication. "Easy, there."

"Yes, cower before its might and power!" Miranda exulted, as she and her followers retreated from the circle, to the edges of the chamber. The demon beat its stone-encrusted fists repeatedly into the cracking floor with a screeching, pained howl. It tried to lunge out of the circle, but bands of light encircled and squeezed its ankles, keeping it leashed and under Miranda's power.

Mina stepped closer to the circle, ignoring Miranda and the other witches to focus on the demon. *You know me, friend,* she mouthed silently, lowering herself to one knee, just outside the circle. "You are not meant to serve weaker beings, Ba'ermun."

*Weaker and arrogant,* Mina thought to herself, studying the stone tiles underneath her, as the demon took swipes at her that she easily dodged. Digging her nails into the spaces left by the broken stones, she began ripping them from their settings, concentrating on the ones that supported and were marked by the witches' circle.

Miranda and the others began to suspect that their plan had gone wrong, as the demon Ba'ermun did not move against Mina with the murderous fervor they expected. By the time Miranda and the acolytes realized what she was doing, Mina was almost done breaching the circle, and the demon gnashed his fangs at anyone who dared to interfere.

"What are you doing?" one of the witches cried. "It'll kill us all!"

"No, not all," Mina said, as the magical shackles fell from Ba'ermun's legs. "Just the ones that tried to enslave him, and anyone who gets in his way."

As Ba'ermun stepped easily over the broken circle, Miranda's followers scrambled for the exit, no longer trusting her ability to safeguard them as they once had. *Their faith may be absolute, but not their courage.* Mina let them flee, standing guard at the entrance to ensure that Miranda wouldn't get past her, too.

Miranda was left alone, but she was not helpless. As the demon barreled towards her, she flicked her hand, as towards an annoying bug, and Ba'ermun toppled with a pained grunt. Mina snapped into a fighting stance, preparing herself to battle Miranda herself, if she had to.

"I'm not stupid enough to call forth a demon I can't control myself," Miranda sneered. "Until next time, Mina. You may have your pets back, for now." She turned and vanished into her usual veil of black, choking brimstone smoke.

"Ba'ermun, are you okay?" Mina asked, helping the demon to his feet. His stone-encrusted chest was scored, and fine lines of lava seeped through his wounds. He batted her hand away with an irritated snarl, and she stepped back. "Alright, no 'witchy-stitchies,' no problem."

Mina turned at the sound of yelling and approaching footsteps, a lot of them, heading towards the chamber. "What the fuck is this now?" she muttered.

The demon warbled, inquiringly, as it stood next to her. It translated roughly as: *Kill all for you?*

Mina pulled out her dagger. "Hopefully, it won't come to that. Just watch my back, and I'll get you home as soon as I can."

# Chapter 14

With Morgan and Jonah at his heels, Adam couldn't stop short in the corridor, but the sight of Mina with her dagger drawn, with a giant glowing charcoal briquette looming next to her, gave him pause.

"Adam?" Mina cried, eyes wide, as she stepped back, and the oversized smoldering beast moved aside as well, more agilely and gracefully than Adam would have expected from a pile of burning rocks.

Morgan followed Adam into the chamber, but Jonah stopped in the doorway and turned to face the horde that had pursued them. In the time it took to get from the server room to the basement, the trio had accumulated more than a dozen pursuers, that they could distinguish, from a variety of unearthly, nightmarish reptilian and insectoid species. Glancing at Morgan's bugged-eyed, ashen face, Adam was amazed that Morgan was still conscious and able to keep up with him and Jonah.

"This is a surprise," Mina said. "I was going to look for you."

"We were coming to rescue *you*," Adam said, glancing at the gargantuan figure moving past Mina, who seemed to burn more brightly now.

"So much for that idea. Behind you, Jonah!"

Jonah jumped back in time to avoid being singed by the massive lava creature, as it charged past him, tucking its arms and legs to barrel down the corridor like an oversized bowling ball from hell. Some of their chasers were crushed or trampled, others fled from the corridor, and a couple managed to slip past, only to be tackled and rent apart by Jonah's newly-sprouted fangs and claws.

"We need to talk about your new boyfriend there," Adam said, crushing one of the demonic, human-faced cockroaches with a well-placed nightstick between its eyes.

"This is not the time!" Mina shot back, beheading one of the imps that buzzed her, with a swing of her dagger.

"I didn't mean now!" Adam said, slapping the nightstick against another imp, crashing it against the wall. "He'd probably set me on fire."

Mina stopped and looked at him in confusion, then drove the dagger deep into the scaled belly of one of the serpent guards, disemboweling it. "Are you talking about Ba'ermun? The fire demon?"

At the mention of his name, the fiery creature returned to the chamber, baring its sharp blackened fangs in either a smile or a grimace. It snarled a few terse syllables of something like speech.

"What he said," Jonah said tiredly, leaning against the stone wall to take a breath. "All clear. No one else left on the floor."

"He's not my boyfriend, either, *ge-ge*," Mina smirked with a subtle nod towards Jonah, as she stepped up to the demon. "Could I just trouble you to open *that* for me, pretty please?"

Mina was pointing to an iron-barred and locked space at the rear of the chamber. The demon wedged its powerful claws between the bars and the hinges holding them in place and ripped them out like a sheet of newspaper. The demon nodded with a satisfied grunt and returned his attention to Mina.

"Thank you," Mina said, with a bow of the head. "Ready to go?"

It peered at her inquiringly and warbled a question.

"What, for sending Ba'ermun-ti home?" Mina waved her hand dismissively. "No worries, I didn't mind that at all. I would hope, if my spawn ever ends up in your realm, that you do the same for me."

The demon muttered a guttural response, and Mina laughed, pulling a stick of chalk from her pocket, which she used to trace a tight circle around the demon, who stood patiently as Mina went around it. She traced a symbol in the air and whispered a few words under her breath, causing the chalk circle to glow brightly.

Adam stood with Jonah and Morgan to watch the glowing circle erupt into a cylinder of light, like a flashy Las Vegas fountain, and vanish just as suddenly. The demon was gone, as well, with no sign of it ever being there, aside from the destruction it had wrought.

Mina pocketed her chalk again with a bemused smile and stepped into the tiny room that the demon had unlocked for her.

"Was that an actual demon?" Morgan asked,

still staring at the faded chalk circle.

"Demon, elemental, spirit… He is a creature from another dimension, another realm; let's leave it at that," Mina answered, as bottles and jars clinked and smashed inside the nook. "He was yanked from his home abruptly, so he was in a hurry to get back to his family. It's his turn to put his spawn to bed."

Adam looked towards the empty corridor. "Did everyone leave?"

"There's nothing preventing them from leaving. I undid all the security coding I started for them," Morgan said, "so their system's offline, and nothing's locked down anymore. It's just the manual key locks that the building had originally."

"I'm sure Miranda and her followers have their own secret entrances, not listed on the schematics," Mina said, emerging from the closet. "I wouldn't expect Garrison or the sisterhood to share all its inner workings with you, even as their prospective security provider. Speaking of which," she said, holding out a vial filled with a small amount of thick, dark maroon liquid, to Morgan. "This is yours. It's labeled with your name."

Morgan took it warily. "This is my blood? This is how they were controlling me?"

"Otherwise, it wouldn't be called 'blood magic,'" Adam commented.

"I wouldn't dispose of it here," Mina advised. "But once you get it home, you can get rid of it however you want."

"Home," smiled Morgan, pocketing the vial. "God, that sounds nice."

"Yes, it does," Adam answered. "Let's go while we have a chance, and talk on the way. Should we leave everything intact here?" He looked around at the profane and grotesque artwork installed in their stations around the room. "These are the symbols and gods of the sisterhood, aren't they?"

Mina looked around disinterestedly. "They're icons and idols, nothing more than stone, wood or fabric. None of the subjects are inherently evil or malicious, and most of them just have public image problems," she said. "If they don't bother me, I don't bother them. Let's go home."

As they neared the front door, Adam smelled the cloying incense and candle-permeated scents yield to fresh, crisp autumn air coming from outside. Mina found a ring of keys on a stand near the front door, that she pocketed.

"What are you planning to do with those?" he asked. "You're not planning to come back here, are you?"

"No," Mina said resolutely. "But I should return the keys to the owner."

"You think we've seen the last of the sisterhood?" Adam whispered as they reached the sidewalk in front of the brownstone.

Morgan was already texting Xani to let them know that everyone was alright, while Jonah turned his face towards the breeze, relishing the cool autumn air in a way that the others couldn't.

Mina looked at the others and smiled. "No, definitely not," she said easily, "but the idea doesn't scare me as much anymore. Miranda has followers, but I have friends." She hooked her arms around Adam's elbow and leaned her head on his shoulder. "And I have my awesome *ge-ge,* watching my back."

From the street, the brownstone looked like any other rowhouse, well-maintained but unremarkable. Tourists and locals crowded the narrow pavement, unaware of the horrors and carnage lurking inside walls of the vintage building, but a patrol car rolled to a stop in front of it, just as the group reached the corner.

They looked at one another, then Morgan spoke. "Nothing in the system was set up to notify the police, and none of us called them, right?"

They shook their heads in unison and watched the police officers cautiously approaching the front door. "I think we left just in time," Jonah murmured. "We should probably leave the area."

Adam looked across the park, at the white arch of Washington Square Park, almost glowing in the light of the afternoon sun like a beacon. "My place," he offered. "You guys can wash up and crash for a while. Text Xani back," he said to Morgan. "See if she and Cindy are still free for dinner. We never did officially cancel for tonight."

Morgan leaned over the glass-enclosed railing of Adam's balcony, peering down to the traffic and lights of the street level, and he considered how just a little distance could provide so much perspective. He was maybe less than a hundred feet above the noise and pollution of the street, but it was enough to let him now focus on the beauty of the skyline against the night sky.

Similarly, standing on the balcony looking in,

he could study the connections amongst his friends as an observer. Seeing Mina sitting on Adam's couch, giggling with Jonah and Cindy, he saw how much she cherished them, and how deeply she was loved in return. Given the horrors and challenges of her work—which he had now witnessed first-hand—it was no wonder that she maintained a cold and tough demeanor, but now, embraced by love and companionship, she actually seemed happy, in a way that he had never seen, in all the years he had known her.

Morgan looked over his shoulder, as Xani and Adam shared a quick stolen kiss by the balcony door, and Xani took their empty glasses inside, almost prancing in her step. His big sister was happier than he had seen her in a long while, too, and he had Adam to thank for that. He also had Adam to thank for all the salacious, cringe-worthy details of their time together, that he would never be able to expunge from his memory, for as long as he lived.

"Are you good out here?" Adam asked, joining him on the balcony. "Another drink, or more *lokma*?"

Morgan held his full stomach with a gracious nod. "All good, thanks. Just enjoying the fresh air and admiring the vista," he said, pointing towards the partial view of the park between two neighboring towers.

"Better than some others," Adam laughed. "Maybe this year, I'll actually get to see the leaves finish changing color, and real snow. Depending on when and where I start working again, you may see me around a little more. I thought you should be aware," he said wryly.

245

"Thanks for the warning," Morgan grinned. "It'll be nice to see more of you. Just don't give me any more play-by-plays of your time with Xani, okay?"

"It's a deal," Adam smiled. "You're a nice guy, Morgan. If I had another sister, I'd definitely set you up with her."

"What's wrong with the one you have?"

"You're too kind." Adam shook his head with a grin. "Mina would destroy you."

"Harsh," Morgan muttered.

"Hey, I'm just being honest." Adam watched the interactions inside his apartment with Morgan. "I taught her how to throw punches and kicks, from the time she could ball her fist or balance on one foot, but even beyond the physical stuff, she can still be a little intense."

"Yeah, I've noticed," Morgan said. "These past couple of days, I've discovered a new appreciation for her dedication to her craft. She deals with some terrifying shit."

Adam nodded. "Some monsters are easier to fight than others. She tells me about some of her work, but she doesn't like to share too many details."

Morgan thought of the exchange he had with Mina, in her apartment the night before. "Back when I was under the sisterhood's control, I said some cruel things to her. I didn't mean most of it, but some of it, I did. Sometimes, I think she does more for others than they deserve, and cares more for some than they care about her."

Adam followed his absent stare, and Morgan realized with shame that he had been looking at Jonah. "Shit! I didn't mean it like that!"

"I know," Adam said mildly. "And I agree, to a certain extent. That may be why the universe has put me here, now that I think about it."

"I don't follow," Morgan said. "I thought you were here because you got downsized and decided to take a break."

"This isn't exactly my idea of a break," Adam said. "In any case, I was having a little bit of an existential crisis even before my accident, which completely blew up once I got back home. The more I've seen of Mina's life these past few days, the more I realize that she needs some regular support."

"And you don't mean the emotional kind, I'm guessing," Morgan said.

"No, I think you guys have that covered. I'm thinking about the kind of field work she has to do, and that she needs someone to watch her back." He snickered. "I guess that makes me the sidekick."

As Adam went back inside, still tickled by the idea of becoming his little sister's wing-man, Cindy passed him with a flirtatious smile. Morgan was always struck by how easily Cindy could warm up a room with her dazzling simper. Not struck, really, more like enthralled or bewitched.

And now she turned her smile on him, and Morgan forgot about the chill evening breeze, as Cindy joined him on the balcony.

"I'm glad you were able to make it," he said. "You didn't have to bring over dessert from the Lotus. I know the *lokma* take a while to prepare."

Cindy shrugged her lean, slender shoulders. "Perks of being the boss: you get to call your own hours and raid the kitchen at will. Besides, the salamanders had made extra for tonight; they had set aside two dozen for Micah alone."

Morgan could always tell when Cindy had something on her mind, even back when he was a guy and struggling to maintain a tough, stoic persona. "You're okay with Adam and Xani, right? It's not too weird for you, seeing them together?"

"Weird?" Cindy laughed. "Hell, no! They're both gorgeous, genuine and sweet, and they're perfect together. Xani hasn't glowed like that since she was with me," she said, then caught Morgan's eyes slipping back to Mina and Jonah. "Now, *that's* weird for you, right?" she asked gently.

"I'm trying not to be a dick about it," Morgan said. "But yeah, it feels a little like Jonah swooped in and got her before I had a chance."

Cindy rolled her wide brown eyes and turned around to enjoy the view of the street and other buildings. "Honey, you had four years to 'swoop.' Admit it: you were either too chicken-shit to speak up, or you thought she was going to laugh her ass off. The truth is, she thinks you're a nice guy who deserves a nice girl, and she knows she'll never be that."

"Nice guys finish last," Morgan sniffed.

"But they get to finish," Cindy rejoined with a saucy smile and wink.

Morgan laughed and took Cindy's hand. "You always know what to say to make me feel better." He gave her hand a kiss. "You're amazing." *And nice, and sweet.*

Maybe it was his tiredness from the long day,

or the Japanese whisky finally hitting him, or just the way that Cindy's mahogany skin reflected the golden glow from the streetlamps far below, but Morgan felt helpless and frozen in place.

She was looking at him with concern, waiting for him to release her hand. "Are you okay?"

"Yes, I'm fine," he said, pulling her into his arms and kissing her for the first time. He tasted the sweet *lokma*'s honey and rosewater syrup on her lips, and it felt like tasting heaven. "Better than fine."

"Wow," Cindy murmured, wrapping her slender arms around him, as he tugged her closer. "You certainly are."

As he kissed her again, he accidentally brushed the fine scars on her back, and she startled. "I'm sorry," she said, withdrawing, her face reddening.

"No, it's my fault," he said, keeping his hands around her, but more gingerly. "I'm sorry, I didn't know how much you still felt your wings."

She stiffened and flashed her eyes up at him. "You knew about my wings?"

"Of course." He pulled her closer. "I work in security, and we've been business partners for years. Even if you hadn't been with Xani, I wouldn't have done my due diligence if I hadn't researched you, thoroughly."

"You've known that I was fae," Cindy said, "and you've known me since before your sister and I were together, when I was still a dude."

"Yes," he confirmed.

"Despite all that, you kissed me anyway."

"Is that a problem?" he asked, wondering if

he had overstepped.

"No," she said. "I just want you to be sure about this, Morgan."

He liked how his name sounded from her lips. "Cindy," he said, tightening his embrace, as he leaned over for another kiss. "I've never been more certain about anything in my life, than wanting to be with you."

"Okay," she said, returning her hands to his shoulders as she received his kiss. She grinned teasingly. "Took you long enough to make up your mind."

Mina woke up in her bed, with her socks and shoes off and her hair loosened, but otherwise dressed. She glanced at the bedside clock: *4:45 AM*. She sat up slowly, expecting some kind of headache or nausea, but then remembered that Adam had provided the drinks, so no hangover would be forthcoming. *God, I love my ge-ge*, she smiled, getting slowly out of bed.

As she crept quietly from her bedroom, she pieced the night together. She had drunken and eaten a little more than usual at Adam's, but she had had a wonderful evening watching her brother and her friends enjoying one another's company. She was particularly glad to spot Morgan and Cindy kissing on the balcony—they looked beautiful and happy together. When Cindy had to leave, to return to the Red Lotus to close for the night, Morgan left with her. Xani had told Mina to go home and get some sleep, and that she would stay to help clean up; it was her unsubtle way of telling Mina to leave so that she could be alone with Adam.

To make sure she got home okay, Jonah had accompanied Mina back to her apartment. Xani had also conveniently "forgotten" to bring Jonah's bag with her when she met them at Adam's apartment, so Jonah had to go back with Mina, anyway.

Jonah had intended to pick up his scant luggage and find a hotel for the remainder of the night, but Mina offered him the couch, "for old times' sake." With her inhibitions lowered by drinks and tiredness, it was possible that she had said other things, that she no longer remembered.

If she had, it couldn't have been too awful, because Jonah had accepted her offer and was stretched out asleep on her couch. She recalled that he had stayed sober all evening, since one of the remnant effects of Miranda's last shifting curse, was that he could no longer have alcohol, chocolate or any of the other foods that were toxic to dogs and wolves. Aside from that, he seemed nearly perfect.

*He kind of is, isn't he?* He was thoughtful, kind and smart—not to mention handsome, in whatever form he took—and he could protect himself in a fight, if the situation called for it. As the relative newcomer to their circle of friends, he had blended in wonderfully with the others—after that initial friction with Morgan, which was history now. Who could say how things would've turned out, had she met Jonah before Malcolm?

She saw his phone on the coffee and recalled when he had gotten his late night texts. One was from his uncle, Malcolm's father, letting him know that Malcolm's remains had arrived back in

Boston, and asking Jonah to deliver the eulogy for Malcolm's services next weekend. The other text was from an ex-girlfriend, Jonah said, but he didn't give additional details, nor did Mina ask. *None of my business*, she reminded herself.

Mina set her tea kettle to boil, as she emptied her pockets and sling bag and laid out the supplies on her counter. Some of them reminded her of the small recent victories that she could savor, while others reminded her of tasks that still ahead, the thoughts of which prevented her from going back to bed.

Jack's spirit wavered into view on the other side of the kitchen counter. *I never thought I'd miss being able to sleep.*

Mina stared at him incredulously. "What the hell are you still doing here? We figured out what happened to you, so your grievance is resolved."

Jack looked pained and panicked. *I'm not ready to go.*

"I can't help you with that," Mina said sternly. "You're dead. There's nothing left for you here."

*I know, but... I don't want to go to hell.*

"That's not my call," she said with a sympathetic frown. "You can plead your case during your review, or whatever Christian souls usually do, but it's too late to undo all the pain you caused. For what it's worth, I forgive you for what you did to me, but I'm just one person."

*You said everyone deserves a chance to make amends.*

"Yes, and you had it," Mina said evenly. "And you wasted it, by refusing to take responsibility for your own actions. I can't help you, if you can't recognize your own sins."

As the kettle came to a low boil, Mina turned to turn off the flame. When she turned around, Jack's spirit was gone. In his place, Malcolm's ghost was perched on her coffee table, exchanged in a hushed exchange with Jonah, still stretched out on the couch but wide awake. Mina allowed them some privacy by preparing her tea quietly in the kitchen area.

*And the other message was from Ellie?* Malcolm whispered.

Jonah craned his neck and met Mina's eyes. "There's no point in whispering. Mina's right there. Yes, the other text was from Ellie. Rambling booty call text, which I'm ignoring."

*It doesn't sound like Ellie's done with your relationship.*

Jonah sat up on the couch. "I've made myself as clear as I can: I said to her face that I'm done, and that I don't love her. She even keyed my truck, afterwards, so I think she got the hint."

His voice was sharper and colder than Mina had heard before, and Malcolm glanced over. *Ellie cheated on Jonah, a lot. They weren't engaged, but it was serious—*

"It's over. Done," Jonah said tersely. "I blocked her number."

*Okay, but she might show up at my funeral and offer you condolence sex.*

Jonah shot a quick glance at Mina. "Ellie can offer all she wants. It doesn't mean I'll accept."

*That's fair. Hey, at my funeral,* Malcolm began sheepishly, *when you deliver my eulogy…*

"Dude, I'm not going to be an asshole," Jonah said. "I loved you like a brother, and I'd rather remember the good times we had. If our places were reversed, I'd hope you'd do the same."

*I only had good times with you*, Malcolm said. *Even when you tried to set me straight, you were never a dick about it. I'm going to miss that.*

"Me, too," Jonah said.

Mina watched the wispy edges of Malcolm's ghost dissipate, then the more solid-looking form fade, with the last view of Malcolm's ghost being his wry, handsome smile.

"I don't see him, anymore," Jonah said. "Is that it?"

"He said everything he wanted to say to you," Mina said, realizing that that had been Malcolm's final piece of unresolved business that kept him from moving on, and now Jonah could, too. "You can go home and resume your life."

"I already ordered my ticket on-line last night," he said, getting to his feet. "Um, this morning? Anyway, I'm on last train out of Penn Station, tonight."

"Oh," Mina said, trying to hide her disappointment.

"I'd stay longer, if I could," Jonah said apologetically. "But, my family is going to need some support preparing for Malcolm's services."

Mina shook her head. "Of course, sorry. That was thoughtless of me."

"Not at all. You've been more than generous, about everything," he said. "Malcolm and I owe you so much, I don't even know how to start repaying you, personally, and for your expenses..."

"You don't owe me anything," she smiled. "Personally, I needed this closure with Malcolm, too. Financially speaking, he took very good care of me, so from my perspective, he's covered it all."

Malcolm hid himself from view to watch Jonah and Mina's cordial, slightly melancholy conversation with exasperation, and waited for Jonah to leave the room to brush his teeth and get dressed before he popped up again, so suddenly that she nearly dropped her teapot.

"Shit, Malcolm! Why are you still here?"

*You were right, I did have something to say, and I've made my peace with Jonah*, he said. *I even talked things over with Adam last night, at his apartment. But I told you, when you restored my clarity, that there was something else, that I didn't want to say to you, yet.*

Mina set down her teapot and dried off the counter where she had spilled her tea. "Okay, I'm listening."

*I wanted to tell you: you married the wrong cousin.*

Mina laughed. "Now, you tell me! If I were smart, I wouldn't have gotten involved with any of you Gideons."

*No, I mean it*, Malcolm said soberly. *The night before our wedding, Jonah told me, that if he were in my shoes, he'd swear off alcohol and never miss it, because he'd want to remember every single moment he had with you, perfectly.*

"That's sweet, but that was years ago," she said. "Why are you even telling me?"

*Like I said, you married the wrong guy. You deserved the one who would treat you better, and I was an asshole because I was jealous and didn't want to give you up. I thought that I would do the*

255

*noble thing by asking him to visit you, as a
possible second chance for both of you, but I was
chicken-shit and fucked it up, again.*

"I guess you did love me, in your way," she
said. "But you just sucked at it. So badly."

*Yeah,* he admitted. *I'm sorry, Mina. For all
the pain I caused you.*

"Thank you. That's all I ever wanted,
Malcolm: just one sincere apology."

*Does this mean I'm forgiven?*

"I forgave you a long time ago," she said.
"The moment I left Boston, I left you and all the
emotional baggage behind. We gave each other
six months and didn't owe each other anything
more than that."

*You need to forgive yourself, too, babe,* he
said. *You deserve someone who'll be good to you,
but you have to be open to the possibility. It
doesn't have to be Jonah, but he still loves and
respects you. He didn't even try to feel you up
when he put you to bed last night.*

His comment made her chuckle, and he liked
that his last memory of her would be her
laughter. *I'm going to go, but promise me you'll
think about it. Not all of us Gideons are crazy, or
assholes.*

"Okay. I'll think about it."

Malcolm leaned closer and touched her face.
He wasn't sure that he could, but he felt her
warmth, energy and love seeping into him. Not
romantic love like what they had shared briefly
in life, but an overall harmony and connection to
everything around him. Instead of feeling
disconnected from the corporeal world, he finally
felt like he belonged to something larger.

256

He felt her warmth dissipate and retreat from him, but then he realized that he was the one dissipating and retreating. He no longer felt as though he had or needed a body, so he let himself become enveloped in the energy and light that flooded him. He was losing cohesion, no longer contained by his spirit, but in letting go, he felt his presence expand past the limits of what his body had been, to become part of the energy and light.

A voice called to him from out of the light: *Malcolm Gideon, will you stand for your judgment?*

*Yes, I will.* He was at peace, finally. He had taken his Jonah's advice and tried to do some good. He wasn't sure if he had done enough, but his time was up, and now, he was going home.

## Chapter 15

Mina went to the Red Lotus before its official opening time, because she had received a response from Cindy letting her know that the VIPs had arrived. She left Jonah and Adam to figure out their lunch plans, as she went to tend to business.

As she approached the bar, she saw an empty stool between the two well-dressed, elegant customers, so she took it.

"I finished the purification on the duplex downstairs this morning," she told Cindy, sliding a keyring across the bar to her. "It's ready whenever your visitors need it. You can get the front door code from the twins."

"Thank you," Cindy smiled, slipping the keys into her snug front jeans pocket. "Can I get you a drink?"

"Maybe later," Mina said. "It's barely one o'clock."

"Suit yourself." Cindy shrugged and set a glass of ice water in front of Mina. "But even now, it's happy hour somewhere in the world."

As Mina took a sip of her water, she slid another key ring towards the blond man to her left.

He grinned. "Do you often hand out keys to

your apartment to men in bars?"

"Keys to the Garrison brownstone," she said. "It's vacant now."

Lucifer did not pick up the keys, and instead took a sip from his drink. "Keep it, as spoils of war, with my compliments on a well-fought battle. It's prime real estate, worth tens of millions in today's market."

"I pay enough taxes for the building I already own," Mina said. "I don't need to be saddled with another one. Besides, I think it's an active crime scene right now. There's a copious amount of blood and remains that will need to be examined and sorted, that may take some time."

Lucifer seemed annoyed by the inconvenience, as he finally pocketed the keys. "Fine. I'll find some other use for the space. You have my assurance that Garrison Brothers will abandon its expansion efforts into New York and will remain headquartered in Boston."

"Why did you give me the front door code?" Mina asked. "You made it that much easier for me to get inside and confront the sisterhood directly."

"I did it to move the plot along," Lucifer said flippantly. "There was no reason to drag it out. Besides, if you have to endure trials and challenges, my followers should, too."

"And Miranda?" asked Gabriel, glancing over from his seat on Mina's right. "What will happen to her?"

"I've recalled her," Lucifer said, "and will be keeping a close eye on her. She will be assigned to other projects and should not trouble Miss Xing again." He moved a little closer to Mina.

"Unless there is someone else who is inconveniencing you who needs to be displaced?"

She glanced to one side of her, then the other, and she snickered at the position in which she found herself: with a devil on one side of her, and an angel on the other, literally. "Who needs metaphors, Cin?" she muttered under her breath, and Cindy smiled.

"I think Miss Xing prefers to deal with her nuisances more personally and directly," Gabriel remarked. "And even with her oversight, she can't be held accountable for the decisions of others that impact her, as with Mister Mackay."

Lucifer snorted with disgust, and Mina looked at them both. "What about Jack?"

"He's a pain in the ass," Lucifer said. "As he was in life. He invoked your name this morning during his review, in order to be granted a stay, but unless you claim him, we'll reschedule his review."

"What do you mean, that he invoked my name? He tried to pledge himself to me?" she asked distastefully. She would rather take Malcolm than Jack. *Hell, I'd sooner accept one of the dead sisterhood witches over Jack.*

"Clearly, he is trying to avoid his sentence," Lucifer said, rolling his eyes. "Just release him, and I'll be happy to take his soul and add it to the overflowing, writhing pit of pedophiles and rapists. He'll fit in fine and get a taste of his own medicine, so to speak."

"But I'm not a deity," Mina said. "I have no authority to interfere."

"You already have, Miss Xing," Gabriel said, taking a sip of red wine. "You claimed him as one

260

of your *yuan gui* and stayed his initial review, pending the resolution of his grievance. As of this morning, Mister Mackay renounced his Christian affiliation and can no longer be judged unless you release him back to us."

Lucifer nursed his clear, colorless drink; knowing him, it could be water, or 190-proof Everclear, or anything in between. "Mina, you've seen for yourself that Jack is clueless about his failings, so if he's incapable of change, wouldn't it be better to just be rid of him?"

Mina looked at Gabriel, with his serene doe eyes and beatific, enigmatic smile. "Your doctrine offers hope and forgiveness, from an ever-loving god, but you wouldn't take Jack as he is, now, would you?"

"No, Miss Xing, he is far too corrupted and unenlightened," Gabriel replied. "But there is still hope. It takes some souls longer than others to find their path, but wayward believers are still welcomed if they follow their faith home to God."

Lucifer snorted his disdain. "You know why Peter's guarding those pearly gates, right? It's to keep the pathetic fools from escaping their colorless, pedantic, pious eternity."

"Oh, Luci, how you kid," Gabriel said lightly, with a slight edge to his tone. "But there is even still a place for you, if you choose to repent and seek His forgiveness."

"Go fuck your halo," Lucifer said, with the same light tone. "Ah, that's right. You can't, because you're a dickless tool. Go fellate your fucking trumpet, then."

"Alas, it appears that Luci's civil tongue has run its course," Gabriel said. "So, it's time for you to decide, Miss Xing."

*Shit.* She missed the days when the worst she had to deal with, was facing down a horde of necro-demons. She wasn't suited to be anyone's caregiver, certainly not qualified to be Jack Mackay's spiritual keeper, and knew she lacked the patience and wisdom for the task.

Mina tried to map out the options in her head. "It seems like Jack's going to some form of hell, regardless of whose judgment is executed. Either way, he's doomed to eternal damnation," she said to Gabriel. "How would he find his path to redemption, if he's stuck in hell?"

"He should've thought of that, when he was alive," Lucifer said impatiently. "And for his numerous misdeeds, he had plenty of time to consider the consequences. It's not your problem to solve."

Gabriel seemed to sense Mina's vacillation. "Would you like to speak with him?"

Mina nodded. She didn't owe Jack anything, and she still thought he was an asshole, but she wanted to understand his rashness in invoking her name.

"Miss McManus," Gabriel asked Cindy gently, "would you mind terribly if we manifested him here?"

To Mina's surprise, Cindy's countenance turned serious, almost hostile. "You have five minutes," she said, pivoted on her heel and went into the office, slamming the door behind her.

Jack's spirit appeared in the lounge, and he immediately smiled with relief at seeing Mina, then looked around in a panic, as he recognized the devil and angel flanking her. *Wait, is this judgment again?*.

"I never agreed to claim you," Mina said sharply. "I did you a favor by giving you an extension, but I will not be your loophole for avoiding your afterlife."

*I need more time*, Jack cried. *I haven't even been dead four days!*

"More time for what?" Mina challenged. "Your body is gone, your time on earth is over. You don't get to go back and hurt more people."

Jack struggled for words. *I need time to fix what I did wrong. I know that what I said and did hurt others.*

"It doesn't always work like that," Mina said. "Even if you knew that what you did was wrong—which I'm not even convinced you do—not all damages can be fixed or undone with an apology or a good deed. Certain scars will never heal."

*I understand that better, now*, Jack said. *I've spent the past few days listening and watching people, since I can't talk or do anything to most of them, and I think I could help, if I had another chance.*

"I'm not a divinity," Mina said, as patiently as she could manage. "I can't absolve you of what you did, or restore your life. You have to accept judgment."

*Then I'll accept your judgment*, Jack said, raising his chin.

Mina noticed that Jack wasn't looking at her, but past her, at Cindy, who stood in the doorway of the lounge, watching them all with her arms crossed sternly, her eyes steely and cold.

*I'd recognize those eyes anywhere. Cyril*

*McManus. You've changed, a lot.*

"You're still a cock-sucking piece of shit, Mackay," Cindy said. "Still refusing to take responsibility for your own actions. If the authorities here accept my decision, and I sentence you to hell, whose name would you be cursing for all eternity, hmm? It might be Mina's, most likely mine, but it certainly wouldn't be your own, would it? It's always someone else's fault."

Mina was unaware that there had been any history between Cindy and Jack, but the mutual animosity was clear in both their expressions.

*If you want to send me to hell, just do it*, Jack said. *I deserve it. Back then, I thought you were a freak, and I knew you were queer. I wanted you to fight, so that I could beat the shit out of you, but you wouldn't. Even when I...*

Jack's voice stalled, and Cindy waited for a moment before she finished, "Even when you sodomized me? No, you were bigger and stronger than me—I knew I'd never beat you in a fight, and I thought you'd get tired of fucking me, but you came faster than I expected. Was it the rush of domination, or just lack of self-control?"

Mina fought a sob and a growing queasiness. *Oh, shit.* She didn't want to imagine the brutality in her mind, but Cindy was deliberately, unapologetically frank.

Lucifer and Gabriel were more stoic but looked similarly disgusted at what Cindy had suffered. Lucifer, in particular, looked as though he was ready to obliterate Jack's soul on the spot.

"Despite what you did," Cindy said, "I will not judge you because I don't care what happens to you. I will not be saddled with the guilt of determining your fate."

*This was a mistake to call him here.* Mina hadn't meant to reopen old wounds for Cindy, or was even aware that those scars existed. Looking up at the red pumpkin lights to control her furious tears, Mina felt a kind of serenity overtake her, and she realized that she was subject to the same peace-inducing protections and enchantments that prevented the more powerful beings from tearing each other apart. *Motherfucking enchantments.*

Mina took a deep breath and unclenched her jaw. "Take him," she said to Gabriel and Lucifer. "Give him his review first, or just send him straight to hell. I don't care."

Jack looked stricken, and Lucifer looked smug, but Gabriel looked raptly curious. "You'd allow him to plead his case with us, rather than dictate his fate now? He may receive a lesser punishment with us."

"Then that's your choice," Mina said, "but you have more information to make your decision, and more options for sentencing. Besides, the house rules of the Lotus prevent me from sending him directly to his damnation, even though I'd very much like to."

"Your five minutes is up," Cindy announced stonily.

"So, it is," Gabriel said. "We will see you soon, Mister Mackay."

Jack's spirit vanished in a wink, before he could protest or argue.

"I'm so sorry, Cindy," Mina said, reaching across the bar for her hand. "If I had known, I never would've gotten so involved with helping him. He was an asshole who deserves to suffer for everything he did."

Cindy squeezed Mina's hand. "Thank you, honey, but you know how you always say that people deserve a chance to make amends. I'm glad he found you—few others would've bothered with him. If he couldn't turn himself around with your help, then the blame is solely his. You have nothing to apologize for."

Lucifer and Gabriel watched the women's exchange with interest. "Cindy's human side certainly has a mollifying effect," Lucifer remarked. "If she were pure fae…"

"If I were pure fae, Jack would have been castrated and dead in a ditch, with his own severed dick crammed down his throat," Cindy said darkly.

"To be fair, your adopted human father would've plotted a similar form of justice," Mina remarked. "If he'd known, he wouldn't have let the crime go unpunished."

"True, which is why I never told anyone," Cindy said. "Had my father known and attempted such an act of vengeance, his conscience would've plagued him. A fae would do it and never get caught, and never lose a wink of sleep over it."

By the time Mina left to deal with an emergency in her tenant's apartment, the Red Lotus had opened its doors for business, but Lucifer and Gabriel stayed to watch the variety of customers who came and went. Cindy continued to top off their drinks, without bothering to keep tabs on how much they drank.

"Why *are* you here, today?" Lucifer asked his angelic counterpart. "It's not your day off."

"I've decided to take your advice, and research these modern humans and their company a little more," Gabriel said. "I think I understand the Master's affection for them better now."

"Not all of them are equally deserving of his regard," Lucifer sniffed.

"It's not my place to say," Gabriel demurred. "You seem to find them useful and engaging enough, however, to get so directly involved with your followers' dealings with their adversaries."

"I don't consider Miss Xing an adversary," Lucifer asked, noticing Cindy's watchfulness. "My followers may see her as a threat, but to me, she is a potential resource, so she must be tried."

"You subjected her friends to their own trials," Gabriel said amiably, returning to his half-empty glass of wine. "That's not very fair, is it?"

"Mackay was not her friend, Malcolm Gideon's penance is finite and equitable, and there was no lasting harm done to the others," Lucifer said, then riveted his eyes on Gabriel. "And you are in no position to lecture me on becoming involved in mortal matters, given what you've done these past few weeks."

*Past few weeks.* Cindy looked at Gabriel sharply, and the dark angel simply drummed his manicured fingers against the counter. "What did you do?"

"I may have dabbled in matters of fate," he admitted.

267

Lucifer slapped down his empty glass. "You sycophantic wretch! Just say it: you stepped in to save Adam Xing's life."

Cindy leaned on the counter. "That's why you said, the last time you were here, that Mina wasn't alone." She held her tongue on the matter of Adam healing from his injuries at a supernatural rate.

"It seemed only fair," Gabriel said, finishing his wine. "We can't very well leave Miss Xing without some assistance, can we?"

Lucifer's handsome features twisted into a sneer. "You overstepped your authority. Adam Xing isn't committed to you or your master."

"Neither is his sister, yet you continue to court her allegiance, openly, with your favors and hints," he said evenly. "While manipulating your own minions to help you without their knowledge. Tsk, tsk."

Lucifer vanished in a puff of sulfurous smoke, with barely any reaction from the mixed clientele, and Gabriel blew a gentle puff through his full lips to clear the air. "Always the sore loser."

"That was sneaky of you, to bless Adam without telling anyone," Cindy said, setting a new glass in front of Gabriel. "You might have gotten a conversion from him for saving his life, perhaps even one from Mina."

Gabriel shook his head. "Faith should entail more than a mere exchange, Miss McManus. If they choose to align themselves with us, it should come from somewhere inside them that transcends their logical minds, that moves them to believe without the burden of proof."

"Miraculous healing is hard for logical minds to explain," Cindy said, then noticed Gabriel's look of confusion. "Adam's speedy recovery?" she reminded.

"That was not my doing," he admitted. "I prevented Adam from dying in Singapore, and may have manipulated events to have Ba'ermun be the demon summoned to fight Mina, but I don't grant powers."

"Maybe Adam's just very lucky, then," Cindy said breezily, but she surmised there was more at work, possibly other interested parties. "Besting Lucifer at his own game, even temporarily, is a baller move," she smiled. "Your drinks are on the house today—no favors or blessings needed."

Gabriel nodded gratefully. "Without angels, there would be no devils," he reminded. "Lucifer was one of us for eons, and we learned a great deal from each other until his fall."

"You know, Luci's a regular here," Cindy said. "You're welcome to stop in whenever you'd like, even if you don't want to drink, and just want to chat."

"Thank you," Gabriel said in earnest. "I do see the appeal of this place, now," he said, looking around at the strings of glowing red lights, and the varied assortment of customers from across different divinities and cultures. "It really is a safe haven for all types."

"I'm glad you see it that way," Cindy said. "That was our vision."

"You still don't see it as a little piece of heaven?"

Cindy shook her head diffidently. "No, we're too imperfect for heaven. We are all unruly, emotional, carnal beings on this earth, and this is where we can find acceptance and succor, despite our failings and weaknesses." She cast her warm, generous smile to whomever met her glance. "The Red Lotus is a home, for anybody in need of one."

In the bustling, dingy metal concourse of Pennsylvania Station, Adam waited by the assigned gate with Jonah, watching the board for any delays to the train schedule that would impact Jonah's homebound route. Over the past few days, he had become friends with Jonah, closer than they were when Malcolm was alive, and he was going to miss his company. Aside from Mina and Cindy, Jonah was the only other person he knew who could see and hear spirits and easily as he did—another one of those lingering enchantment effects.

He was going to miss swapping science fiction trivia and references with Jonah over beer and tongue-searing wings and rib racks, while watching New Yorkers—especially the spirits, but some live ones, too—go about their business unaware of being noticed. He and Jonah even had a discussion over whether Bostonian ghosts would look and sound different, and Jonah promised to update him.

He stole a glance at Jonah and noticed his blue eyes, almost predatory in his gaze, as he scanned the crowd, with his nostrils occasionally flaring at something in the air. Even Jonah's gait and stance were a little different—more alert and self-assured—but Adam wasn't sure if that was due to his enchantment, or because his experiences over the past several weeks had changed him. Either way, Jonah was going to have an interesting time readjusting to his old life with his new senses.

It was past seven o'clock, and Mina had texted that she would meet them at Penn Station, to see Jonah off, but she was running late. She said only that the situation with Mrs Krantz was taking longer to resolve than expected.

"You're welcome in Boston, anytime," Jonah offered. "The wake is Thursday night, and the burial is Friday, if you want to attend the services," Jonah offered, "but there's no expectation. The family would just be happy to see you and Mina again—they've always liked the two of you."

Adam nodded. "Maybe. I'll have to talk to Mina about it." He extended his hand. "And you're welcome to come back to New York, anytime. You'd have to stay somewhere else, though—not Mina's apartment."

Jonah looked at Adam's hand, then pushed it aside and gave him a brotherly hug. "It's a deal. I wouldn't expect any different." He tried mussing up Adam's hair, the way he used to with Malcolm, but the black locks fell back into perfect place. "Damn fae dust."

Adam laughed. "Take care of yourself."

"I'll try," Jonah said, then paused. "You know, if I do start something with Mina, you don't have to worry. I'll never hurt her, never in a million years."

Adam nodded with a wry grin. "I'm not worried. I appreciate your gallantry, but you do know that Mina's perfectly capable of kicking your ass without me, right?"

"I'm starting to get that impression," Jonah said drolly.

They turned towards the approaching figure. "I'm going to get a coffee," Adam said, bowing his head and stepping back, and Mina came closer. "Safe travels, Jonah. See you around."

Mina cast a look over her shoulder at her brother's retreating figure, as Jonah waved farewell to him. She was thankful for the extra few seconds, as she was at a loss for a witty, memorable comment to send off Jonah properly. On the way down to Penn Station, she had crafted a number of platitudes and quips, as well as a couple of heart-felt confessions, but all the planned words abandoned her, as soon as she found herself standing in front of him.

She started with something simple: "What did Adam say?"

Jonah smiled. "He told me he'd cut off my balls, if I look at other girls."

Mina laughed. "He did not!"

"No, he didn't, but he didn't have to," he said. "He knows I wouldn't, anyway."

"Look all you want. Go, live your life," Mina said. "It was nice to see you again, Jonah." She spoke with a wistful finality, since it was anyone's guess when they would meet again, if ever. "Thank you."

"For what?" he asked.

She wasn't sure why she had said it, except that it had felt natural. "I don't know. For coming here, for staying through the fight. For just being you." *For helping me feel something that I haven't felt in years*, she refrained from saying.

"I'm glad I could help," he said. "We should get together again, sooner than four years," he said, reaching for her hand. "It was good to see you again, regardless of the circumstances. I told Adam that you should come visit. The family would love having you around again."

"Maybe," she said noncommittally. She grasped his hand and kissed his cheek. "Take care of yourself, Jonah."

He turned his head and caught her mouth before she could pull away. His kiss was hot and sweet, and it reminded her of how mind-blowing such a simple gesture could be, executed skillfully. "Don't forget me, Mina," he whispered back, as her head still reeled.

"Not a chance," she said breathlessly, when she recovered her voice. She released his hand when the intercom announced the initial boarding for the train, and she missed the warm strength of his touch.

"If you ever need anything, I'm just a call away," he said, taking a tentative step towards the platform stairs.

"I know. Same here," she said, managing a smile. To keep her emotion from choking her voice, she sifted through the absent-minded banalities that she and Adam would say to each other. "Text me when you get home, so I know you're okay."

Jonah laughed, pausing at the top of the stairwell. "Yes, 'Mother,'" he teased, as the other passengers crowded past him to file down the stairs.

"Remember: no alcohol or chocolate," she

273

said, remembering his new canine allergies.

"I know. Sucks to be me." He curled his lip.

"Raisins, too," she smiled.

"No problem. I hate raisins, anyway."

"Love you," she blurted, then caught herself.

Jonah raised his brow, but he smiled, knowing that it was a slip of the tongue. "Love you, too," he returned laughingly, as someone shoved past him. "I should go," he mouthed, smirking at the irritated, impatient faces around him.

Mina nodded and watched him disappear into the crowd flowing down the stairs, to the train that would take him home, back to his family and his normal life.

"Hey," Adam said, standing with her. He handed her a wax-lined bag from one of the station donut kiosks and put his arm around her shoulder. "You okay, kiddo?"

"Yeah," she said a little shakily, setting her head heavily on his shoulder. "I will be." She peeked into the bag. "What did you bring me?"

"Boston cream, in Jonah's honor," he said, then chuckled at her mock outrage. "Just kidding. Chocolate glazed."

"With sprinkles?" she asked hopefully. Spying the rainbow-colored jimmies on top of the shiny brown glaze, she closed the bag and gave her brother a hug. "You know me so well."

"Still learning," he said, giving her a peck on the forehead. "Ready to go home?"

Mina shook her head, thinking of her empty apartment building.

"Is Missus Krantz okay? You said she fell?"

"She'll be okay, just a bruised hip. I had to

make sure she settled in okay at the hospital and waited for her daughter to get there before I left," she said, as she wrapped her hand around Adam's elbow. "That's why I was a little late."

"You could probably use a drink," Adam hinted.

"Actually, after last night, I should give my liver a break," she said, recalling all the whisky and wine she had at Adam's. "I'm starving, though," she said, sniffing her donut through the bag.

"Let's eat, then. I promised Xani and Morgan that I'd help them later tonight, to freshen up their mom's apartment before she comes home from vacation this week."

"Sucking up to the Crain matriarch, already," Mina grinned. "This sounds serious."

"We'll see," Adam said. "There's steak and stout pie on the Lotus's menu tonight, and carpaccio."

"Beef?" Mina asked warily.

"Knowing the elves working the kitchen, it's anyone's guess," he muttered. "Does it matter?"

"Nope, not at all," Mina laughed, grateful for her *ge-ge*'s expansive outlook, grateful to be able to enjoy his presence without worrying about keeping secrets—grateful for all the blessings in her life, near and far. "Raw mystery meat sounds scrumptious," she said ironically.

"I'm sure the kitchen can concoct something for you, *mei-mei*," Adam said, as they finally reached the street level of Penn Station, the sidewalk teeming with evening commuters, tourists and transient souls, both past and present.

"Back to the Red Lotus, we go, then," Mina said. "It's starting to feel like a second home."

*Thank you for reading!*

*If you've enjoyed this story, and the series so far,*
*please connect with me or drop me a line!*

*Ande Li*

# About the Author

Ande has lived in Hong Kong, China, and the various boroughs of NYC, and has settled in the NJ suburbs with her husband and occasional co-writer Maurice X. Alvarez, their children, their free-range budgie and incredibly forgiving and patient shelter dog.

### Discover other titles by Ande Li

#### *The Xonen Archives*
Book One: The Healer's Girl
Book Two: The Children of Xon
Book Three: The Second Life of Cyrus Ex
Book Four: The Trickster's Game
Book Five: The Souls of Stars *(upcoming)*

#### The Gideon Files
Book Two: White Jade
Book Three: Gold Peony
Book Four: Black Rose *(upcoming)*

co-written with Maurice X. Alvarez
#### *The Trouble with Thieves*
Book One: Return to Averia
Book Two: Trials of Halgarin
Book Three: Elmar of Tranquility

## Connect with Me!
On Twitter: twitter.com/andeliauthor
On Amazon: amazon.com/author/andeli
On Facebook: facebook.com/Room808Press
On Smashwords: smashwords.com/profile/view/andeli